Saoirse

A Novel

Charleen Hurtubise

CELADON
BOOKS
NEW YORK

This is a work of fiction. All the names, characters, organizations, places, and events portrayed in this work are either products of the author's imagination or used fictitiously.

 For information, address Celadon Books, a division of Macmillan Publishers, 120 Broadway, New York, NY 10271. EU Representative: Macmillan Publishers Ireland Ltd., 1st Floor, The Liffey Trust Centre, 117–126 Sheriff Street Upper, Dublin 1, D01 YC43.

www.celadonbooks.com

The author received financial support from the Arts Council of Ireland in the creation of this work.

The Library of Congress Cataloging-in-Publication Data is available upon request.

ISBN 978-1-250-40064-2 (hardcover)
ISBN 978-1-250-40065-9 (ebook)

First Edition: 2026

10 9 8 7 6 5 4 3 2 1

For Sue

Saoirse

(Sear-sha)

Irish female name, meaning "freedom"

Part One

The Prize

Early October 1999

The front door is open and the full length of Daithí fills the frame. He leans against the doorjamb, soaking in the unexpected heat from the autumn sunshine. The mid-morning brightness splits the surface of the bay into shards of light below the house, dazzling Saoirse for a moment as she pulls the car between the gate piers, past the slate sign Daithí has fastened to the wall. Here, in their remote corner of Donegal, houses have no numbers, only names. *Teach Cuan na Míolta Móra.*

Eloise is slumped in her car seat; she has fallen asleep somewhere along the winding coast road. Saoirse can't bear to think of her youngest daughter's face when the public health nurse cooed, tickled her thighs, and then surprised her with an injection in the arm. The child had jumped at the sting, her bottom lip quivering. Eyes, soft and dark as her father's, filling with tears, looking at Saoirse as though she was the source of the betrayal, her own mother the cause of her now broken heart. She wept inconsolably as the nurse turned to her paperwork while Saoirse gathered the child in her arms, comforted her between sobs.

Saoirse pulls into a patch of shade at the end of the house, barely coming to a stop before reaching for her bag, rummaging for a sketchpad, a receipt—anything she might use to capture this moment, the light on Daithí's face. Something about his position reminds her of the first time she sketched him in the garden at the Byrnes' house. She fishes out a repurposed Altoids tin, prying open its lid, selecting a broken piece of charcoal—she finds an old bill in her bag, turns it over and blocks in the lines of his shoulders, his arms. It is not the first time she has considered painting a series using him as her sole subject, simply title the exhibition *Daithí*. Add it to the growing canvases of her daughters playing at the sea, climbing the rocks, placing their tiny hands in the crevices of the walls surrounding the house.

Whichever her next series, it will be a happier collection than the one she is due to install in the Raymond Frank Gallery in Dublin next week. A van collected the canvases days ago. She was happy to see it move off down the road, her *dark period* as she knows it, as though it is all behind her now.

She will follow the paintings up to Dublin in a day or two. Daithí will drop her into Sligo town to catch the train. Fiona, the curator, no longer trying to hide her irritation, is insisting the paintings have a descriptive title at the very least. *Gan anim—without name*—will not suffice.

"They speak for themselves," Saoirse has argued, borrowing the curator's own lingo. "You either connect with the work, or you don't." But this exhibition is different from all the others that have come before. The smaller galleries allowed her what they saw as the eccentricities of the artist, leaving her to her own devices. She is aware of the scale and prestige of this upcoming exhibition—but what she hadn't reckoned on was the scope of Fiona's ambitions, her plans to not only curate the work but also to document Saoirse's journey, to make a big deal of the trajectory that has brought her to this place most artists will only ever dream of reaching. Her resistance to this success, she fears, will bring its own suspicions.

Now Fiona has requested her sketchbooks to put on display, she will use them to write detailed descriptions for a catalogue in the absence of Saoirse's cooperation.

"There are no sketchbooks," Saoirse has lied. But she does, in fact, have books full of drawings, graphic depictions, like untold confessions, events that happened just outside the frame. She keeps them locked in a secret place. When this is all over, and the exhibition is dismantled, Saoirse envisions herself burning the sketchbooks. The past can haunt someone else now, she thinks, and turns her hand back to this drawing of Daithí, back to the things in her new life which can be named.

Leah on the Rocks.

Daithí on the Threshold.

She breathes him in as she works.

Every happiness that is hers is right here, in this corner of the world. The slowness of the day, the blue sky rising tall above the house—a house Daithí has built for her and their two girls—Eloise, their baby, will sleep here, in the shade, windows open to the sea air. Her older sister, Leah, builds a fairy castle on the rock beside the sea wall, draping seaweed for a bed; shells become the characters of her invented world. She stops now to wave to her mother pulling into the driveway.

Saoirse plans to go immediately to her studio; she will make larger sketches of this scene, of this man, and then she will turn to the canvas already drying on the easel—the girls barefoot amongst the rock pools. He will find her here—*Mind your sister*, he will say to Leah. He will come in and close the door, she won't need much coaxing away from the easel where she is painting them into this corner of the world. The two of them, imposters in a country that reminds them, at many turns, they do not belong. But here—they are four now. They are one.

Daithí unfolds his body in the doorway, crosses his arms. And as he does it dawns on her—he is still home. He is home when he should long be at work, he should have Leah dropped at school by now—that was the plan while she took Eloise for her appointment. But here is Leah, in her uniform playing at the rock, here he is in the doorway, waiting for her return. She is unwinding the window, opening the door. A recognition passes through her. She feels the warmth leaving her body. *He knows.*

"What?" she asks. "What is it?" She tries to keep the panic from her voice. It puzzles her, then, when he smiles, in spite of this strange look in his eyes.

"Tell me!" she demands. She wants to rush to him, shake him, make him quickly say the thing she has dreaded hearing all these many years.

His voice is low, almost a whisper.

"Your man rang this morning."

She feels the blood draining from her face.

"I told him you weren't home. He left a message." He comes across the gravel to her, takes her forearms in hands so large and comforting they could hardly belong to a human. It is then he sees the fear on her face.

"No, love. It's all right. There's nothing to worry about," he reassures her, caressing her, trying to unseat the panic. "It's good news. Hey. Look at me." He takes her face in his hands. "You've won a prize. That's it. That's all."

Panic gives way to relief. She is rattled by her own sloppiness. If she is not careful, she will give herself away. She moves out of his grasp so he will not feel her shake, busying herself with lifting the groceries from the boot.

Daithí opens the door and unbuckles a still-sleeping Eloise, lifting her out of her car seat. She shifts and settles onto his shoulder, he smells the back of her neck, gives the folds of fat a soft kiss. He watches Saoirse, puzzled by her reaction.

"It's good, babe," he says. "It's all good."

"Okay," she says flatly. "You should get Leah to school."

"That'll wait. She's happy for you. Come inside," he says gently. "I'll make a cup of tea. I've the details written down—"

"Give me a minute." Her Midwestern accent comes through in full force, the American accent is not something she can turn on or off. She finds, when she is happiest, she has the song of the language, fragments of someone who has lived in this part of the world forever. Now, she hears the syllables fall dead and flat, and fearful.

"I've to put these away." She nods toward the shopping bags, the handles cutting into her palm. She can't afford any further attention brought to this exhibition. She turns to the sea, breathing, convincing her body it is not time to flee.

When she turns around, he is watching her, raising a question with the twist of a brow, a shake of his head. She knows he will ask questions later, but for now, for the children, he will play this out, and she will play along, too, feigning delight when he gives her the details of this latest prize she has won.

"You coming?" he calls to Leah out on the wall. "Remember?"

"Oh yes," Leah shouts, abandoning her castle, suddenly remembering something important she must do. "Dotty took a phone call, Mammy—" She is jumping off the rocks, running toward Saoirse.

Eloise is waking, lifting her cheek from Daithí's shoulder. She sees her big sister and startles into full excitement, kicking at Daithí, rocking with glee. *Dotty*, Leah calls him. *My girls* he says and treats them as though they are both his own, even though Leah must be driven to Dublin every other weekend, to keep her bargain with Paul.

She watches the three of them walk toward the house, Leah has climbed onto his shoes and wraps her arms around his waist, he hoists his legs stiffly, giving her a lift, balancing the baby in his arms. They move as though they are one entity.

Saoirse places the bags down on the gravel and steps beyond the shelter of the house, the wind off the sea catches on her inhale. She can't put this off any longer. She has to tell him and tell him soon.

"Let's have chocolate biscuits!" Leah calls up to Daithí.

"No way," Daithí tells her. "Biccies are for ordinary mammies. Clever mammies must have cake."

Saoirse smiles.

Leah pokes her head out around his legs, her eyes wild with excitement. She beckons to her mother.

"Come on, Mammy, something good is happening."

IRISH ARTIST WINS £50,000 ART AWARD

Irish Times, 14 October 1999

Donegal-based artist Saoirse Byrne has become the first Irish woman to win the prestigious Margaret Dowling Art Prize which recognises emerging artists around the world. The aim of the prize is to discover and financially support promising artists, allowing time and space to focus on their work. Byrne's first solo exhibition opened in 1996 at the David Davis Gallery, and since then the artist has gone from strength to strength, holding several solo exhibitions across the country, including in Cork, Limerick and Donegal. Her work is featured from next month at the Raymond Frank Gallery in Dublin and runs through into the millennium in an exhibition entitled *Lost Was Found*.

The Margaret Dowling Art Prize was established in 1984 and there is no submission process. Artists are unaware their work is being considered for the life-changing prize.

The judges were impressed by Byrne's current exhibition featuring a collection of eight pieces, an array of oil paintings and other mediums capturing everyday objects. Appearing as mundane, simple objects at first: a vial of lavender, lines on a road. They exhibit sculptural qualities, an intensity of colour, while the use of light adds both a weight and a lightness, dependent on the directional aspect. The judges describe the work as having 'a complex directional gaze,' remarking on 'the tension this creates, an uncertainty, as though the object isn't the subject at all, that it is perhaps only a clue to something imminent and unsettling awaiting just outside the frame'.

Her paintings first came to the attention of critics at the

Annual Exhibition of the Irish Academy of Arts where she won the Eugenia Lawrence Scholarship. From here she went on to continue her studies and earned a BA in Fine Art.

Ms. Byrne has established a reputation for maintaining a deliberate silence about her work and is generally unavailable for interview or comment.

Flight

Early September 1990

If her heart wasn't already beating in her throat as she boards the plane, her blood pressure spikes when she notices a man sitting in the seat she has been assigned. She doesn't trust herself to speak, to interact with another human, to tell him to move. Instead, she stands in the aisle, double-checks her boarding pass, compares the number and letter with the decals on the overhead bins.

"This you?" the man asks, rising halfway from his seat.

She nods, grateful she doesn't have to engage.

"Sorry, sorry," he apologises. He is compact, dressed tidily, a white shirt with sleeves pulled up to his elbows. His sport coat hangs on the button knob in front of his seat. He stands out into the aisle, making space for her to pass.

"Take the window seat." He gestures, as though his act is somehow what she desires, a sacrifice he will make for her, a stranger. She moves past him, pulling her overnight bag into the seat with her.

"Will I put that up above?" The man gestures to take it.

He has the same Irish accent as her friend, Sasa.

"No, you're fine," she tells him.

She wishes she had used the bathroom before she sat down but it feels too late now since she has settled in her seat, crushing her overnight bag into the space at her feet. She is still clutching the stolen passport, amazed by the fact that she wasn't stopped. She opens it to the middle pages, placing her boarding card inside when she notices the folded piece of paper, her original birth certificate, bearing her real identity. She should have destroyed it in the bathroom before she went through security.

"I hate to tell you, but they're going to ask you to stow that," the man points out. "Give it a shove, under the seat."

She resents that he feels he should instruct her on a basic point of flight—but the bag is too tight for where she is stowing it and the air hosts are cross-checking the doors. He extends his hand with a patient smile, waiting to take it. She gives it over and he arranges it in the overhead bin for her. He folds his sport coat and lays it beside her bag. She wedges her documents into the seat pocket in front of her and turns to watch the vehicles on the tarmac.

An air host moves down the row, banging overhead bins closed as he passes.

"Seatbelts," he says and continues moving down the plane.

For all the stupid things she has ever done, this is the biggest disaster she has engineered. She wonders if there is still a chance to slip off without drawing further attention to herself, attention to her mistake, to the crime she is committing by boarding a plane under a false identity. Is *this* a felony? she wonders. She will add it to her many others. This can't be any worse than everything else that has come before. Once she disembarks into this unknown country, presents herself as Sarah Walsh, the woman on the stolen passport, there is no turning back. So far, she has gotten away with it, the similarities are there. Everyone had noticed how much they looked alike. Still, she lets her long dark hair fall around the lines of her face, covering her ears, so there is less to compare.

The man beside her clears his throat.

"First flight?"

"Mmm," she says coldly.

"Paul," he says, stretching his hand out to shake. Tiny lines show around his eyes when he smiles. She looks at his hand but doesn't take it. He pulls it back and keeps talking as though he hasn't noticed her slight. "Or Pól. Some people call me the Irish version of my name."

He launches into an explanation about some language he is allowed to use, whether it is on his passport or not. Something about the English and colonialism, and his birthrights as an Irishman. She has stopped listening. She is staring at the dark hairs covering his arms to his wrist, examining his clean fingernails, neatly manicured, noticing his nervous manner, the way he is talking with his hands.

"But call me Paul," he says decisively. "Keep things simple."

She wishes she had bought a book in the airport, to fend off conversation.

"You have a name?" he asks, eyeing the seat pocket where she has stashed her Irish passport.

"Sarah," she tells him, firmer than she intended.

"Sorry," he says. Settling back into his seat. "You sound more American than Irish."

"Long story."

He looks at his watch. "We've roughly five hours, forty-nine minutes. Go."

She smiles despite herself, quickly concealing it.

"Let me guess, rather."

"Please don't."

"You're not from Boston."

"Hmm." She is noncommittal.

"But your mother is Irish. Your father is American born."

"You're a psychic," she says dryly.

The plane lurches and pulls away from the stand. Her hands sweat. She is relieved to see Paul lifting a book from his seat pocket.

The thrust of takeoff pushes her back into the seat, she watches the ground leave them, she cannot pull back from this now. The world grows small below, ships in the harbour shrinking to tiny game pieces. They head out over Massachusetts Bay, over the Atlantic, up into a bank of clouds.

Sarah Walsh. Born in Ireland. Twenty years old on the seventeenth day of . . . She chants this information, though she has drilled herself so many times it is seared in her memory. By the time the captain's voice fills the cabin they are in Canadian airspace, though all she can see is a blanket of clouds, a world turned over on itself. She imagines her sister, Léa, somewhere below, somewhere safe—and she knows she must block out those last moments—the way she laid her on the back seat of the car, knowing the next face her sister would see would belong to a stranger. She must train her thoughts away, think of her own survival. She rolls up her sweatshirt, places it in the window, resting her head on the ledge.

SARAH IS STARTLED AWAKE BY a vigorous shaking. She sits up and clutches the armrest.

"Nothing to worry about," Paul reassures her. "Just a little turbulence."

The plane gives another shimmy, and a slight drop like they've sailed over a speed bump, but then returns to a smooth stream, as though they are not even moving. She stretches and looks around. The cabin has darkened. Someone has thrown a blanket over her knees.

Paul points to the meal placed on the lowered tray of the empty seat between them, the wrapper still on.

"Chicken," he says. "Sorry. It's gone cold. I didn't want to wake you."

She feels the depth of her sleep in the knots in her neck.

"Thank you."

"Will I get them to warm it?"

"It's fine," she tells him, pulling back the foil. She can't remember her last meal. She tries not to eat too quickly, giving her hunger away.

"So, what about you," she asks.

He looks up, pleasantly surprised she is initiating conversation.

"What about me?"

"What brought you to Boston?"

"I study medicine." He presses his lips together, as though humbled by his own revelation.

She acknowledges his remark with a lift of her eyebrow.

"Not impressed?" he asks.

"Should I be?"

He folds his arms, amused.

"Definitely not. No."

"Don't they teach medicine in Ireland?"

"Yes, of course. I was on a clinical placement. I hoped to gain a fellowship, stay in Boston a little while longer."

"Nice," she says, uninterested.

He scrunches up his nose.

"Well, not nice. I didn't get the fellowship."

She registers his disappointment.

"Sorry."

"Ah, sure." He tries to brush it off, without success. "It's a pity. Both my father and brother got it in their time. I thought it was a legacy, a sure thing. But—that's the way."

Two small bottles of red wine sit on his tray, he tilts them toward her.

"Anyhow, I grabbed us a drink. To celebrate my failure."

"Very thoughtful of you," she jokes.

He unscrews a bottle and pours the contents into the plastic cups.

She hesitates, deciding if it will help her focus or hinder her nerves.

He notices and pulls the bottle back. Squinting, he measures her up.

"What age are you?"

"Old enough."

Was it only a few weeks ago she had sat up late into the night with her Irish friend Sarah—Sarah Walsh, or "Sasa" as everyone called her—a childhood mispronunciation that had stuck and morphed into something sounding close to *Sasha*. It hadn't been as much of a celebration as a goodbye. She had been devastated her new friend had decided to leave Boston and follow a boyfriend down to Florida. Florida wasn't a place Sarah was willing to go, ever again. It was on this night she had glimpsed Sasa's passport—and the possibility of escaping from this nightmare that had become her reality.

Paul is waiting for an answer.

"I'm twenty," Sarah lies.

"Ah bless," he says, pouring the rest of the second bottle into her cup. "Somewhere in the world, you are legal to drink. *Sláinte*," he says. They tip glasses and she sips the wine. It is warming and settles her straight away, and it also reminds her she must use the bathroom. She excuses herself. It feels good to stand and stretch her legs and move around a bit. The wine has already gone to her head. When she is finished, she washes her hands and splashes her face with water. Looking in the mirror, she tells herself to be cautious about the easy chatter between herself and Paul. When she returns to her seat, he has refilled her glass.

They have each finished three small bottles by the time the lights are turned down in the cabin and he has snagged two more from the galley, for later, he says. The alcohol takes hold of her quickly, loosens her up. Makes her forget. She thinks she should drink more often.

"What's your plan?" he asks.

"No plans, really."

"Visiting relations?"

"I was born in Ireland, but we left when I was a baby." The lies come much easier with a few drinks.

"I guess that makes you as Irish as the rest of us."

"I guess."

"Will you visit your mother's people?"

Sarah shakes her head.

"She hasn't kept in touch with anyone."

"So, you're coming back to discover your roots." The way he puts an emphasis on roots annoys her.

"Yeah, I guess."

"Seeking your heritage."

"Maybe." The audacity of him makes her laugh through her annoyance.

"Or running away."

She stops laughing.

"We are all running from something," he says.

She clears her tray to the middle seat between them, puts her seat back.

"What are you running from?" she asks.

He smirks.

"Nothing really. Success, I guess. Maybe failure, rather. I became engaged in America. To an Irish-American girl. My mother is furious."

"She doesn't like her?"

"She hasn't met her."

"Why is she furious?"

"My mother likes things to go a particular way. Her way. I'm to focus on my studies, gain prestigious fellowships, and not marry American girls. It doesn't matter now. We broke it off."

"Sorry to hear."

"Yeah, well. My mother will be delighted."

"You haven't told her yet?"

"No. I'll tell her in person, I suppose."

"Aren't you upset?" Sarah asks, turning to face him fully, interested in what people with normal lives feel when things go wrong. She thinks of Eddie. Then tries to erase him just as quickly.

"Ah, she wasn't for me, I suppose. You know what they say—"

"Not really."

"What's for you, won't pass you by."

"I hadn't heard that before." She thinks of the things that eluded her and her sister. Like parents who looked after them, kept them from danger. The basics. She isn't sure she believes in his saying.

"Well, no matter, I'm expected to become a doctor. That is the obligation and that is the expectation I shall fulfil. It would have been handy to get the fellowship, but it won't deter me." He sits up tall and puts on a brave face. "Cheers, anyway." And he downs the last of his drink.

"Well, I'm sorry it didn't work out for you," she says. For a moment, she genuinely feels for him. There is something about his demeanour, a glint of charm perhaps, that moves her—or is it the wine?

"I loved America. The people, the lifestyle. Especially if you make money. And that is one thing about medicine. I'll make money."

"Hmm," she says. "A doctor. I am impressed now that you mention it."

"Works every time," he jokes.

He puts his head back on the seat and smiles.

She is sorry when she hears his soft breathing, once he has fallen asleep. She is on her own then, with her thoughts, over the dark Atlantic, flying into the unknown.

The Gallery

Late October 1999

When she arrives at the gallery on Parnell Square, the paintings are already hung. The workmen are tidying the crates, a ladder remains in the centre of the room. The room, like the building, is imposing and Saoirse is bewildered to see her name in such prominent lettering on the exhibition's title panel:

Saoirse Byrne
Lost Was Found

Fiona has intuited something about the order of the collection. It is like she has figured out her *journey*, after all, and to see all eight panels together like this disconcerts her, overwhelms her. She has exhibited paintings before, but not so many, not an entire collection—it is like looking at a puzzle of her life, all the pieces jumbled in a box for so long, now taken out and clicked in place, her story emerging for all to see.

She shouldn't have let her friend Catherine talk her into this. She should have painted, destroyed, painted them again—a therapy of sorts—but they do not belong here, on view. The panic wells up again, a vertiginous sensation enters her head. She closes her eyes, breathes in slowly, but the parquet floor sways and she sits down in the middle of the room on a wooden bench that reminds her of an ornate pew. Her eye moves immediately to the first painting, her earliest memory displayed there for all to see.

Lavender

Oil on board

When I am three my mother drops me off at a house in the middle of the night. I have fallen asleep across the back seat in the watery illusion that life contains my mother and me. I wake next morning in a single bed in a finished basement and my mother is nowhere to be found. Beside the bed is a little table. On it is a tiny bottle, like a small vial. I cannot read the label, the word is too long, but the faint smell emanating from this bottle alarms me, in its unfamiliarity, in its concreteness. Beside this is a photograph of a mother, a father, and on his shoulders, their little girl.

In this house there are long, white hallways and open, spacious rooms. So much space and high ceilings and a view out over a lake. There is a woman who comes to me. She is the woman in the photograph, an older version of my mother; tiny, frail, a sophisticated beauty. She speaks a language I cannot understand. It isn't much use when she switches to English, her accent is strong and the only word I understand most of the time is my name. Sarah.

For me, these are nameless days. I measure time in what is given and what is taken away, and however long I am here in this house, I begin to feel I will disappear into the white walls, as though I am a breeze passing through the open doors.

And one day, my mother comes back. The shape of her stands in the doorway, dark and tan, wearing cut-offs and a pair of sunglasses that fill her face. When she sees me poke my head out of the basement, she steps out of flip-flops, stealthily lowers her shoulder bag to the tiles and chases me.

I have never laughed in this house, never raised my voice. I'm not even sure I spoke a single word all this time. But we are off now—running and shrieking through the big room, circling past the kitchen, past the woman, smoke curling from her cigarette.

My mother chases me down the mouth of stairs leading back

to the basement. I don't know if I am laughing or crying, if this is ecstasy or terror. She catches me and spins me around, tosses me on the bed. Now she wraps her arms around my body, cradling me, and once again we become one.

Sarah, *she whispers my name.*

She picks up the photograph beside the bed.

Mama, *she tells me, pointing to the woman.*

She runs her finger along the younger image of the man who comes home in the evenings, tousles my hair. Sits in front of the television and smokes. She touches the image of the little girl sitting on the man's shoulders in the photograph.

Papa, *she says sadly. She turns the frame upside down on the bedside table and picks up the small vial. With my mother close, there seems to be a meaning, even for this.*

Lavender, *she tells me, and shakes the oil into her palm, rubbing it into my heels, tickling the softness along the bottom of my foot.*

And he is standing there now, a shadow at the foot of the bed. His presence brings an unsettled stillness to my mother, robs her of her playfulness. She has stopped rubbing my feet.

Here is Lou, *she tells me. He stands there looking at me as though he is waiting for something. His eyes are arresting, sparkling blue, lined with thick, dark lashes.*

Mama is calling down the stairs. My mother shouts up to her, she knows her language. Lou speaks it, too, they are shouting at one another. My mother shifts my weight and rises, moving toward Mama's angry words. My body feels cold where she has pulled away. She runs upstairs. I want to follow but I would have to pass this shadow, this man, so I lie still, hoping he'll go away. His forehead wrinkles as he studies me, he jams his hands into the pockets of his leather coat. His unkindness diffuses through the room, strong as his aftershave.

My mother pounds back down the stairs, shouting and laughing—but it is not the joyful chasing laughter. It is frightening and angry. She opens the little set of drawers and throws my things into a laundry basket. She throws the photograph on top, leaving the vial of lavender behind.

She is leaving again. I rush for her legs and hold them. She pushes me away and grabs my hand, pulling me roughly up the stairs. Mama comes toward us, she holds tightly to my wrist, they are struggling over who will keep me. I wrangle myself away from Mama, feel my wrist slipping out of her grip and fold myself into my mother's arms, wrapping my legs around her waist, clinging to her with all my strength. Outside the car is running. My mother places me on the back seat. Mama stands on the step. Her face austere.

My mother cries and swears. She raises her middle finger to Mama, saying unkind things to her. Lou laughs. He is putting the car into drive. He is pulling away from the house. And now my mother is in the passenger seat, she is laughing, too. She reaches into the back and takes my hand. We are laughing and holding hands through hot, fiery tears.

Landing

Early September 1990

Sarah is ready to ditch Paul once the plane lands in Dublin, but he walks beside her along the jetway commenting on the damp, cold morning air they feel but cannot see. She doesn't have a jacket. With every step closer to passport control, that sense she has always relied on kicks in, and a calm takes hold. She is in control. It unnerves her, then, when Paul begins issuing advice, as though he somehow suspects an uncertainty around her entry. He guides her by the elbow as they reach the channels, moving her toward the lane for EU citizens.

"Keep moving," he whispers, and Sarah feels unsure about his closeness, this sense he is doing her a favour.

"Open the passport, hold the photo toward your man, and don't stop moving."

The officer barely glances up as she holds the maroon passport book for inspection. With his nod, she is through.

"That was easy, so," Paul tells her.

She doesn't dare reply. She sees her moment to escape, moving through the hall toward baggage collection. Paul waits for the luggage carousel to start, but she moves toward the exit. She is through the customs channel, walking out the security door when she hears him calling her name. She doesn't turn back.

Inside the arrivals hall, the eyes of the waiting crowd turn their eyes to Sarah, and like a murmuration, turn away again as swiftly, toward the next passenger. Groups of young people who have no one to greet them cluster together and stream toward the exit. She follows them onto the street.

A green double-decker bus rattles past, the destination blind promising: *An Lar | City Centre | Via Connolly Station*. The young people board the bus, digging into their pockets for change. She only has a few crumpled dollars, along with a stack of cash buried deep in her overnight bag. She turns back inside, to figure out currency exchange.

"You nearly escaped," a voice tells her.

She lifts her brow, annoyed to see Paul.

"I was wondering—" He hesitates.

"What?" She hopes her rudeness will hide the worry that is beginning to take over, overwhelming her with the sense that she doesn't know how to move around this foreign city. Once on her own, she will find a seat, absorb her surroundings, figure this out.

"—where are you staying?"

Her face is blank.

"I realise I sound like a serial killer."

"I need money. For the bus."

"Oh right. Here." He rummages around in his pocket, hands her loose change.

"I mean, I need to change money." She hands the coins back, shows him the crumpled dollars.

"Right."

They return inside to the Bureau de Change. He waits with her in the queue.

"I don't want to hold you up," she tells him.

"Well, if you're getting the bus, I'll wait."

"Are you going my way?"

Her sarcasm doesn't thwart his persistence.

"I'd know the answer to that if you answered my first question. Where are you headed? Not so much to murder you, as to meet up? Show you Dublin?"

She smiles at his bumbling awkwardness.

"How about if you give me your number," she tells him.

"Right." He rummages in his bag for a pen, finds one, scribbles on his boarding pass. "You do have somewhere to stay?"

She says nothing.

"That looks like a *no* to me."

She shrugs.

"I hate to tell you this, but you won't find a place at this late stage."

"No? Well, I'll figure it out."

He gestures to the hordes of young people filling the airport, queuing for the buses outside on the pavement. "*Youth Jamboree* mean anything to you?"

She shakes her head.

"The Pope's Cult. Young papists converging on Dublin this weekend from all over the world. Every affordable room from here to Tipperary is booked since last year. You haven't a hope."

She studies him to see if he is exaggerating.

"Ask your woman," he says.

They have arrived at the front of the queue. The lady behind the counter agrees.

"You've little hope without a booking."

Sarah closes her eyes.

"Right. Then it is settled. You have no choice but to come home with me for a night. Or two. After that, you can hike the untrodden pathways of Ireland, search for your roots."

"I couldn't—"

But she does.

SARAH WAKES TO THE SMELL of crisp sheets in a room so white she thinks she has awoken once again in the Lavender House. She slept heavy, she doesn't know if it is night or day, light or darkness, except for a crack of light coming through the closed blackout blind. She remembers where she is now, the taxi had brought them here, to this street lined with red-brick houses, each with an arched recessed doorway mirroring the attached house next to it, a double-story bay window at the gabled end.

Bugle, Paul's dog, had run out to greet them. His mother, Nuala, filled the space of the hallway wearing a bathrobe. She placed her hand on her expansive chest and scolded Paul for giving her a fright, coming in this hour of the morning without warning. If Sarah had thought it too easy coming through passport control, she hadn't expected the scrutiny this woman placed her under at the threshold to her house. She had scanned every inch of Sarah with interrogating eyes, not a single word said. Paul introduced her as his Irish friend he met in Boston.

After a terse breakfast, Paul brought her upstairs, to this room, his sister's bedroom.

"Vivienne," he explained even though she hadn't asked. "I hope you don't mind."

"I hope she doesn't mind."

"She's off travelling at the moment."

"When is she back?"

"God knows. When she runs out of money or runs out of a story to chase. She is an amateur journalist, though don't tell her that. She likes to think she is an investigative reporter, an intellect." He chuckles. "We might see her at Christmas. You never know with Viv."

The room is neat and ordered. There is a desk and a small bookcase full of books arranged by genre and filed alphabetically. The only books in the many houses where her family lived were the ones she had borrowed from the school's library.

The librarian in third grade had recognised something in Sarah she had wanted to reach. But the first books she gave her, about babysitting, and then about a pioneer girl, all went unread. The librarian tried again with *A Wrinkle in Time*, and with this she was hooked. By the time they had moved again, she had found a theme that kept her devouring novels: survival, resilience, and escape.

Here, from Vivienne's shelves, she chose an Irish author, *Light a Penny Candle*, and promptly fell asleep reading it. She is certain the central character, a timid evacuee, and the girl's mother were somehow wrapped in her dreams. She can feel the book buried now in the covers near her toes. She reaches for it and opens the page, aware only of birdsong in the tree outside her window, and a hammering in the background. She would like to stay in this room, continue reading, or maybe get out of bed and sit on the window ledge overlooking the garden. If only her thoughts could stay like this, blank, as though nothing is written on her own conscience, as though this is all happening to a character somewhere in a book she cannot put down.

There is a tapping at the door. Paul enters with a cup of tea balanced on a saucer. He brings it to her bedside. She lays the book on her chest and sits up against the pillows, taking the steaming cup from his hands. He lifts the blinds. The late afternoon is grey and dingy, threatening rain.

"Sorry about the noise. Mam has a builder in, converting our garage to a studio."

"It didn't wake me."

"I think they plan on banning me from the house," he laughs.

"I would, too—dragging a stranger home." She smiles, and then apologises. "Your mother doesn't seem happy I'm here."

"She's grand," he dismisses her concern. "Did you sleep well?"

She snuggles down into the covers.

"I slept like the dead."

"I warned you—one-hour nap, maximum. You'll never sleep tonight."

"Look, Paul," she begins.

She can't stay here with his family, his mother is uncomfortable with the idea, that is clear. She noticed, on their way from the airport, the landmarks on the left of a bay. Paul pointed out the Pigeon House, a power plant, two chimney stacks striped red and white like candy canes. Plumes of steam rose from their towers. The tide was in the bay, touching the sea wall in places. She will find this again, she thinks, follow the road until she reaches the city centre. If she can't find a hotel, or a hostel, she will buy a tent. She has been in worse situations before. She'll work it out. That is what Lou always told her—*You'll figure it out.* And despite him, she always did.

But Paul is holding up his hand.

"Are we all that bad?" he asks.

"No, sorry. I'm so—"

"Awkward? Yes you are—" He stretches his hand out to her and helps pull her up to sitting. "Now stop. Just accept a night or two of our hospitality, say *thank you very much* and come have dinner. If you still feel awkward, I'll drive you to the nearest park bench."

She laughs, then lifts the rectangular cookie he has placed on the side of her plate and nibbles the corner, washing it down with a sip of tea.

DOWNSTAIRS, THE FIRES ARE LIT. Bugle is asleep at his father's feet. Joseph, Paul's father, is warm and charming and invites her to sit by the fire. Nuala warms dinner, and though her tone still holds a degree of coldness, her disposition toward Sarah has thawed. Joseph is briefly interested in Sarah, in a polite way, but his focus turns to Paul, talk of Boston and the internship. Paul skirts around his father's questions and Sarah can see he is giving nothing away, about his future, or the fiancée who didn't work out—though he dodges his father more respectfully than he did his mother's questions at breakfast. Eventually, Joseph gives up trying to retrieve information from his son and their chatter turns to the building work in the garden. Sarah listens to them without taking any of it in, her shins and cheeks and hands grow rosy from the heat of the coal fire crackling in the grate.

THAT NIGHT IT TAKES HER a while to fall asleep, and when she does, she is startled awake to find her stepfather, Lou, has come to her bedside. She smells him first, a whiff of aftershave, senses his shape looming above her in her sleep. Once fully awake, it takes some time to slow her pounding heart, to convince herself he was only a dream.

A faint light washes across the sky. She is wide awake now. She reaches for her book, to keep her company, to settle her nerves, to begin to move her thoughts away from the trouble she left in the past. To move them away from Lou.

ChapStick

Oil on canvas

Put it back, Lou. *The pharmacist stands at the end of the aisle. I have seen him standing there for a while now, watching us. Watching Lou.*

Oh, hey Tom. *Lou doesn't look up from examining the box of pills in his hand.*

I am eight. The school has called Lou to come and collect me. My mother, Fleur, has been in bed, ever since the difficult birth. She was snorting lines of cocaine to ease the labour pains until Lou practically carried her to the car, brought her to the hospital. She is home now with my new baby sister, Léa. Fleur has stitches in her tummy which she tells me is what makes her sleep all day but I watch Lou give her more pills and he hands Léa to me. Léa is sweet and quiet and I wrap her in a blanket and rock her in my arms. I learn to make bottles. I don't want to go to school, I want to stay here and watch over my baby sister and my mother, but Lou says all he needs is for the police to show up at our door again, threatening social services.

The principal comes into the classroom after lunch today with a nit comb. He starts at the top of the classroom, works his way down, examining scalps through thick bifocals. I try not to itch my head. When he comes to me, he barely moves a strand before tapping me on the shoulder. All the children watch me cross the classroom. One of the Deborahs (there is a Deborah in every class, in every town, wearing lemon jeans and matching tops) lifts her brow at me, knowingly, she expected this of me.

I wait an hour in the secretary's office. The principal, who had been leaning over the secretary's desk, flees to his office when he spots Lou coming through the door. Lou curses the secretary out when she tries to give him instructions for treating my hair.

On the way home, he pulls into the pharmacy not to buy a bottle of the insecticide the secretary said would kill my chronic lice, but because my mother needs more pills.

Put it back, Lou, *Tom says again.*

What? *Lou is defensive.*

Put it back. *Tom stands in front of him, his arms crossed over his white coat, blocking Lou's progress down the aisle. Lou's hands are behind his back.*

Take it from me, Tom. *Lou sets his jaw in a smile.*

You can't keep robbing me blind, Lou. Put it back and I won't call the police.

Do it, Tom. *Lou smirks.* Call Bill. I'll give you his number. *Lou shoves something up the back of his leather jacket. Tom reaches for whatever he is stashing.*

Lou smiles as though congratulating Tom. Put your fucking hands on me, Tom, I'll sue you. *He steps aside, a can of baby formula falls to the floor. Tom sees me now, standing behind Lou.*

He looks shocked at first, then softens. Hey, little miss.

Lou walks away. Tom picks up the baby formula. Is this for the new baby? *I nod.* I'll get you a bag. *He smiles one of those fake smiles adults use on children. I follow him to the counter.*

I'm putting this on your tab, Lou. *Tom takes up a clipboard, his hands shake.* And I'm charging you for the two packets of Tylenol in your pocket.

In front of me is a box of ChapSticks. The kind the Deborahs keep in their pencil cases. I reach out and take one, slipping it into my back pocket. Tom puts the clipboard down and hands me the bag with my sister's formula.

Don't forget to say thank you to the nice man, *Lou tells me. He raises an eyebrow in triumph, there is a brightness to his eyes. He has seen what I have stolen.*

You have a good day, Tom. *Lou holds the door for me.*

In the car, I take the ChapStick out of my pocket, twist off the lid. I roll it up and roll it back down. I hate to use it, it is so new, hate to think of spoiling it. Lou leans against the car door, watching me. He shakes his head in disbelief.

Good one, kid. *He turns the key in the engine. He is still shaking his head, smiling to himself as we pull away.*

Soon after, Lou begins collecting me at least once a week from school. He drives me to a park, a beach, a shopping mall. A person, usually a man, a new one every time, appears with a treat, usually an ice-cream cone. The man sits down and hands me the cone and takes the backpack I have brought into his lap. I remember to tell the nice man thank you. *I learn to eat the ice cream quickly before the drips run down my hand. I learn not to ask what is in the bag. I watch the man rise from the bench taking the backpack with him. I try not to think about how much I would like to keep one of these backpacks one day. What a shame it is to give another one away. I think about this all the way home.*

The Artist

29 September 1990

Down across Sandymount Strand, the tide pulls out of the shore leaving welts of silver and black behind in small pools. On the horizon, beyond the vanishing point, container ships appear docked on dry sand. This is an illusion, of course. Sarah rotates an imaginative painting knife through the air as though cutting a swath across Howth Head. Bringing it around the bay, and behind her, a Martello tower, the houses forming a tidy line across the coast road. The light still stuns her, the way it settles on the landscape. She would like to paint these scenes.

It has been a month since she arrived in Ireland. It is calm here, predictable.

This past month she has felt herself letting her guard down, perhaps for the first time in her life. She feels minded. There is a structure, a civility, and though she hasn't quite figured out exactly what all the rules are or how to navigate around them yet—she knows there is an invisible architecture of sorts, a politeness, keeping everyone in check—and even though some days she senses Nuala would be happy if Sarah walked out her front door and never returned, she knows she would never vocalise this, as long as Paul wants her here.

Paul walks ahead, throwing a stick to Bugle. The dog brings it back, her paws matted with mud and water. Paul scratches behind her ears and throws the stick again. When he forgets himself, Sarah thinks, she can almost find him attractive. It isn't magnetic, the way it was with Eddie, but there could be something there, she imagines. She smiles and runs to catch up with him, to tell him about this idea she has—she wants to buy some paints and canvas, to paint the local scenery.

Terns hover above the water, diving for small fish. The beach is strewn with strands of kelp and decaying algae. A pair of oystercatchers pick at the sand. They walk past a girl building in the mud, a snowman of sorts out of silt, patting it with her spade. They stroll to the other end of the bay, find the path leading back toward the Pigeon House. They are passing the factory when Paul stops.

"What about you. I've kidnapped you all these weeks. What are your plans?" With Paul's encouragement and Joseph's kindness, it has been easy to stay. But she is certain she hears Nuala's instructions now in his words. She has overstayed her welcome.

"I probably should head off soon, shouldn't I? Travel."

"What's your hurry? We're happy if you stay around."

She is confused. Isn't that what he is asking? When she's leaving? But he is taking her hand, watching her, expectantly. She studies him. His square jaw, his small, sharp eyes. She leans in and kisses him on the mouth, and this, she thinks, perhaps is the answer to his question.

He pulls her into him and kisses her hard, like he has been waiting for this moment, and she is pleasantly surprised by the strength of the kiss. Bugle yaps at them from the path. They laugh. He slips his arm around her waist. It is awkward, walking like this, along the path leading back behind the factory, leading toward the Poolbeg Lighthouse.

"You could do worse than landing with us," he tells her. "You've fallen on your feet."

She agrees, she could do far worse. She has done so much worse. Before all this.

THE NIGHTS ARE CLOSING IN earlier suddenly and darkness has already fallen as Nuala and Joseph leave the house that evening, meeting friends for dinner in the village.

"Don't stay out too late," Paul calls to them from the kitchen. He is making dinner for Sarah. He won't let her inside to help, but she smells the garlic and hears sizzling in the pan.

"It smells delicious," she calls. "What can I do?"

He hands out a bottle of wine, already uncorked.

"Pour that," he instructs. She does, and takes a sip, then another. She touches one of the keys on the piano. Paul has come through the door with a steaming bowl of rice, he places it on the table.

"I like it here." She smiles at him. "You have a nice family."

He comes to her side, touches a key on the piano. Runs his hand up the scales, elegant in the way his fingers move.

"Play," she demands.

He laughs. She has unnerved him. He pulls out the bench and sits down, resting his hands over the keys, closing his eyes, centring himself. She waits for him to play, expecting a classical piece, pretentious—possibly boring—to emerge. She is surprised, then, when a wave of melancholic notes fills the room, threatening in the emotion they evoke. But as the mood of the piece changes, she becomes more interested in Paul, certain she is glimpsing a side of him she has not seen before.

As the music builds, she finds herself lost in his playing, thinking of the sun lighting on the steeples at the strand, the brilliance of the stone shining in platinum, its clearness wraps her, pulls her toward its centre. Overcome, she sits down beside him, feeling the movement of his body as the intensity of the piece reaches a crescendo, and then gradually subsides. He brings the song so gently down to its conclusion, his fingers still on the keys as the notes fade into the room. Her body is tuned to his playing, she follows this urge to place her head on his shoulder, to reach around and overlay her hands onto his. He turns his hands upward to take hers and she kisses the back of his neck where he is still bowed over the keys; she waits for him to touch her the way he has touched the keys.

He turns now, facing her on the bench, and the urge she felt quickly dissipates as his elegant fingers become twitchy and grabby at her breasts. He stands and pulls her to standing, reaching for the zip on her jeans, tugging at the waistband. She is surprised at how fast he is moving; and she wants to slow things down, tell him to stop, instruct him to play again, but her jeans have dropped to the floor, he is lifting her shirt, fumbling with her bra and it all feels a bit frantic and too late to change her mind as he takes her hand, leads her to the sofa.

"Wait," she tells him, pushing him gently backward. His look is expectant, she thinks of Bugle at the strand, poised, waiting for the stick to be thrown. She reaches up and takes off her shirt herself, unhitches her bra, hoping this act will reignite her desire. She lets them drop to the floor. He takes off his own shirt, throws it on top of her pile. His fingers feel mechanical on her skin.

"Lay down," he instructs. She perches on the sofa wishing she knew how to back out of this without offending him.

"Wait," he tells her. "Get up." He takes the throw blanket folded so neatly over the back of the sofa and spreads it across the cushions. The act has brought Nuala to both of their minds.

"Should we—" she is asking, not sure how to finish this sentence. If she doesn't sit back down, they won't have to move ahead.

"No. Right here," he says, anticipating she will want to go upstairs. "They won't be home for a while." His breathing is heavy, and he is moving toward her again.

Eddie floods her thoughts. The sense of wild abandonment she felt with her first lover, the freedom of undressing, moving toward one another. Now with Paul, all she wants is to repel him, slip out of his reach, retire upstairs to read her book. She knows it will upset him, though, if she has brought them this far and doesn't see it through. Her repulsion, she reasons, is probably less about Paul and more about what happened to her in Florida. This is the first time she has slept with anyone since the *incident*. She had pushed that away, or so she had thought, tried to forget. She can't help wondering if this is the way it will be, going forward, this sense of standing in front of Paul in the ill-fitting underwear she has stolen from his sister's dresser, feeling exposed. Violated.

She sits back down on the sofa now, folding her knees, clutching them to her breasts to cover herself. He is unbuttoning his pants, and she realises, with a sense of self-loathing, giving in to Paul is the quickest way out of this, and perhaps the easiest way to test if her enjoyment of sex is gone, taken from her, left behind in a Florida bungalow.

Paul is clinical, the way he opens her legs. Eddie was always careful to use a condom and she assumes Paul will pull back, put one on. But he doesn't. He enters her, unruly and undirected like a bird flown in through a window, wildly trying to escape, and as she begins to protest, he is finished. He collapses on top of her and lies there for a moment. When he stands, he covers her with the blanket, gathers up his clothes. He watches her face for a reaction, but she can't even pretend to smile.

"What?" he laughs, unsure of himself now.

He dresses, and when he sees she is still lying there, covering herself, waiting for him to leave, his confidence returns.

"Come on," he tells her, almost playful, trying to force the sense of closeness he felt at the piano. "Get up. Dinner's gone cold."

SHE IS UPSTAIRS IN BED when his parents return but she is not sleeping. She can hear the television and the key in the door, the murmurs of their conversation. When she hears footsteps on the stairs, she turns the bedside lamp off and pretends to sleep. Paul moves around in his room across the hall, she hears him opening a window, the creak of his bed, and when there is stillness, she moves back the covers, carefully steps onto the floorboards, switches on the lamp at Vivienne's desk.

She is overcome with thoughts of Eddie, he circles inside of her head, there is no relief as she listens to the sleeping house.

She turns to a blank page in a notebook, selects a pencil from the drawer, and begins to sketch. She is hesitant at first, feeling the danger of these scenes emerge under her pencil, as though she is opening a portal back to a time better forgotten. She starts with Eddie's face, the corner of his mouth, the way one side tugs up when he smiles as though he is permanently laughing at the world. Whatever this force that comes through her drawing—she forgets herself, forgets time—and in this forgetting, a remembering takes over. The night wraps itself around her once more. No malice emerges in these sketches, no sense her friend will have the capacity to betray her.

Summer Triangle

Gouache and ink on paper

Eddie stands against a chalkboard in this painting, mathematical figures floating off the surface behind him. Only his back pocket is in the frame. Eddie notices me the first morning in this new school, as I slide into the seat next to him in Algebra I, wearing my new dark jeans, a peek of cleavage cresting the line on the white blouse. The top was easy to steal, and the leather choker I slipped in my pocket with little effort at hiding the fact I was shoplifting. I feel Eddie studying me. We recognise something in each other. We are from the same caste of imposters.

Eddie couldn't give a fuck. He really. couldn't. give. a. fuck. Blame it on fetal alcohol syndrome, or the fact he is raised by a mother, a granny, and two much-older sisters. Who knows what conspires in any of us to make us what we are, but this first day Eddie is staring at me and Mr. Blackburn, an ex-Marine, senses he doesn't have the rapt attention of everyone in his classroom.

Gags, *Eddie is saying.*

I know I look cool in my eyeliner-ringed lids, looking sideways at him like I could care less.

Gags. *Eddie repeats, smiling dully, pointing to my last name on my notebook. His elbow rests on the desk, leaning on his open palm.*

I tell him my last name is French Canadian.

The girl in front of me turns and with a look, instructs me to shut up. Eddie curls his top lip and the girl flips him off and turns back around.

Mr. Blackburn teaches math and PE. He has the arrogance and physique for both. He writes an equation on the board. I know the answer before he has finished.

Edward.

He says Eddie's name with the expectation of failure. Eddie couldn't answer the equation last year, he won't do it this year, ever after onward until finally he gets to an age or a sense where he drops out of school altogether.

He takes his time walking to the board.

Failing algebra the first time wasn't enough? *Mr. Blackburn smirks. Eddie doesn't answer but doodles on the board, writing pi and square roots and not even attempting to answer the question at all.*

Back for more. *Mr. Blackburn chuckles to himself.*

Eddie's smile is sly and his words barely audible, something about Mr. Blackburn's wife also wanting more.

Eddie is hoisted up by the collar, Mr. Blackburn drags him to the classroom door and throws him against the lockers outside. Eddie's a big guy and anyone his size with his background would have at least taken the opportunity to pop a shot at this man, and truth told, all of us wish he would. But Eddie straightens his flannel, flicks up the collar, and strides back into class, smirking. He folds his large body back into the desk.

Mr. Blackburn composes himself outside in the hall.

The girl in front rolls her eyes and turns back around. Eddie winks at me. He waits for me in the parking lot after school.

Eddie has two settings. Slow motion, and sex. This is what catches me off guard. I have only seen the one side of Eddie, until now. The way he speaks, slow and surly, out of the corner of his mouth. The way his words trail behind a conversation like a toy pulled on a string.

I slip out my rooftop window, climb down the side of the house. Eddie and I drive around the back roads with a six-pack and cigarettes, listening to classic rock on the radio, passing cornfield after cornfield. We talk about everything and nothing. Though I don't like when he asks about Lou. Eddie used to come to the farm, hang out with Léa and me. She came out of her shell when he was around, he could make her laugh.

But Lou doesn't like Eddie. He blames him for robbing the crop of weed planted between the rows of corn. Someone dug it up in the middle of the night. He suspects Eddie, or the people Eddie works for. I laugh at Lou, at his paranoia, because Eddie doesn't work for anyone. He's just Eddie. But Lou is convinced, he's been our only visitor to the farm, and an acre and a half of weed is a lot of money.

Eddie pulls down an irrigation road, pulls his seat all the way back. He is so easy, there is a pull to him which I try to ignore. I am curious about sex, curious to see if it will do anything for that deep-down ache.

It starts when we both reach for the car's cigarette lighter at the same time, he pushes it in, catches my fingers on the way back, and some energy that has been simmering between us ignites.

His hands are all over me, pulling at my hips, moving into all the right places. But it is more than what he does. *It is how he feels doing it. His big droopy eyes close and his mouth opens as though he is touching something that burns him deeply, consumes him. His wanting is an invitation, his yearning allows me to want what I want, too.*

We meet almost every night, sip beer, and talk about getting the fuck out of this town. Then I follow him into the back seat, and we lift our heads to the stars, our hands and mouths all over one another, emptying ourselves into the heavens. Then we lie there, fingers twisting together, listening to the radio and the crickets, clocking the stars out the rear window. Watching the shift of the night sky.

The Builder

6 October 1990

Sarah trawls through Vivienne's closet looking for something decent to borrow, a blouse or a shirt, her own wardrobe feels shabby, but Paul's sister seems two sizes smaller than her. She takes an oversized sweater from a shelf, it will just about fit, she guesses. Someone is hammering outside her window. The builder has returned, no doubt to Nuala's exasperation with the timing of her oldest son arriving for the weekend, his family in tow.

Down in the garden, planks lie on the ground. The builder leans over a bench, hammering a loose arm back into place. Joseph chats with him, even while he works, and when the arm of the bench is secured, he stands and folds his long arms across his chest, the hammer held upright like a flag. Sarah hides behind the curtain, noticing his statuesque build, his copper jawline, short black hair. Every inch of him is beautiful. He laughs with his whole body, amused by Joseph, the timbre of which resounds across the garden and up to her window.

She pulls the sweater on over her T-shirt, pulls her own jeans on, checks her reflection in the mirror, she moves downstairs.

Paul's brother Simon and his family have arrived. They assemble, ceremoniously, around the table Nuala has set with salads, side plates for bread, real silverware, speaking in low voices, a formality the table setup seems to force.

"Paul's friend—" Nuala whispers.

"The fiancée?" Simon asks.

"No, I don't think so—you wouldn't be sure. He tells us nothing."

The talking ceases when Sarah enters the room. She considers retreating upstairs but Joseph has come through the kitchen door, encourages her to come inside and take a seat.

"Ah Sarah, you're as welcome as the sunshine. We've been summoned for lunch."

There are hugs and kisses all around for Joseph, though there is not a place set for Sarah. Simon's wife, Mary, jumps up and offers her seat. She is unmistakably pregnant, her belly rounding out beneath her dress. She moves slowly into the kitchen for another place setting, while Sarah reluctantly takes her seat; when she returns, Mary pulls up a stool beside her. There is much of a skirmish as Sarah insists she trade places with her so Mary can rest her back on the chair.

"Ah, you're too good, thank you, Sarah," she enthuses.

"I didn't know—Paul wasn't here," Nuala defends her oversight to no one in particular.

Mary is introducing her two young daughters now. They smile shyly at the stranger and Sarah tries not to think of her own little sister, who is about the same age.

Simon stands and reaches his hand across to shake hers.

"You're very welcome," he says. He reminds her of Joseph, more so than Paul.

There is much clicking of cutlery and little small talk while the rolls are buttered and salad plates passed around. Sarah is self-conscious eating with the entire family looking on, she knows they are curious about her. She has tried, but cannot manage, the elegant way they eat, scooping their bites onto the back of their forks. She is relieved when Nuala stands to clear the dishes and make tea, but Mary insists she'll do it.

"Sit down, Mrs. Byrne," Mary says, lifting Nuala's plate and scraping it onto her own. She reaches for Joseph's. The others begin to scrape their plates and hand them over to Mary. "Sarah and I will look after the tea."

Sarah is happy to help, but in the kitchen, she can see Mary has been tasked with a mission.

"Come here to me, what's the story?" She lifts her brow. "Are you with Paul, or what?"

"Paul?" She laughs, hoping the shame she feels at her mistake in sleeping with him doesn't show on her face. "No, we're friends."

Mary lets out a sigh of relief.

"Thanks be to God. I didn't think he was your type."

Sarah isn't sure what this means, but she thinks it is in her favour.

Mary is spooning cream onto the plates of rhubarb tart. The builder is tapping on the window beside the kitchen door. Seeing him up close, a jolt moves through Sarah. Mary lets him in, delighted to see him.

"Daithí!"

"My timing is good, yeah?"

"Ah, Daithí, couldn't be better. Come in. Come in."

He moves inside and he leans down to let Mary kiss his cheek.

"Are you well?" she asks, and you can see, she is genuinely wanting to know.

"Not a bother," he says. "How're you keeping?"

"You know yourself," she says, patting her bump. "I'm twice the woman I was when you last saw me, Daithí."

"Every woman counts, Mary." His smile is crooked. "You're looking well."

"Go away with that—"

"How's Simon? In there with his feet up?"

"Sure, it's only the tea," she reassures him. "Your one's at the hospital but Simon's inside. Go on in, I'll bring you a plate."

"Don't be bothering with me," he says, winking hello to Sarah, turning on the taps to wash his hands.

"That's Sarah. She's American."

"How ya, Sarah?" Daithí asks, smiling sideways at her. Sarah feels dazzled by his presence, at his attention turned toward her, and then she worries it shows.

He dries his hands carefully then holds one out in greeting. She takes it and feels the size of her own swallowed into his. "Are you well?"

She can only nod. He is already smiling at her, but there is a movement across his mouth, it is subtle, and Sarah feels he is looking carefully at her now, noticing more than what can be taken in at a glance. An intense warmth grows from within.

"She's Paul's friend."

"Is she now?"

"From Boston."

"Paul's friend from Boston," he repeats.

Sarah doesn't correct any of their assumptions.

She feels herself trying to adjust her body, so it is not obvious she is stunned, she leans on one hip, tilts her head sideways, absorbing the power in his voice, feeling every bit of his presence, his height, his focus tuned on her. She feels her own smile curving, turning crooked.

"That's Daithí," Mary tells her.

"Dah-hee?" she repeats, checking the pronunciation if only to be saying something, and instantly feels foolish.

"That's right," he says and leans back against the counter. He looks between Sarah and Mary. "Are you—" Making a little swirl indicating the ring finger.

"No, she's not," Mary answers urgently.

"I see."

"Apparently, there is no longer a—" Mary returns the gesture, indicating a wedding ring.

Daithí grins, knowingly.

"Go on in, say hello." Mary puts a teacup into Daithí's hand and spins him out of the kitchen. Sarah is sorry to see him go. She hears the family's chorus of greetings; smiles to hear him berate the party—a guest and a pregnant woman serving the tea.

Mary and Sarah turn to each other in the kitchen and laugh.

"Now, there's one worth catching, if you can," Mary says. She turns to the kettle, pours the boiling water into the pot.

Paul is coming home from work, arriving in the front door.

Sarah busies herself with rinsing dishes, attempting to recover herself from meeting Daithí.

"Is there something set aside for me?" he asks.

"Hello, yourself, Paul." Mary bristles, giving him the tray to take to the table. "And get yourself a plate," she tells him coldly.

Sarah helps Mary deliver the desserts.

Daithí's presence has lifted the formality of the room. Sarah sits back and listens to the banter crossing the table, weaving a web of conversation.

"Daithí is building the mews," Nuala announces.

"Are you staying on awhile, then?" Daithí asks Sarah.

"You embarrass us, Mam, I thought we agreed to call it a studio," Paul says.

"Sorry I embarrass you," Nuala says tersely.

"Are you planning on moving into it when it's finished?" Simon asks his brother.

"I am not."

"You ought to," Mary says, pouring out a hot round of tea. "Let your parents have their empty nest."

Paul gives his brother a look as though to tell him to keep his wife in line.

"You're a man, now," Simon antagonises, having a laugh with Mary.

"Shut up, Simon."

"I am, staying," Sarah answers Daithí. He hasn't looked away from her all this time. "In Dublin, anyway. I'm looking for a place."

"No need, no need," Joseph tells her.

Nuala purses her lips.

Paul sits back and folds his hands patiently. The morning after they had slept together, Sarah had told Paul she only wanted to be friends. He had smiled at her as though he would humour this suggestion and she knew he was still waiting for her to come around. She had been scouring the adverts ever since, hoping to find a job and a place to stay, but there didn't seem to be the same demand here for live-in nannies the way there had been in Boston. She didn't know what else she could do.

"It's actually going to be quite nice." Daithí turns to Paul. "Your mother's mews." Sarah can't quite tell if he is taunting Paul or standing up for Nuala, or both.

"Imagine, Nuala," Joseph says. "You didn't even know what a mews was when you came up from the country."

"I'm not from *the country*," Nuala says indignantly. "I'm from the town."

"Culchie," Paul laughs.

"Feck off, Paul," Mary scoffs.

"Here now, Mary, I'm only joking."

"Has he shown you around?" Simon wants to know.

"Some," Sarah says.

"Not enough," Nuala says.

"I've been working," Paul says defensively.

"You must come to Cork," Mary invites her.

"We're always extending the welcome, but we don't ever really mean it, do we now?" Nuala says, then seems surprised herself she has said this out loud.

Daithí suppresses his puzzlement with a laugh as though she is joking.

Mary looks at Nuala sideways.

"Well, *I* do mean it. You're very welcome," she assures Sarah.

"Thanks." Sarah gives her a grateful smile.

"I'm taking her to Gal-way." Paul mocks the way Sarah had pronounced the city, and Sarah reddens.

"Galway's a lovely city." Daithí says the correct pronunciation, eyeing Paul.

He accepts a hot drop of tea from Mary, pours a stream of milk.

"You're full-time based in Donegal now, I hear?" Simon asks Daithí.

"I am. I'm in Dublin more frequently than I want, though, these days."

"Do you get to speak much of the ole Gaeilge?"

"Of course," Daithí says. "It's surprising how much of it comes back."

"Daithí learned Irish the natural way," Simon explains. "The rest of us had it beaten into us at school."

Nuala clicks her tongue.

"No one was beaten."

"Daithí grew up in a Gaeltacht," Mary tells Sarah. "They speak only Irish where he lives."

"Do they really, though?" Paul asks, sceptical.

"They do," Daithí tells him. "If you speak decent Irish yourself."

Paul, irritated, mimics his words.

Joseph chuckles to himself.

"More Irish than the Irish themselves," he says absentmindedly.

Mary looks at Joseph, disapprovingly. Simon picks up on her look.

"Daithí *is* Irish, Da."

Daithí's mouth curls into a diplomatic smile. He blinks patiently at Joseph.

Joseph chuckles.

"Of course he is," Nuala scolds.

"When will you head back?" Simon asks.

"I'll finish the job here this weekend. Then we've a few nights at the beach down in Wicklow before I return for the winter."

"Wintering in Donegal," Mary says dreamily. "Sounds lovely."

"Beach?" Paul asks suspiciously. "Who's *we*?"

Daithí looks caught out.

"Gus and Liamo, some of the girls. You know yourself. You coming?"

"Not that I'm aware," Paul says, annoyed.

Mary looks at Simon, amused.

"It's pretty late in the season, isn't it?"

"We're promised a warm spell." Daithí is telling Sarah this, even though it is the answer to Paul's question.

"Go, Paul," Nuala says. "That part of the coast is gorgeous, you'd love it," she says to Sarah. "Go on, Paul, bring your American friend."

"Is the accommodation booked?"

"Yes—" Daithí tells him tentatively.

Paul puts his fork down with a clatter.

"Are you not going to tell me?"

"Camping in the dunes."

"Not my thing," Paul scuffs.

"Suit yourself," Daithí says.

"Well, maybe you'd like to go, Sarah?" Mary asks, devilment in her voice. "Is that your kind of thing?"

"I'd love it. I'm up for anything, really," Sarah says.

"There you go." Mary is sitting close enough to elbow Sarah. "You go, Sarah, and then Paul can spend the weekend doing the things that suit him."

Paul stiffens.

"Paul should focus on his internship," Nuala suggests.

"You're welcome to come," Daithí tells her. She has this sense of intense warmth when he looks at her like this. "There's a good crowd. Some of the girls will have room in their tent."

"Thank you."

Mary presses her leg into Sarah's underneath the table. Sarah tries to keep from smiling.

"Yeah, we'll see," Paul says. "It would have been nice if I had heard about it earlier."

Daithí speaks to Sarah then.

"I can swing by for you, give you a lift."

"No need, I'll be bringing her." Paul bristles.

Mary smothers a giggle.

Daithí drinks his last slug of tea, smiling behind the mug. He rises, biting his lower lip to conceal the smile.

"That was lovely, thank you," he says to Nuala. "Back to work." He brings his plate and mug with him to the kitchen.

"Isn't he gorgeous?" Mary whispers to Sarah once they see him pass by the window.

"Mary! Not you too." Simon pretends to be affronted.

"It's Daithí," she teases. "It's always been Daithí. I'm a little bit in love, to be honest."

"Bit of a lady's man," Simon explains.

"Bit of a loser," Paul says.

"Ah, here," Mary says.

You have no idea what a loser is, Sarah thinks.

"He's just a builder."

"He isn't *just a builder*, he's a craftsman. An artisan," Mary says.

Simon rolls his eyes playfully.

"You'd do anything for cabinetry," he accuses his wife. Sarah can't help but feel they are putting on a little show for her benefit.

"Daithí's a carpenter, by trade," Simon explains.

"I wish I married a carpenter." Mary frowns.

"I wish *I* married a carpenter!" Simon raps her on the wrist with his teaspoon.

"Jesus was a carpenter," Joseph says.

They all laugh.

"Exactly," Simon says.

"Jesus wept," Paul says.

"Don't blaspheme," Nuala scolds.

"Didn't I turn you a bowl once?" Simon asks Mary.

She rolls her eyes.

"He spent two years in New York City, working on the old brownstones."

"He's after telling me he's restoring a distillery in Leitrim and an old mill in Sligo," Joseph adds.

"He can turn his hand to anything, all right. His house in Donegal will be beautiful. He's a restoration specialist."

"Don't mind them," Paul tells her. "He's a builder."

The others protest his throwaway remark. But he defends himself.

"Do you know what he is capable of? He could have studied medicine; his points were higher than mine."

"And?" Mary asks.

"And he goes and throws it away on this builder's course in Donegal."

"Now, I wouldn't be running down the trades," Joseph warns.

"So what?" asks Mary.

"If he is happy, it isn't wasted," Simon says. "The quiet life suits Daithí."

"We'd all like the quiet life," Paul sneers.

"Would we, now?" asks Mary.

"So, you're going camping, then?" Simon laughs at his brother.

"I didn't say we'd go for certain. Maybe we'll go west, instead?" He asks this question in Sarah's direction. "A hotel city break?"

"I think I'd like to see this coastline," Sarah presses.

"You can't have the car, Paul, I need it," Nuala tells him.

"You could take the Morris Minor," Joseph volunteers.

"Deadly!" Mary says.

"Impractical," Paul says.

"Maybe you should let Daithí collect Sarah," Nuala suggests.

Mary gives a robust agreement.

Paul sighs.

"I guess we're going camping."

One by one, after the lunch is cleared, the men follow Daithí outside. They stand in the sunshine, watching him work. Simon has pulled a table out of the garden shed at Mary's insistence. She has brought paint boxes of watercolours, brushes and paper. When Mary calls to the girls, who are leading Sarah around the garden, showing her where the fairies hide in the rosebushes, they pull her by the hand, insist she sit with them at the little table while they paint.

Sarah admires the flowers they draw. They hand her a brush and insist she make a picture, too. Upstairs, inside one of Vivienne's notebooks, are the scenes she drew of Eddie. Every night for the past week, she has sketched late into the night. When she had exhausted him as a subject, and his car and the summer triangle, she had started drawing scenes of her art teacher, Mrs. Jones. She drew her classroom, Eddie with his chin in his hand, his elbow propped on the desk watching her draw. Sarah drew into the darkest part of these nights, until the gold of sunrise streaked the sky, until she was nearly falling asleep at the desk. She hasn't lost the touch, she thinks.

The girls watch her with great anticipation as she lifts a brush, dips it into the water, and begins.

Yams

Oil on board

Not all teachers find Eddie threatening. Mrs. Jones, or JezaBelle, that's what the art teacher—somewhat inappropriately— tells us to call her when other adults aren't in earshot—perches on the edge of her desk in a flowy skirt, high-heeled boots, and bangles rattling up her arms, her red curly hair ratted out to here. She is one of the smallest figures in school, she could be mistaken for a pupil, and by far the most popular teacher with the students.

Up close, her teenager resemblance ends. She is weathered and thin and her fuchsia lipstick does nothing for her nicotine-stained teeth. What is still intact, however, is the essence of the young woman she brags she once was. Whatever that spark, it remains—the spark that made every important Midwest professor and visiting artistic zealot paint her into their portraits, according to herself.

She tells us we'll visit the Art Institute in Chicago and find the paintings that feature her, all splayed in her glory. Eddie gives an involuntary snort of laughter when she says this, which only encourages her.

But, on the other side of things, she encourages me to develop concepts within my paintings, and she takes me seriously. She says I bring raw sexuality to the page. I point out I am drawing still life: a bowl of red apples sitting on a blue stool.

Doesn't matter, *she says.* It's there. The inexplicable. The je ne sais quoi, *she titters, and I roll my eyes at Eddie.*

Gags has no natural talent, *she says to the class.* Natural talent doesn't exist—in anybody, *she explains.* Gags is simply good at looking, paying attention, and then trusting what she sees.

And something about this is right.

She brings her finger down my jawline as though she is contemplating something, measuring me for some other use—and I wonder if Eddie has told her about our sex life.

At the end of the term our assignment is a collage, and she is our muse. Most of the class arrives with images that flatter—they render her in petals, arrangements of diamantes reinstating her youth. Acts of adoration piled high on the altar of her desk.

My idea comes to me in the vegetable section of the supermarket. I buy yams and peel them, I cut small shapes from the peel with a razor blade Lou uses to cut his lines of cocaine. I let the peel wither and crack, then I arrange it, leaving negative spaces and textures to suggest a chin, cheekbones, unflattering neckline, a mouth I paint in a fuchsia lipstick I have stolen from the pharmacy.

I lay the piece in front of her, awaiting her critique.

She studies it and says nothing at first. When she looks up at me, she has narrowed her eyes.

You are vicious, *she whispers with genuine excitement.* Vicious. Like the Greats.

In the Garden

6 October 1990

Sarah draws the apple tree in front of her, the girls cry out when an exotic bird perched in the branches emerges from beneath her brush. They abandon their own pages and begin to instruct her on what to draw. The girls take charge of each new piece she finishes, setting them on the lawn to dry, charging her with a fresh page, watching with anticipation.

Sarah picks up a pencil now and boxes out the garden scene in front of her. She includes the lawn, the brick wall Daithí has begun to build, a ladder. And there is Daithí, fitting a board onto the sawhorse, billowing clouds above the garage.

Paul is moving in and out of the shed near the side passage, pulling objects out onto the lawn. He has pulled out a camping lantern, some mats, a gas cooker, strewing them across the lawn.

"What are you doing, Paul?" Mary comes to the back door, watching him.

"What does it look like?"

"Mammy! Look!" the girls call to Mary.

Mary picks up the girls' abandoned pages, praising their drawings.

"Not ours—" they tell her. They point to the mini exhibition they have created with Sarah's drying pages. By now, Sarah has finished the sketch of the garden, dabbing sparse colour across the scene. While it is drying, she takes a new page, draws the curve of Daithí in close-up, climbing the ladder. Sketching in his flannel shirt, the pockets of his cargo pants, his soft brown eyes.

"Wow," Mary whispers under her breath. "It's as good as a picture book. You're an artist."

Simon is helping Paul pull out camping chairs. Mary calls them over.

"Draw me, draw me," both the girls cry.

"You've got to get into the scene," Mary tells them. "Silly little feckers, go play in the garden." Sarah quickly sketches them running between the late stalks of sunflowers. The youngest girl climbs into the bough of the apple tree and hangs upside down. Sarah captures her quickly with little effort.

"Can I keep these?" Mary asks. "I'll frame them!"

"Of course."

Paul comes over now and is watching her draw.

Nuala has finished tidying the kitchen and joins them in the garden.

"Look at this," Simon calls to his mother.

Nuala reluctantly moves to the table. She examines the drawings. Gives her verdict.

"Lovely."

Joseph wanders over now, too, to see what the fuss is about. He doesn't comment. Instead, he goes into the garage. He returns with an old, battered easel, aged with cracking, faded paint. He sets it up in the grass.

"That belonged to my mother, God rest her," he says. "She loved painting in this garden."

Sarah is touched by his gesture.

"This garden?"

"Right here where she reared me and my six brothers and sisters. And she found little time for her craft," he tells her. "But when she did, she was like a magician. The roses above the mantel are her very own. You are welcome to the easel," he tells her.

"You're giving it to her?" Simon asks jealously.

Mary shoots him a look.

"Not your mother's easel!" Nuala says, and her tone is like nails on a chalkboard.

"Borrow it—as long as you'd like," Joseph corrects himself.

"Aw, that is lovely," Mary says.

"Thank you," Sarah tells him. "I've got to get proper paint first."

"It's in hand," Paul says, full of his own self-importance in the matter. "First thing Monday morning."

"Coffee, Daithí?" Nuala calls.

"I'll have coffee, Mam," Paul says.

"You might make it yourself," she tells him tersely.

"Are you in art college?" Simon asks. A cloud comes over the garden.

"It's spitting," Mary calls to the girls. "Tidy up, now."

Before Sarah can answer Simon's question, Paul interjects.

"She studied in Boston."

"Emerson?" Simon asks.

"MassArt," Paul replies.

Sarah doesn't confirm this, she doesn't counter his untruth, either. She feels it may even bring her up in Nuala's esteem, in all their esteem. Paul returns to his task, pulling the equipment off the lawn, bringing it to the Morris Minor which he moved from the back lane into the driveway. Simon helps him. The girls have run off to hang their paintings on their grandmother's fridge. Sarah tidies the little table, closing the paint box, swirling the brushes in the water.

Daithí is packing up for the day. He comes up the path. Joseph beckons him over to look at her paintings, and then moves back inside the house.

Daithí stands in front of Sarah. They are alone in the garden.

He turns one of the drawings around. It is speckled with drops of rain. "There I am," he says, surprised.

She can feel the heat on her cheeks.

"I couldn't hardly ask you to get out of my way."

"Fair enough."

He picks up the image of himself on the ladder.

"I enhanced that one, to flatter your features."

He bites his lip, amused. He looks at her. She doesn't break his gaze.

His words are barely audible.

"Will you come? To the beach—"

She nods.

"I'm glad."

"Me too," she mouths.

He lays the image on the table and taps it once, his crooked smile turning up, revealing a dimple on his cheek.

He leaves out the side gate, and she hears him calling to Paul.

"You're getting out the wheels for the coast?"

"It has to be done."

"Does it?" Daithí asks.

Sarah lifts her paintings off the table, she grabs the easel from the garden, carrying it under her arm, dragging it into the conservatory, just as the heavens open and it begins to pour.

Becoming Saoirse

12–13 October 1990

The weather is mild and the sun shines out of the bluest sky when they pull out of Sandymount and drive south down the coast road. The Morris Minor is fumy and loud, but Sarah is glad to be driving out of Dublin. They wind through small coastal towns, passing large houses overlooking the sea. Paul tells her which rock stars live where along the coast road.

Sarah is carsick by the time they reach Bray, and there is still a distance to go. On the other side of Greystones, they pull over so she can throw up on the side of the road. They aren't long moving again before the car begins to thump, everything vibrating.

"Shite." Paul hits the dashboard. "What now?"

He pulls over and inspects a flat tyre. It takes him some time to work out how to pull the jack out of the boot, hoist the car, release the nuts. She has done this before, had to do it for Lou, and she offers to help, but Paul is strained when he tells her to let him think—so she walks away, sits on the edge of the road, cursing herself for not borrowing a second tent.

At the seafront, the warmth of the day has drawn families from Dublin. They converge at either end of the beach in front of the lifeguard shacks. The middle of the strand is empty apart from figures kicking a football. Paul sets out toward them, lugging the camping equipment. Sarah's shoes are full of sand by the time they reach the lads.

"How's the form, Paul?" one of the men asks as they approach.

"Where are the others?" Paul asks tersely.

"Nice to see you, too," the man says and kicks the ball back toward his friend, nodding up into the dunes behind him.

Several tents are dotted haphazardly around the bottom of a bowl-shaped dome. Hummocks of grass at the top of the dune cliff wave in the stiffening breeze, but here in this slope of land, there is shelter from the wind. A group of young women cluster together on piles of blankets as though sitting on nests in the sand. A woman with sleek dark hair paints her nails.

"You'll get sand in your manicure," a woman with blond hair points out.

"Deadly. Glitter, like."

They turn when Paul comes down the trail, bringing their attention to Sarah, looking her over, giving one another the eyes. Daithí sits a short distance from them on his own, strumming a guitar, he nods to Paul and Sarah.

"Daithí," Paul acknowledges sternly.

"Come over here, Daithí, and give us a song," the nail painter demands, he smiles and continues playing.

Paul walks around inspecting tents, noticing their anchor points are secured with bricks and large rocks.

"Great," he complains. "No one told me to bring bricks."

"Did no one tell you there'd be sand?" the blond woman asks innocently.

"Sorry for ya," the nail painter says flatly.

He ignores them and searches for a site to pitch, away from the others. He commands Sarah to hold this pole, no—*push it this way, you're bending it, clip it—clip it*. His voice rises and the others look over toward them.

Liam introduces himself, shaking Sarah's hand. They chat about the weather, which part of America she is from, how she is getting on at the Byrnes' house—they both pretend to ignore the quiet fit Paul is throwing, trying to wrestle the fly sheet onto the tent.

"I better help," he says. "Emily," he calls. "Come say hello to Sarah."

"I'm painting me nails," Emily calls back. "Tell her to come here." Liam nudges his head in their direction, encouraging her, and she strays over, beginning to wish she had gone west instead.

"Hey," Sarah says.

"How ya?" Emily asks, squinting up at her, the sun bright in her eyes.

"Are you well?" a woman who introduces herself as Sinead asks, but she doesn't wait for an answer before she returns to her conversation with Emily. Sarah shifts from one foot to the other, looks out to the sea, half smiling as though she is content, her cheekbones strain with the forcedness. She looks back to Paul who is searching, and failing, to find something heavy to tie down the tent.

A sandy trail leads up through the undergrowth, into the dunes. Sarah steps out of her runners, the soft grains of sand pack like brown sugar underfoot, and she slips away, rising with the trail until she is standing on a cliff, looking out over the sea, surveying the expanse of rolling dunes. The sun is moving in behind a cluster of gathering clouds, not foreboding or threatening, but soft and marbled with a hue of lavender. The sea moves like silk underneath a changing sky, capturing a patch of sunshine out beyond the distant cloud, flowing with steel and lavender where it turns and rolls onto the shore. Around her, the seagrass rustles in the wind and the burnt oranges of autumn seep into stalks of ragwort and fern. She closes her eyes against the beauty of it all.

There is a swish in the undergrowth. Daithí has put his guitar aside and followed her up the trail.

"You all right?" he asks.

"Long drive," she says, relieved someone is talking to her. Thrilled it is him.

"I don't doubt it." They smile easily, understanding one another.

"It's beautiful," she says, turning back to the vista. "Worth the drive."

He comes up alongside her and they stand in silence, absorbing the coastline.

"Will you paint this?" he asks after some time.

"I'd like to. I try, but lately, louder, more demanding subjects get my attention," she tries to explain.

He is surprised, intrigued by the process she describes.

"You don't choose, it chooses you?"

"Something like that." She nods, she doesn't quite understand it herself.

"That's . . ." He makes a gesture of awe. "Surprising."

She is moving her finger, at this moment, at her side, sketching the line of his face against the expanse of the sky.

"Is it?"

They smile at one another self-consciously.

He makes a gesture suddenly, as though he has forgotten his manners. "You must be famished. Will you have lunch?"

"I will," she says.

"The offerings aren't amazing," he laughs. "Sausages."

"I'll eat anything," she says, grateful. "I don't mind."

"Come on, I'll introduce you properly. The girls can be awkward at first, but they'll warm up."

The sizzling juices from the cooking meat are tantalizing, and it tastes even better on an empty stomach. The women drag their blankets over, Emily blowing on her nails as she walks. They talk about outfits, and weddings, hat rental, fascinators. They never seem to run out of things to discuss, and though Sarah doesn't have anything to say about these matters, they nod toward her, including her this way, and she doesn't feel awkward now. She knows she has Daithí to thank for helping her cross this line.

Behind her, something is happening. Sinead is hissing with laughter, and Emily covers her eyes. Paul has come out of the tent wearing a Speedo. Sarah, when she turns and sees him, is clutched with embarrassment.

"Oh. My. God." She stares at the fire and whispers under her breath. Emily grabs her hand in solidarity, and they shake with hidden laughter.

"I don't know where to look," Sinead whispers.

"Are you coming?" Paul calls to Sarah. She pretends not to hear.

"Can I borrow your nail polish?" she quickly asks Sinead.

"Work away."

"Come for a swim."

"I think he is waiting for you," Emily warns.

Sarah concentrates on painting her thumbnail, refusing to turn. She can feel the heat in her neck, her ears. The girls suppress their giggles, but they come out like hisses. Daithí holds a neutral face, but she can tell he is amused, more so at the women's reaction.

Paul is hovering now, waiting.

"She's eating—" Emily calls.

"—sausages," Sinead adds.

The women can no longer contain themselves, their suppressed laughter bursts, ringing out across the dunes.

"Seriously?" Paul asks, and Sarah knows she will hear it later. He marches toward the water on his own, towel in hand.

DAITHÍ KEEPS BEES IN DONEGAL, that is what Emily is telling her.

"Isn't that lovely?" Sinead asks.

"It's not right." A young man has joined them, squatting on a camp stool.

"What do you mean *it's not right*?" Sinead challenges.

"It's animal exploitation."

Emily sucks in her breath.

"Don't be ludicrous," Sinead says. "Bees make honey for us."

"Bees make honey to feed their brood, you eejit."

Emily calls on Daithí to dispute the facts but he only smiles. He has returned to strumming the guitar.

THE EASY CHATTER OF THE afternoon has given way to a more intense, beer-fuelled debate, a single conversation with many opinions that seem to be leading to the same conclusion, but Sarah doesn't have the background to know for certain. What she is surprised to find, though, is there is no option for divorce in this country.

"That's right," Gus assures her. "We've no get-out clause."

"Beware," Emily whispers, looking sideways at Paul, who has returned from his swim and is standing at the edge of the fire circle, seemingly making a point of avoiding Sarah.

"That's why we all wait until we're nearly forty to marry, half the time served—" One of the women laughs.

"How can this even be—" Sarah thinks aloud, she is beginning to feel the buzz off the cans they offer her.

Paul rolls his eyes at her and tuts as though she is embarrassing him.

She ignores him. Divorce is such a commonplace thing in America, she thinks, it is a pity her mother and Lou never opted out of each other, though she supposed they had never even married. They had opted out of parenting instead.

"Is it true they have drive-through divorce in America?" someone asks her. She shrugs.

"Of course they do!"

"Careful where you tie the knot."

"Constitutional ban," Gus continues to explain. "Welcome to Holy Catholic Ireland. Step inside, leave your condoms at the door."

"At least we've that one sorted," Sinead says.

"Five years ago you couldn't buy condoms without a prescription," Gus tells her.

"In fairness, it wasn't impossible to obtain them," Paul interjects.

"Just impossible to use them, right, mate?" the bee man jokes. Laughter echoes across the dunes and Paul forces a laugh, crosses his arms, looks at Sarah. She looks down at the sand.

"That's not the point," Emily argues with Paul. "Ireland is infantile. As a woman, I am treated like a child. It is 1990, for God's sake, and I still can't divorce you, I am forced to have your babies—"

"Ireland needs to grow up," Sinead agrees.

"As a medical professional," Paul interjects, trying to sound measured, "my opinion—"

"Fuck off—Paul," Sinead interrupts. Daithí and Sarah exchange amused smiles.

"No need for that, Sinead," Paul snips. "I'm saying as a medical professional—"

"Red flag," Emily whispers beside her. Sarah wants to tell her she has nothing to worry about where Paul is concerned. She cringes though, feeling deeply embarrassed she has slept with him, wishing she had been more forceful in her *no*.

"A medical *student*," one of the men corrects Paul.

"You doubt I'll earn my title—"

"This isn't about you, it's about fundamental human rights."

"In my opinion, I question the right—" Paul begins.

Sinead cuts him off.

"Also speaking as a medical *student*, Paul, I beg you—don't have an opinion on my body."

"Fine. It's not an opinion. It's the Eighth Amendment—"

There are groans around the fire circle.

"Weren't you out canvassing with Mammy and Daddy in '83?"

"Jaysus—" someone calls to the sky.

"No wonder another of your *fiancées* didn't work out."

"That's a bit unfair, Sinead," Liam defends Paul.

"Be careful." Emily leans into Sarah, continuing to coach her. "You know he's been engaged twice?"

"My point is—"

"Your point, my body—"

The ethical bee man interjects.

"Look, mate, we're exporting our own questions abroad—"

"Life is life." Paul is shaking his head vigorously.

"Scarlet for ya," Sinead tells him.

Daithí has changed the capo, he picks up the tempo.

Dissention in the group turns to clapping. The chords echo through the dunes. Suddenly, all around, everyone is singing about power and life. The tune is catchy.

Paul is the only one not joining in.

"I was making a point." His persistence annoys Sarah. The singing swallows his argument. She claps along, delighted by the humour of it all.

Emily puts her arm around her shoulder, and Sinead sits down on her other side, swaying.

When the song is over, Paul is poised ready to continue arguing, but Daithí moves one song into the next without a pause. Liam has picked up a mandolin and sings the harmonies. They have sung these songs before, together for many years.

When there is a lull, Paul erupts from across the fire circle.

"Where did your own mother stand—"

"Jesus Christ," Gus mutters.

Daithí half smiles.

"Fuck's sake, Paul," Sinead says. "Let it go."

"Can you not say?" He is staring intently at Daithí, challenging him. "You know what I'm asking—" Paul says confidently.

"I don't," Daithí says, shaking his head, biting his lip. Sarah can see his confusion is genuine, and she can also feel Paul's frustration building.

The women are ferocious in protecting Daithí from whatever he is insinuating.

"What the fuck, Paul?"

"Shut the fuck up."

Kicked sand skitters toward Paul, landing in his eye, he wipes it, continuing to draw out Daithí, while the others argue him down.

It only takes Daithí putting up a hand for quiet.

"I'm not sure what you're on about, mate. Do you want my mother's medical opinion, or is your point she was unwed? Or that my father is Black? Or foreign?"

"Why don't you just say it—you're a racist, misogynistic git?" the bee man challenges Paul.

"Forget him, he's winding you up."

"No surprises there."

"That was a long time ago—" Paul defends.

"Fair—" Daithí agrees.

"I didn't know what it meant—" Paul isn't doing himself any favours, labouring some point.

"You really are an arsehole," Sinead tells him.

"Talk about calling names, Sinead. Can't I make a point?"

"We're just not sure what point you're making there, mate," Liam chimes in.

Sarah watches Daithí's fingers move along the fretboard as he picks out individual notes on the strings. The others have turned from Paul now, there is a sigh of approval at the haunting air Daithí has begun to play, others shush the last of the talkers.

"Go on, Sinead," Daithí says gently.

And into this quiet, Sinead begins a song of parting and loss; words so vivid they tighten the muscles around Sarah's throat. It is impossible not to think of her sister, of the things she has left behind, all she has lost.

"You're shivering," Emily whispers, rubbing her arm. She brings a blanket over her shoulders. Sarah is relieved when the song ends and the amphitheatre of sand fills with a chorus of conversation and she can breathe again. She hasn't noticed, until now, Paul has left the fire.

The sky darkens and more friends arrive with instruments: a bodhrán, accordions, uilleann pipes, even a trumpet, and the music continues without ceasing while the embers fly into the night.

Sarah is feeling quite drunk now. She watches Daithí's hands, he catches her eye as he sings. When she stands the whole of the dunes shift underfoot and she falls back to the ground, laughing. She thinks she better go to bed.

Paul is awake when she enters, but he is not sleeping.

"Enjoying yourself?" he asks, and she knows by his tone he is not waiting for an answer. She rummages around for her sleeping bag in the dark. It is still in the sack. She fumbles with the string but cannot loosen the knot.

"At my expense," he continues.

"Stop—Paul. Everyone is having fun."

He springs up, she can feel him near her face, a looming presence in the darkness.

"*Everyone* didn't beg me to come down here and then flirt with my mates."

"Jesus, Paul, calm down."

"*Pól*, I told you my fecking name is Pól."

She is frightened now, by the quietness of his rage. The emotions strangled just below an audible register, like a pulse flowing toward her, the way he whispers so only she can hear.

"And what should I call *you*?" he hisses.

She is uncertain where this is leading.

"Sarah," she says timidly. "Look, let's just go to sleep. You're tired." He ignores her plea.

"Oh yes, Sarah the Paddy, Sarah from Ireland," he laughs cruelly. "Is that who *you* really are?"

A spike of fear paralyses her. She blinks at his awful smile, his eyebrows raised, waiting for an answer he thinks he already knows.

She takes her sleeping bag, moves toward the door.

"Wait," he says, and some of the steam goes out of his rage.

"I'm going to sleep with the girls," she whispers.

His anger drains, he is softer now.

"No, come back. I'm sorry. I'm just tired. And a little upset, if I'm being honest. I thought you came here with me."

She hesitates, seeing things from his angle, then cringes to realise she has embarrassed him in front of his friends. For a moment she takes pity on him.

"I'm sorry, Paul. I've told you already—we're only friends."

He takes the sleeping bag from her. Unknots the string and pulls it out.

"You smell like booze," he taunts.

He lays her bag on the ground, and she is relieved when he slips into his own and turns away. She lies down, shivering, wide awake. Her buzz has worn off, but now she feels the spin of the earth underneath her back. It is the drink she has taken, she reminds herself, the change in Paul, it must be her own skewed perception, her own paranoia. And yet, a recognition is rising inside of her. She has travelled this path before. And she knows very well, from here there is no easy departure.

Sarah wakes to the sound of the waves. The air in the tent is stale and smells of breath and beer. Her head is pounding. Paul is still sleeping. She unzips the tent carefully hoping not to wake him. A cool breeze is fresh on her skin. Liam and Emily have emerged and are sitting at the embers of last night's bonfire, sharing a blanket, speaking in whispers. She wonders if they ever even went to bed. Daithí stands in his jeans, no shirt, barefooted at the entrance to his tent, rotating his shoulder blades, stretching his arms. He smiles when he sees her head poking out of the tent. Sarah tries not to notice the shape of his torso, the muscles of his arms, the warm colour of his chest.

"Morning swim?" he suggests.

The group sidestep in a line down the dunes and onto the beach. The retreating tide has left driftwood and shells scattered on the smooth sand at the water's edge. It is cleaner here than Sandymount Strand. Gannets dive into the waves, impaling their breakfast on sharp beaks. The beach is empty apart from these morning swimmers. Daithí is first to step out of his jeans, he walks into the water wearing boxers, dives into a wave and swims out; Liam and Gus follow suit. Sinead and Emily have waded in up to their thighs, they cling to one another, shrieking from the shock of the cold on their skin. Sarah shimmies out of her jeans, abandoning them in a pile on the sand. She braces herself and tip toes out into the water.

By late morning, small crowds are arriving to enjoy the last of the autumn sun. Daithí has drifted away. She watched him follow a trail above, disappearing into the dunes. Emily brings out a pint of vodka, a carton of tomato juice, Sinead squeezes slices of lemon into their drinks. They sit in the sun, down on the beach, watching the others volley a ball.

"Someone has to go to the shops," Emily calls to them, holding the empty vodka bottle upside down.

"Not us," Liam tells her, dodging a ball. "We're still pissed from last night."

"Paul's on call," Sarah volunteers.

He shoots her a warning look.

"Are you?" Liam asks.

"Yeah, afraid so."

"Well, you drew the short straw, my friend. Off you go!"

They abandon the game and gather around him, giving Paul their drink orders.

"Don't forget charcoal," Gus reminds him.

"Sure."

Paul is in good humour today, a decent night sleep sorted him out, he keeps telling everyone. Recovering from the stress of rotations.

"I'm on rotations, too," Sinead reminds him. "But I don't go around offending anyone—"

"Let it go," Liam tells her gently.

"And grab some crisps," Emily insists.

"Right, fine. Ready?" Paul asks Sarah.

Sarah shakes her head.

"I'll stay."

He looks surprised, but if he is angry, he recovers quickly. Sarah hopes his beeper will go off, calling him back to Dublin.

"You sure you won't come?" he asks.

"Go on, don't ruin her fun, too. She's not on call," Sinead harasses him.

"I'll go," Gus volunteers.

"Good man, Gus," Liam tells him.

It is chilly and some of the party have scattered to look for firewood. Sarah walks along the strand, toward the headland at the far end of the beach. She stops to examine a red frond of seaweed, a piece of driftwood lies nearby, bleached from the sun. When she looks up Daithí is coming toward her from the opposite direction.

"Heading this way?" he asks and falls into step beside her. They continue along toward the headland in the distance, walking closer, the waves swivel onto the shore, moving like a satin veil, leaving a lace of foam along the sand.

Farther down the strand, he stops and pulls something clean of seaweed, swirls it in the receding wave, it is a lens-shaped capsule, translucent brown with winding tendrils. He brushes it off with his thumb. Stretches it out toward her.

"Mermaid's purse."

"Hmmm." She smiles, and takes it. Their fingertips touch. There is a joy spreading through her, she feels it could open like a chasm and pull her into its centre.

"Shark's egg case," he explains. She watches his mouth when he says this. His eyes. The sand at the corner of his temple.

"Daithí," she says. Their fingers are interlacing now. He moves slowly up her wrist, traces her mouth. She touches her fingertips to his chest. His friends are silhouettes moving in the distance, high up in the dunes. He turns to watch them.

"Daithí." She says his name again.

He turns back, full in thought, and half smiles at her.

"Daithí," she says for the third time, and the more she tries to stifle her laughter, the harder it is to control. Before she knows it, she has tears running down her face and she can't even remember why she is laughing. Daithí laughs with her, amused.

She shouldn't have smoked so much hash. Someone had pulled it out and lit it up the minute Paul left. She doesn't want this high to end.

"Daithí," she says again, recovering herself. "I like saying your name."

"Daithí is the Irish equivalent of David," he tells her, and she giggles at how solemn he sounds.

"Spell it," she commands.

He takes her other hand, turns it over, scratches the letters into her palm. The tips of his fingers are rough with callouses. "The last 'i' has a fada, like this—" He draws a line over the *i*; they would call this an accent in French. "Dah-hee," he pronounces his name. "The fada makes the *i* say itself."

"Daithí," she repeats, exaggerating the last sound. "Why i-father?" she asks, wilfully misunderstanding his grammar lesson. "Shouldn't it be *e-father*?"

"Now that's enough of that," he laughs. "Say my name," he insists, and his smile is irresistible.

"Daithí." She smiles. "I like your name."

"I like you saying it." His finger is circling her palm.

"Paul says I should call him Pól, that's his Irish name," she says.

"Paul's name is Paul. Paul's an arsehole."

"Why don't we just call you David, then, if that's what it means? It's easier to say."

"Easier for Americans?" he laughs.

"I'm Irish," she tells him.

"Are you?" he asks, his brow twisting in a question.

"Are you David, or Daithí? It's so hard to know. Men are not always who you say you are."

"Are we not?"

Her smile reveals three dimples. He touches each one.

"My mam actually named me Daithí."

"You could name me." She is serious now. They have stopped at the edge of the water. There are large stones in the sand. She pries one loose and picks it up, throws it out to sea. "Give me an Irish name."

"I could. Sarah." He thinks for a moment. "Sorcha is the Irish for Sarah. We could call you Sorcha."

"Wouldn't I be an arse, then, like Paul?"

His laugh lines crinkle at the edge of his eyes.

"Paul's not an arse because of his name. What are you doing with him, anyway?"

She ignores his question.

"Sorcha," she repeats. "No, it doesn't feel right."

"It won't do? No?" He is amused.

"No."

He thinks for a moment.

"Saoirse."

"Saoirse," she repeats, closing her eyes to the sound. "I like it. It sounds like the waves."

"I suppose it does."

"Does it mean something?"

"Freedom."

She repeats it quietly to herself.

"It'll do, yeah?"

"Yeah."

She examines a constellation of pebbles, smooth and clean and embedded in the sand, unsorted. She picks up a pure white stone and a polished round one the colour of onyx. She opens her hand to show him, then brings them to her lips. There is the taste of the sea at the corner of her mouth. He puts his thumb there now, stroking softly as though rubbing away a smudge. She runs her fingers along the back of his hand.

He moves closer, his eyelids lower as the sun emerges from behind a thin cloud.

"Come west," he says as though he has been thinking about this.

"Why?"

"You'll like Donegal. It is beautiful, and wild—"

"Would you like me out there?"

He comes in close.

"I'd like you right here."

He kisses her, she moves into the kiss, rotating the pebbles in her hand—the waves washing up over their feet, the tide coming in fast and heavy.

She pulls away first.

"We better go back," she whispers.

He lays his forehead against hers and closes his eyes. She closes hers, too, and they stay this way for a moment, feeling the quiet between them, the heaviness of their breathing.

"Whoa," he exhales, pulling away. She places the pebbles in her pocket. He puts his hand to the small of her back, manoeuvres her away from the water, follows her up into the dunes. They walk the narrow, sandy trail. She feels the warmth of his hand until they are nearly at the crest of the hill. When they can see the others through a curtain of marram grass, he lets her go, the space where his hand has left hers grows cold.

Grey Sky

14 October 1990

The unseasonal weather breaks the next morning and grey skies return. All the way back to Dublin the wipers clear the fine drizzle on the windscreen. It forms again, dot by dot, and it is hard to make out the road ahead. Saoirse doesn't say anything to Paul, about his increasing speed on the wet pavement or the slowness of the wipers. She tried to apologise again when they first got into the car. And to hear herself, she is embarrassed for him, the way he holds on to his anger, in a secret way in public, in this aggressive way in private. The way he waited until they were alone, how he yelled at her the moment the doors were closed. Calling her a fool for letting Daithí convince everyone her name was Saoirse, for not correcting them when it caught on, but Saoirse knew his anger was over something else entirely. She had not come to his tent the second night on the dunes.

It had been a quieter night. Most of the musicians left by late afternoon. Sinead brought sleeping bags to the fireside, gave Saoirse a spare so she could avoid facing Paul. Daithí left his guitar in his builder's van and fetched his sleeping bag; he had returned wearing a woollen hat. He brought one for her, pulling it snug over her ears.

"For the midges," he said. "They'll eat us alive."

He settled down beside her and a few of them stayed out by the fire all night, sleeping under the stars. There was light chatter, and she and Daithí opened the bags, wrapped them around themselves, found each other's hands in the folds of their covers. At first, it was a thrill, then a settled warmth of feeling from his constant touch. She had fallen asleep, and when she woke, the light of dawn was coming into the sky.

He left first thing that morning for the long drive back to Donegal. She had walked him down the path to say goodbye. They were disappointed to find Liam and Gus in the car park, disposing of their rubbish, looking guilty for disrupting the moment even though it was Daithí and Saoirse who had come upon them.

"See you, man." Liam waved.

"You legend, Dot," Gus called. "We'll come out your way next."

"Deadly. Come anytime." He was looking at Saoirse when he said this, the pull of him close to an ache. He slipped a piece of paper into her hand. She placed it in her pocket, alongside the pebbles from the beach. He leaned in and kissed her cheek while Liam and Gus turned away, walking to the crest of the dune, waiting for her. Together the three of them waved to Daithí as he started his van and pulled away.

THEY ARE NEARLY HALFWAY HOME before Paul stops shouting at her and turns silent. They take the N11, a much quicker route than the coast road, and she is glad. It is time to leave the Byrnes'.

Today, though, on this cold, drizzly Sunday, Joseph will have the fires lit. Paul won't dare raise his voice in front of his father. She thinks of the book she left turned upside down on the bedside, she will climb into the bath and then straight into bed for the rest of the day. She will search in earnest tomorrow, for a way out.

Back in Sandymount, Paul parks the Morris Minor on the street. Puffs of smoke stream from the house's chimney. Saoirse grabs her bag off the back seat while he unlocks the front door, Bugle scutters up to greet them. Paul moves into the house, past the dog. She leans down and scratches Bugle behind the ears.

There are voices coming from the little dining room off the garden, in the room where Saoirse had breakfast that first morning. A young woman sits at the table with Nuala, she holds a teacup in her thin, birdlike hands. Her fringe is red and thin and falls across her eyes. She brushes it aside. Her legs are tucked up under a black tunic and the severeness of her face matches her dress. Her first words are to Paul.

"Will you take off your shoes, you're dragging muck all over the house."

"Welcome home, Viv." Paul's voice lifts and he drops his bag on the settee and kisses his sister's cheek.

"Here she is," Nuala accuses. "Here's the painter staying in your room."

Vivienne moves her head around Paul and looks Saoirse up and down.

"She's wearing my cardigan."

They all turn and stare at Saoirse.

Vivienne turns back to her mother.

"That's mine."

Stubble

Oil on canvas

I pull a razor blade over my outstretched leg, cutting a swath through the white foam. A patch of skin emerges, smooth and stubble free like a cleared road through a snowy landscape. I flick the razor and the blobs of foam fall onto the bathtub floor.

It is the first day of summer vacation. The screen door slams. Lou's voice booms through the house, I ignore him. He calls up the stairs, calling with great urgency. I roll my eyes and grab the towel from the rail. It is damp and smells mouldy. Whatever Lou wants, I'll make it quick, and then I will finish shaving my other leg, and start a wash. Léa deserves fresh towels.

Lou persists. His footsteps are overhead in the bedroom. He is loosening the fresh-air vent, a Victorian remnant of this old farmhouse, a grille embedded into the floor. He shifts something in the floorboards. I know what this means.

He finds me in the bathroom, wiping the foam off my unshaven leg.

He is impatient to leave. His mood is euphoric, a state which can easily turn to violent anger. I tell him Léa is on her own.

Fleur is here—that is what mothers are for.

His eyes roam over my tank top, my shorts.

And wear something decent.

Coming out of Michigan on I-75 into Ohio, the setting sun is a ball of red to the right, and to the left, pink lightning flashes cloud to cloud in the anvil storm hanging over Lake Erie. Before Lou falls asleep, he tells me to wake him up once we reach Lexington. The farther we drive away from the Michigan border, the deeper my despair, the stronger my terror. I hold my breath and pass eighteen-wheeler trucks, kicking up water from the steadily falling rain. We've never gone this far before. I think of a prayer, the only one I know, which was on the back of a funeral card stuck in the one book my mother owned. She kept it in her underwear drawer, along with a pistol. La Sainte Bible *etched in gold on the black leather cover. I whisper the prayer to myself now, from memory, I whisper it for Léa:* The Lord is my shepherd, there is nothing I shall want. He makes me lie down . . .

There were folded documents in this Bible.

Documents in French and English.

```
Birth. Naissance
Ontario
Sarah Roy.
December 7, 1974
Mother's name : Fleur Roy
```

The name where my father's name should be was blank.

It is a surprise to see my legal name: Sarah Roy. I've only ever been known as Sarah Gagneux, registered at my many schools under Lou's last name. I don't know how they got away with it, but there is freedom in seeing my birth name. I am a Roy. Lou is nothing to me.

But he is something to Léa.

Her document was issued in the State of Michigan.

```
Léa Gagneux.
Mother: Fleur Roy
Father: Louis Xavier Gagneux
```

By morning, we are in Jacksonville, a block away from the bus station. Lou had swapped seats with me, taken over the driving somewhere in the middle of the night. His knees jig up and down now against the steering wheel.

You know where you're going? *he asks.*

I eye him, then the two-story totem sign rising above a flat roof. BUS *is written vertically, and atop this, a greyhound lurches perpetually forward toward an unseen hare. I give him the look he deserves.*

Eddie has told me I have nerves like a psychopath. I never give myself away. I had laughed when he said this, but I have to wonder. I am seventeen years old, running some form of illicit materials across state lines, and I feel calm as hell.

You're not coming? *I ask, only to provoke Lou.*

Somewhere between Lexington and Jacksonville I have begun to feel a power over him.

Of course he is not coming.

The worst you'll face is juvey. *He is sweating.* Do you know what happens in prison to people like me? Do you want to see me done for a felony?

Do you want me to answer that? *I ask.*

He stares at me hard.

Felony. *I mutter.* Nice knowing the level of crime I am assisting with today.

Smartass.

I raise an eyebrow.

Get the hat on.

I am already taking the red baseball cap out of the bag, pulling my ponytail through the hole, opening the car door.

I'll see you in twenty-four hours.

Twenty-four hours? *I pull the handle of the door closed again.*

I've got business associates to meet.

I shake my head, staring at the street ahead.

You want me to leave you here? I'll drive home today and move your sister and mother so far away you'll never see them again. You want to support yourself? You're sitting on a million bucks, baby, why not use it?

I don't even flinch.

Where will you go? *My voice is steady, but inside my confidence has turned to jelly.* Back to Canada?

His face is easy to read.

You commit felonies and you're undocumented, *I remind him.*

Are you fucking with me? *he asks, smirking. It reminds me of the way he looked at me when I stole the ChapStick. Like he has discovered a new layer he can exploit.* What do you want out of this? *he asks.*

I just want to go home.

Lou leans all the way over now, I can smell coffee and stale cigarettes on his breath.

What would it be like to live in the world without your mother? Your sister?

I stare ahead at the BUS *sign. I imagine blocking the letters on the page. Graphite. Charcoal. Hard lines and dark colours.*

Did I ever say I wasn't doing this?

Good. Because guess what? You're deep into this now, just as deep as I am. They are watching you and me. Right now. And if you don't do what they ask? They'll kill you. And you know something? *He leans back in his seat, and I can tell he has been wanting to say this thing to me for a long time now.* I couldn't care less. You're not my daughter. Not by blood. Not by anything.

I go cold inside. This is the thing I have been needing him to say. I laugh.

You don't think I know that?

The way he looks at me then, I imagine I will end up dead in a ditch somewhere. I think he might be capable of this.

Just do what they ask.

I focus now, curling my toes, releasing them, curling them again. All my mental energy goes into this. When I am calm, I open the door and walk up the street, the bag slung over my shoulder.

Inside the bus station a man sits in a row of plastic chairs attached to a metal base, his shopping bags gathered around him as though they are his children. A woman waits on the other side of the station with two small boys. It is not clear yet who I will meet. Another bus arrives. Passengers wait for their bags. A girl my age saunters in from the sunlight. Her hair is blond and straight, and she is tan, she looks ready for the beach in her shorts and T-shirt and flip-flops.

Martha! *she calls to me.*

This is what I'm expecting, this is the name I am waiting to hear. I breathe out, uncurl my toes.

Jane? *I ask.*

She hugs me.

The bus station has emptied.

Jane is easy and free, opening a locker, putting quarters in the slot. She shoves the bag I gave her into the locker and turns the key. She places the key in her bag and smiles.

Easy enough? *She winks.* Ever been to the ocean?

We take the bus across town as though we are two friends on spring break.

Jane has towels and bikinis for us both in her shoulder bag. She turns on a small radio and we lie on the beach listening to the music, waves, seagulls, and the children screaming as they run in and out of the water. And before I know it, I am asleep.

When I wake, Jane is rolling up her towel. It is after four o'clock.

You need a proper sleep.

A Jeep with its engine running is waiting for us. Jane hands the driver the key to the locker. That is my job done now. What will happen to the gear in the locker is anyone's guess—but probably another child will be sent to collect it, deliver it to its next destination. The driver places the key in the console and drives us to a house, a bungalow, with a horseshoe driveway lined with palm trees. Kids' voices drift from somewhere at the back. There is a woman in the kitchen. I recognise the dull look in her eyes, it reminds me I need to call home to check on Léa, to check our mother hasn't overdosed again, or forgotten to feed my sister.

I follow Jane outside; we sit beside one another in lounge chairs by a pool.

A man wearing bathing shorts and flip-flops has come out the sliding door. His hair is silver, and he is about my height, his stomach plump and hardened, his chest covered in hair.

Kenny. *Jane has been lying down sunning her back, the spaghetti string of her bikini untied.*

He sits on the lounger in front of her, she sits up and her bikini top slips away. She presses her chest to his back. They lean back together, and she wraps her legs around his waist, rubs his shoulders. She looks over at me—I can't see her eyes through her sunglasses but I don't believe she could enjoy this; I don't believe her smile. I look back out toward the pool, the wind ripples on its surface, I pull the towel around my body. The man stands and takes Jane by the hand, leads her into the house.

By the time I am called to dinner, Jane has disappeared. The last I saw my clothes they were in her shoulder bag. I eat dinner in my bathing suit and a man's button-up shirt I found on a lounge chair. The woman eats staring at her plate. Kenny walks me to the back of the house. It has been twenty-four hours since we left Michigan. He opens the door to a bedroom, shows me the bathroom, a strip of lightbulbs run down the mirror. There are two fresh towels folded on the counter. When I ask for my clothes he tells me they are being washed. He instructs me to take a shower and get a good night's sleep. He leaves, closing the door behind him. I think the woman, the mother of his children, won't let any harm come to me here. I lay on the bed and fall asleep in the bathing suit. I sleep like the dead.

A crying child wakes me at dawn. I am met with a sense that I need to leave this house, immediately. I turn on the shower, step into the stream of water, pull the curtain. It feels like needles on my sunburnt skin. I soap my hair, let the suds run down my face.

Morning, darling. *I freeze at this voice from the other side of the curtain.*

Here's your clothes. *His voice is singsong.*

I say nothing, waiting for him to leave.

He pulls back the curtain and stands in front of me, naked. His dick is hard. He leers at me, reaching for me as though we have an understanding.

Gorgeous tits, *he says, grabbing one of my breasts.*

I pull away, slapping his wrist.

He is no longer smiling. He grabs me by the hair, pulls me violently out of the shower. He puts my face close to the things he has brought with him, they are lying on the counter: a pocketknife, switched open. Underneath this is a photograph, blown up to size, it is my sister. She is standing in the schoolyard, an earnest smile crinkling her face, you can see someone has praised her—she is proudly holding her classwork, daffodils cut out of yellow paper, glued onto the page. It is the same artwork she brought home a few weeks ago, I had taped it to the fridge.

Let's just say this is a little calling card for Lou, *Kenny tells me, pushing me onto the counter.* Make sure he knows you made a down payment on the money he pilfered off the top.

My fear spikes and then slowly, a paralysis moves like a cold wave through my body. Throughout the ordeal, all I can think of is the stubble on my unshaven leg.

When it is over, he takes me by the hand, wraps a towel around me. Pushes my wet hair behind my ears.

If the rest of that money isn't here within the week, I know where to find your sister. *He winks.* She's a cutie, like you.

When he leaves, I lock the bedroom door and then the bathroom door. I shower as quickly as I can then dress in utter numbness. I change into the clothes he brought in—the same clothes I wore driving out of Michigan. I ball up the bikini and stuff it into the wastebin. I have no idea where to find my shoes, so I put on the flip-flops and walk to the front of the house. Kenny sits in a leather recliner in front of the television with the volume full up, watching daytime soaps. The woman watches, too, from the couch. She doesn't look up or watch me leave.

Outside in the driveway, Lou is waiting for me. His cheek is bruised, his eye swollen nearly shut.

What, *he asks. It is more of a challenge than a question.*

I don't answer.

You're sulking? *He pulls away, screeching the tyres.*

We drive in silence until the highway. When we reach I-75 he accelerates onto the entrance ramp, joining the flow of traffic heading north. By now I am shaking uncontrollably. I am thinking of all the people who might have taken that photograph of Léa. A teacher. A parent. My mother. Lou? I can't place who it might be or how these criminals have accessed her—but it is someone she knows, that is obvious, hers is not a smile for a stranger. I am nearly mad with terror.

Lou is pointing at me, giving me a cautionary look. I'm telling you—*he begins, but I cut him off.*

No, *I warn.* I'm telling *you.* Don't say a fucking word.

And he doesn't. Not a single fucking word. All the way back to Michigan.

Donegal

7 December 1990

The suburbs of Dublin give way to rolling hills in the distance. The tension Saoirse has held in her shoulders slackens the farther west she travels. Today is her eighteenth birthday. Of course, no one can know, they all believe she is twenty. Twenty-one at her next birthday, as the stolen passport declares. She bought a backpack, sturdy hiking boots, and a new pair of jeans with the dwindling money to mark the occasion.

Paul had ignored Saoirse the day they returned from camping. She knew he was blaming her for the turn of his mood at the coast; soothing himself from the rejection by attaching himself to his sister. He sat at the table with Vivienne, drinking tea, hearing about her travels, laughing too loudly, intentionally excluding her. Though she didn't entirely blame him, Saoirse had come straight upstairs to get away from the awkwardness and found the sheets were stripped on the bed she slept in all these weeks, the Maeve Binchy books returned to the shelves. Saoirse's own things were placed in a pile in the hallway while Vivienne's towering backpack lay toppled on the naked bed. Saoirse had nowhere to go.

It was Joseph who intervened.

He had called her down the stairs, gently asked her to come for a little walk. He brought her out to the studio. Showed her around, pointed out the solid finishings, as though he were apologetically selling a property no one wanted.

"I'd like to be staying out here myself, if I'm being honest."

"I don't mind," she said, knowing she was leaving soon, it was her only option.

"That's our Daithí," he said proudly. "He makes a weathertight home. It is yours, if you'd like, as long as you wish to stay." He leaned in close and winked. "And I hope you stay."

That night Paul and Vivienne headed to the pub to celebrate her homecoming. After they left, Christopher, Vivienne's boyfriend, arrived late, calling to the house, hoping to welcome Vivienne home. Nuala insisted he take Saoirse along with him to meet up with the others in the pub. Christopher was happy to have her join him.

It was as awkward as it had been at the house when Vivienne and Paul saw her arriving. She was relieved, and then delighted, to see Sinead and Emily, but if she thought she had crossed some line with them at the coast, she was mistaken. Sinead smiled broadly at her and called her *Saoirse* as they had done at the beach, and Emily wondered if she was well. But then they excused themselves, retreated to a table at the back with friends Saoirse didn't recognise.

Mags, the secretary from Joseph's surgery, spotted her on her own and called her over, made room at her table.

"We're the UN contingent," Mags laughed. The group at the table was made up of foreign nationals, a French woman, an Australian, and Mags.

"I don't know about Americans—" Mags talked as though Saoirse was looking for a balm for the humiliation of being shunned. "—but the thing about us Germans is: when we meet, there is a wall. We build a ladder and meet at the top. We climb over and become friends. With Irish women, you might have the craic, but next day: where do you stand? Who knows—it is hidden, this wall—I have never found it to climb."

The others agreed and began to add their own stories. Saoirse was grateful when someone changed the subject.

On the walk home, Paul was a little drunk and jovial, he caught up with her and chatted as though nothing had happened. Saoirse marched ahead of him and even passed up Vivienne and Christopher. When they got to the front door, she refused to come into the house for a cup of tea.

"A quick one before I catch my taxi," Christopher encouraged her warmly. "I want to see this artwork I've been hearing about."

"If she wants to go to bed, let her go," Vivienne snapped and opened the door, moving inside.

Christopher paused. "Goodnight then," he said, and followed his girlfriend into the house.

Paul insisted on waiting while Saoirse unlocked the gate at the side passage. Nuala had given her a key, saying it would be more convenient for her to access the studio through the garden, without passing through the house.

The key jammed, or it might have been Saoirse's hands shaking in anger. Paul fumbled with it, trying to unlock it for her.

"I've got it." Saoirse raised her voice.

He shushed her.

"You'll wake Mam," he whispered, "the neighbours will hear."

"Fuck *Mam*. Fuck the neighbours." She couldn't stop herself now. "Fuck your sister. Fuck you, *Paul*."

He slapped her. A short, sharp sting to her cheek.

"I'm sorry—" he said straight away, reaching for her, surprising even himself.

Saoirse pushed his hand away, touched her cheek.

"You asked for that, in fairness," he said defensively, taking the key and unlocking the gate.

She walked briskly up the garden path.

"You were going to wake everyone," he called after her.

"Good night, Paul," she said firmly, not turning around.

"Don't hold a grudge. Wait—"

She didn't stop.

"What's the matter with you?" he asked.

She reeled around.

"You slapped me. That's what's the matter with me, for starters."

She had reached the studio door.

"I want a chance with you, to start over again," he said suddenly.

She pulled back, wrinkling her forehead.

"Please don't."

He hiccupped.

"You're drunk."

"A little," he laughed. "You've put a spell on me—" His hands outlined her body in the air.

"Go to bed, Paul."

"At the end of the day, you're doing well from this little arrangement." Paul whirled his finger around, indicating the studio.

"You and I don't have an arrangement," she said.

"Do we not?"

"I'm going away."

He took a step backward.

"When?"

"When I can get myself organised."

He smirked.

"You won't be gone long. Will you, *Sarah*? Or are we *Saoirse* now?"

She couldn't help but hear the ominous undertone.

She decided to ignore this.

"I may have to leave my paintings, but I'll come back and get them when I'm settled."

"Are you going to Galway?" he asked.

They both knew she was not going to Galway.

"That night that you and I—" he said tentatively.

"The night we had sex?"

"That, exactly. Yes."

She could hardly believe he had nearly finished medical school and couldn't even say the word *sex*.

"I liked it. I like you. I don't always get it right."

She nodded.

"Any man would be lucky to have you. You bewitch us all." He hiccupped again, bringing his hand politely to his mouth.

"Goodnight, Paul."

She watched him walk, unevenly, up the garden path toward the darkened house.

It had taken Saoirse the rest of October and most of November to work up the courage. It was on a night she stayed too long in the city centre, trying to avoid Paul and the Byrnes. The Christmas lights had come on in Grafton Street; families gathered to watch, full of excitement, and Saoirse was sorry she hadn't left earlier. She walked home, feeling the cold and darkness sink in through Vivienne's raincoat, too small and constricting over the layers keeping out the dampness. She thought of the farm, the phone in the kitchen—was it only months since she'd left? If she dialed the number, would it ring? Ring inside the empty house?

When she arrived back at the studio, it was late and she rummaged around for coins and walked back up to the village in the dark, put the coins in the pay phone outside the shops, dialed the number. It wasn't even his number, Daithí didn't own a phone. He had told her this on the coast at the car park when he put the note in her hand.

Ring Seamus at the pub in Dún Chiúin—he'll let me know when you're coming. Hope to meet again. Dx

Seamus, who she presumed was a bartender somewhere in Donegal, wherever this number was ringing, answered. She had a difficult time understanding his dialect and she had to ask him to repeat himself more than once, much to his patience and her embarrassment.

Seamus assured her it was no bother when she apologised for the late phone call, he was still clearing up from the night. Daithí had only left not long before, and he'd be sure to put the message into his door on the way home. Saoirse told him she hoped to get the bus toward the end of the week, to visit. When she sounded uncertain as to the day, Seamus pulled out the schedule he kept behind the bar, helping her agree on a time he could relay to Daithí.

"The lad'll be glad of the company." The way he said this, she was certain Daithí must have spoken to him about her. "Dot's not going anywhere," he assured her. "Sure, we'll see you then."

And now, here on her eighteenth birthday, she is crossing the country, bouncing over winding roads, nothing but bogland and fields of cows and sheep on either side, over and around the countryside and into the windswept hills of Donegal, hoping Daithí will meet her at the other end.

Nerves, she tells herself when she begins to feel travel sickness from these winding roads. The apprehension of seeing him again is getting to her, she thinks. She has built a picture in her mind, and she doubts now she felt as strongly as she imagines. It was an illusion induced by the freedom of the sea, the cans of beer, the weed. The farther the bus travels into the wilds, the less she worries about how attracted to him she really was, and begins to fear what she will do if he fails to show.

But Daithí is there now, standing in front of his builder's van, waiting for her, his hands stuffed into his jacket pockets. There is a small amount of light left on the horizon. It is late afternoon, and before the dinner rush. He takes her bag, kisses her on the cheek. She is starving, she tells him when he asks if she'd like to grab dinner.

The pub is quiet apart from Christmas music playing on the radio. A sad artificial tree draped in golden tinsel is propped in the corner near a pay phone. They find a table, beside a coal fire, cracking and blazing in the grate. Seamus comes over to say hello and takes their order. Daithí introduces her as Saoirse. She orders fish and chips, and he orders the carvery left over from the lunch menu.

"Ham and turkey and all the fixings?"

"That'll do. I'm starving," Daithí laughs.

"Your man eats like he's sharing the meal with a tapeworm. Where do you get the appetite, lad? Not from a day's work—driving around the country in that van, telling your men what for—it's not like he gets upon the ladder himself."

"What would you know about a day's work—" Daithí mimics the ease of pulling a pint, then opens his hands wide. "Wouldn't I love your job?"

"Now, lad," Seamus scolds, "am I not in and out like a fiddler's elbow already and here it's not even the weekend."

"Ah, you are, Seamí," Daithí laughs, looking around the empty pub. "You're a busy man."

"There you are now," Seamus nods to the couple who have come through the door, as though their arrival proves his point. "No rest for the weary." He returns to the bar to serve them, and after some time, brings Saoirse and Daithí each a pint of Guinness, heads of creamy froth steady in his hands.

"Santa comes early," he says. "These are on the house."

"Go away with that," Daithí scolds.

"Cheers."

"Cheers." Saoirse raises her glass to him.

"*Sláinte*," Daithí says, clinking her glass.

It seems only moments, the discomfort is over, and it is as though they have always been together. They don't feel the hours pass.

Daithí tells her about his parents, how his mother Kitty met his father, Michael—Dr. Kimathi—when Kitty was still a student completing her medical internship in Dublin. Michael was on a visiting fellowship from Kenya, he was her supervisor, and somewhat more. Turns out he had a family already, married with a couple of children back home.

Saoirse raises her eyebrows at the scandal.

"Mam had no regrets when Michael left Ireland. He had always told her he'd return home but she wanted to stay here, raise me in Ireland. She kept journals, I've read them. She was—what would you call it?"

"A free spirit?"

"Liberated, anyway. Maybe Bohemian. I never met Michael after I was a baby. There are a few photographs of us. Mam's mother—Nana—was from out this way, they both had fluent Irish and Mam thought I should have it, too. We lived out here in the Gaeltacht, mostly spoke it at home, and I spent the first years of school learning through Irish."

"The Irish language?"

He nods.

"It was important to Mam. She was, oddly enough for her medical background, superstitious, she thought it gave me a form of protection. In her head, no one could refute my identity if I spoke the language." He smiles at a memory.

"What." She smiles, places her hand on his wrist. "Tell me."

"In Donegal, I was just who I was. Everyone knew us. But when I was quite young, Kitty and I came up to Dublin for Christmas, Nana insisted we go to Midnight Mass with her, and while the two of them were taking their time walking up the steps, saying hello to all the neighbours, I bounded ahead and was waiting at the back of the church—" He gives a preemptive laugh and it doesn't matter what he says, she could listen to him all night. "These old fellas pass me by, they see me standing there on my own, do a doubletake. They must have rolled straight out of the pub and into Mass. They were pissed drunk. One of them reaches into his pocket, hands me a couple of coins—*For the wee African boy*, he slurs. *Save you the postage*, his friend says. *Where you from, lad?* your one asks and I was taught to be polite, so I answer him, of course, telling him we live in Donegal and they slap their thighs, thinking this is hilarious. I'm shrinking away, awkward, embarrassed. They're having great craic at my expense." She cringes at the awfulness of it.

"This isn't funny," Saoirse tells him, but she can't help smiling at the way he holds back his laughter, knowing what's coming.

"Don't worry," he advises. "Kitty is coming up the stairs, and the rage on her face! *I'm* afraid for the old lads." Saoirse isn't sure how this could end.

"*—taispeán dóibh—labhair leo as Gaeilge*. She is scolding me first—*Speak Irish*—her cure for so many things—she turns on the old ones—launches into a tirade, shaming them—through Irish, which they clearly can't understand—*Who are you calling foreign—the fecking eejits can't even* *speak their own native tongue*—Nana has come up the stairs now, onto this scene, she is mortified, frantically shushing her daughter, wrestling her away—all the neighbours skirt around us, making a beeline for their seats, pretending this isn't happening, and meanwhile the lads are shirking away like she is possessed. Mam is relentless, like, berating them—you know that way?" He slaps his knee, pausing to gather himself—his laughter is infectious. "Now she's taking out her own coins, forcing them at the lads, telling them to 'learn a *cúpla focal*,' every other word out of her mouth is *feckers* or *amadáin*, in the back of a church, mind you, while the priest and his entourage are getting ready to make their entrance. Nana is nearly dying, and she's glad to get Mam out of there and in our seats. That's it. It's over. So we think." Daithí is wiping the tears from his eyes now.

"She sat there, fuming all through Mass, so when the lads pass our pew on the way to Communion, Mam lunges, hisses a curse over them: *Bás gan an sagart*!" Daithí's laughter erupts, filling the pub, and other tables look over toward them, smiling when they see who it is. "Their faces! *May you die without a priest.*" He is laughing so hard he can barely translate. "Mother of God—what a curse—the gas thing was, Nana nearly wet herself laughing, too—as did the priest."

Saoirse shakes her head, feeling every bit the indignance along with his mother. "Everyone needs a Kitty," she says.

A crowd has gathered, though neither of them had noticed until now. Couples drifting in for the evening, old school mates have come home early for the weekend and gather at tables, the crowd grows, and the noise levels rise.

"Ah, yes they do. She was something," he says, his laughter winding down.

When he realises he has been dominating the conversation, he shifts it back toward her.

"How about you—are you staying long?" He is still wiping the laughter from his eyes. She wishes he would keep talking but he is watching her now, waiting.

"In Donegal?"

"In general—in Ireland, like. What brought you here?"

She lifts her shoulders, shrugs, uncertain.

"So, you're backpacking—or studying—" he asks helpfully.

"Oh, you know—a bit of both."

He smiles, shaking his head, puzzled at her vagueness.

"You have a return flight or are you staying indefinitely?"

"Open to whatever, I guess." She smiles back at him, puts her chin in her hand.

He tilts his head quizzically, biting his lower lip, and she tries again to move the focus off of herself. It has only occurred to her now that when he takes her back to his place tonight, his mother very well may be there, the way she was surprised by meeting Paul's mother, Nuala, that morning she arrived in Ireland. She isn't certain she wants to meet another strong Irish mammy.

"So—what's Kitty up to these days? Is she here in Donegal?"

"Oh," he says, taken aback, as though he thought she already understood something. "She died." He says this in a way she knows he is trying to protect her from her own mistake.

"Ah, no." Saoirse sits back, bringing her hand to her mouth, surprised. She wishes she hadn't pressed him now.

"Sorry—I guess I thought you knew".

Saoirse shakes her head. "No. I had no idea. What happened?"

"We were living in the village at the time—she had bought a ruin of a house by the sea, a fixer-upper. She had put builders in place, architects—we were fully embracing her bohemian lifestyle." He gave a sad little laugh. "And one afternoon she went off to her shift at the hospital, and she never came home."

Saoirse reaches for his hand.

"I'm so sorry. Why? How?"

"An aneurysm—a burst artery in her brain. It took her like that." He snaps his fingers.

"That is terrible."

"Yeah," he says, inhaling sharply. A gloom comes down over them.

"How old were you?"

"Eleven. My life in Donegal was over. Instead of moving out to the coast, I was settled back in Dublin with my grandparents, put in a private school with the lads, Liamo and Paul and the like—Michael paid my school fees, and sporadically kept in touch."

"No. Daithí, this is terrible. I'm sorry." Her eyes well up for the small boy.

He nods, smiles stoically, shakes his head.

"Your grandparents must have been devastated." She is thinking of her grandmother, at the Lavender House, the look on her face when Fleur was pulling away. Mama must have known what was in store for them all.

"Ah, of course. My grandparents were—conservative. To be fair, it wasn't easy for them. Imagine the times—the shame of their daughter having a child out of wedlock—crushed with grief, and the shock of raising her child—a Black kid in a Dublin suburb. Unheard of at the time. They did their best. It was tough, not having Mam."

Seamus brings them another round; he sets the pints on the table and clears the plates.

"And if his mammy came back today, she'd give him a knock about the head," Seamus says. "He's done feck all with the place—that house is lying derelict—crumbling with the damp, he hasn't even laid proper floors—"

"These things take time—" Daithí grins.

"Never mind *time*. You'd have one of your crews out there tomorrow if you wanted it done. That's the truth." He winks.

Saoirse raises her eyebrow at Daithí.

"He probably told you he's a builder, yeah?" Seamus is full of mischief, the way he says this.

Saoirse nods.

"He's not a fecking builder—he's a construction magnate."

"He's taking the piss now," Daithí warns.

"He's not yet twenty-five years old and your man has building sites all across Donegal and even into Sligo."

"Three." Daithí looks at Saoirse, showing her the number on his fingers. "I've three projects."

"Restoring things left and right, he is. You think he'd look after his own place."

"Isn't that the way?"

"Sure, my father was a mechanic, and we never had a working car," Seamus laughs. "Me mother used to say if he'd been a doctor, we'd all be dead."

They burst out laughing.

"Seriously though, fix it up, lad."

"It'll get there, Seamí. I want to do it properly. It's too beautiful to rush the work."

"She'll be even better when she's finished—" Seamus winks.

Amused, Daithí takes out a bill to pay for the drinks.

"Will that get rid of you, now?"

"Save it. Buy a toilet seat for your girlfriend," he says, winking at Saoirse, collecting the empty glasses.

"Cheers, Seamí."

"*Sláinte*, Dot."

Daithí is still laughing when he returns to the bar. He tells her how Seamus was his coach at the GAA club when he was a boy.

"Gaelic games," he explains. "Hurling and the like."

Seamus hears them across the bar. He shouts over.

"He was our rising star when they sent him back to the Big Smoke. I'd have adopted him myself—could have changed the fate of Donegal. No matter, we still hook him in when we can, isn't that right." A few of the lads at the bar raise their glasses toward him in respect.

Daithí bites his lip, smiling this way she loves. She is warmed by the mutual esteem between the men.

"Come here to me." He nudges her gently. "I want to know about you."

"My parents didn't protect me." Saoirse is surprised this has come out of her mouth. She feels stricken now. She must pull back on the Guinness, she thinks. She has forgotten herself; he makes it too easy, makes her want to tell him things. "I mean, yeah—no. They weren't the stuff of legends, anyway. Not like your mother, by the sounds of it."

He becomes still, watching her carefully.

"I'm sorry," he says finally.

"I'm not sure why I told you that," she says, embarrassed.

He reaches out and takes her hand.

"I'm glad you did."

"I guess, just—you had this amazing mother, your friends, this community." She waves her hand around the bar. "I—I don't have any of this, I never had it. I thought you should know. I'm on my own."

She shrugs, wanting to shake this attention away from herself. But he doesn't look away. Saoirse doesn't think she has looked this closely into someone else's eyes, ever. It is comforting and frightening at once, telling him these small truths, even though she can't tell him the bigger things.

"It might be hard to believe, but I think I've felt much the same way all my life. It can get lonely."

She feels the tears welling up, her throat closing over.

"I think we'd better change the subject, if you don't mind."

"Tell me about your art, then. Where'd you learn to draw?"

She shrugs. Everywhere they turn, there is something waiting for her in the past. She tries not to think of JezaBelle Jones, her art teacher.

"I guess that is something I always had. Art was my escape."

She tells him about what happens to her when she draws, how she loses herself. She thinks she must be boring him to death, but he has his chin in his hand and is listening so attentively to her, she doesn't run out of things to say. He has found a pen, and she draws caricatures of Seamus and some of the locals at the bar onto the beer mats. And before they know it, Seamus is flicking the lights on and off, signalling last call, shouting to the diminishing crowd.

"Right folks, it's time. Move on."

It is only the two of them by the end, and the bar staff turning the chairs up onto the tables around them.

Seamus clears their glasses and picks up the beer mats, delighted by the drawings. "Will I keep these?" he asks. She nods. He offers them a ride out the road.

It is a short drive past the airport, to the strand. He drops them at a car park at the edge of a beach.

"Cheers, Seamí. I'll collect the van at some stage."

"No worries, Dot—safe home," he calls.

There isn't a house in sight. The force of the waves reaching the shore is constant.

"I'm just over the dunes there, we could walk the path or take the strand," he tells her. "In the moonlight."

"So romantic," she teases.

"You'll not find the site romantic, I'm afraid," he laughs. "I guess I should have explained. It's temporary, until I get the house sorted. And I apologise ahead of time for the state of the place. But at least it's not cold. I left a heater on so we won't freeze."

The moon is full over the bay, it lights the sand and the water and the rock formations in the distance, the undulating dunes behind them, dark forms outlined in silver. The effect is surreal and reminds Saoirse of the felt boards from school, how she sat there in the safety of a classroom, manipulating shapes, ordering them into pictures that made sense. Daithí takes her hand, leading her up the strand.

"Are you cold?" he asks. She shakes her head.

He takes off his jacket anyway and places it over her thin raincoat, the one she borrowed from Vivienne's wardrobe. She must buy a new waterproof coat, she thinks, with the rest of the dwindling money. She shakes the thought from her head. She only wants to be here, in this place, right now. The night air and the sea erasing all things that have come before.

It feels they will walk this beach forever, and part of her is shivering, not because she is cold or frightened of this abandoned strand, but because she is so certain of her feelings, and of his. Certain of what will happen next when they reach their destination.

THE CARAVAN IS NESTLED BACK into the rolling span of the dunes. There are other shapes in the distance, more camper vans—or caravans, as Daithí calls them. From here she can see the darkened airport in the moonlight, the orange sock floating in the gentle breeze. Mount Errigal is a dark shape in the distance.

Her insides lurch, and for a moment she is sorry she came. She traces her thoughts, finds Lou at the base of them, the stolen camper van, the way he had made her clean it. How she knew it belonged to another family—she had scrubbed them away with her bucket of bleach. They had lived in it for two months in a field while they were homeless, while Lou looked for someone else in some town to scam, before he found a farmer to let them pay rent in cash for an abandoned farmhouse. She tries to push her thoughts away, but a residue of fear lingers. Daithí notices.

"You happy enough?" he asks. "We can stay in town—I'll get you a B and B if you'd rather, just say."

His outline is silver in the moonlight, his fingers threaded through hers feel strong. It is strange to think—but she has never felt so safe as she has with this man. She breathes in the clear, night air. Lou has taken everything from her, she thinks, he won't take this, too.

"I'm happy." She squeezes his hand.

"Well just say if not—I have a tent I can sleep in, yeah?"

She nods.

Daithí unlocks the door and holds it open; she steps through. It is warm inside. He follows her, there is little standing room, and they are pressed up against one another. He kisses her forehead, pulls her to him, searching her face.

"You good?" he checks. "There's no problem going back—"

The caravan is neat, the bed made. There are no signs or smells of mildew.

She is good. She is certain. She wants to be here. She wants this.

"*Cupán tae?*" Daithí asks, but she is already dropping his coat from her shoulders, unbuttoning his jeans, pulling off his shirt. She is relieved she doesn't have to ask him—he reaches into a drawer and pulls out a box of condoms, tilts them at her as though asking a question. She smiles her consent and he brings his arms around her, she lifts her mouth to his, and he kisses her soft at first, then hard. The electricity coursing through her, as he makes a trail down her neck, her breasts, kneels in front of her pubic bone, is more intense and far reaching than she has ever felt. Their breathing is heavy, her cry involuntary when he lays her on the bed and sinks his mouth into the wetness between her legs.

THEY HAVE FALLEN ASLEEP, AND it is dark when she wakes, though there is a light outside, illuminating the landscape. She follows it to the door, opens it quietly. The moon is full, casting a silver hue over the sandy hills. Daithí is awake now, she hears him turn, lifting on his elbow.

"This is—unreal," she whispers.

"Like you're dreaming?"

She nods.

"It's like that here."

"Is your house far?"

"Directly to the left, about three coves in, at the end of a peninsula," he tells her.

"I want to see it." She smiles, closing the door, climbing back into the bed beside him.

"Seamí is right," he warns, taking her into his arms. "There's not much to see at the moment."

"I don't mind," she tells him, tracing his nose, his lips, storing the curves of his forehead in her fingertips for later, for when she will draw his face.

"It's an hour's walk along the coast. Tomorrow, so, in the light."

To Saoirse, it sounds like the loveliest of all promises.

House at Whale Bay

8 December 1990

It is a bright winter's day, and they walk down from the dunes onto the beach. There are children on the strand, wrapped in army-green raincoats and Wellington boots. The oldest brother, imaging himself a soldier in the Great War, digs a trench with a military-grade shovel while his younger brother scoops the wet sand with a blue plastic spade, tossing it behind him, scattering it to the wind. A hole this wide and deep threatens to swallow them whole. Their sister sits on a rock, reading. The tide is coming in, it will take the trench, breach its walls, spill into the deep cavernous hole.

They continue along the coast until they reach a rocky cove. Saoirse notices the walls first, even before she sees the house. Both have risen out of the stones, strewn as though they've been hurled up out of the sea.

The Famine Wall meets the gable of the house, ominous and towering nearly as high as the first story, and runs parallel to the rocks out along the cove, stopping short at the edge of the land before turning down the length of the fields as far as she can see. These walls, Daithí is certain, led his mother here.

He explains how they were constructed during the Great Famine, built by starving hands, stone by stone, in exchange for meagre relief. There are gaps every five metres or so of the wall, capped by a stone lintel.

"Why are these here?" she asks, reaching her arm through the chasm.

"Mam reckoned they were meant to reach the hands of loved ones, those left on the other side."

A chill passes through Saoirse.

"But structurally, they serve a purpose. They relieve the sheer force of the wind, break its power. It's hard to believe on a day like today, but it is often wild here, the weather. It's a miracle these walls stand." He looks out to sea. "Or a testament to the craftsmanship."

Saoirse feels the unsettled history in their towering presence. She lays her hands upon the stone in the winter light and settles into the quietness they force.

At the front step of the house, there is a hunk of bone to one side of the door, a vertebra of a whale that Daithí found the day his mother took possession of the house. The house had come with no key, and another name entirely on the local map, but from that day they renamed the house and cove: *Teach Cuan na Míolta Móra.* House at Whale Bay.

There is no electricity yet in his house. Daithí builds a fire in the hearth, she walks from room to room, the high ceilings downstairs, the modest bedrooms upstairs, and from every window, a view of the sea. The walls are encrusted in places with a mineral, a salt working its way out of the substrate, Daithí explains. The ceiling is crumbling, the windows rattle in the wind. There is the sense of the house coming down around itself, turning back into the rubble from which it came.

In the kitchen, he has lit a fire, stoking the coals in the firebox of the range and is stirring soup made from a packet. While he butters a turnover loaf he brought from the caravan, he tells her about the dark history of the house. It was built in the 1700s by an absentee landlord for his land agent, whose job it was to collect rent from the local tenants. It is probable, he told her, the house was built from the misery of the landlord's evicted tenants, their houses knocked to source the stone.

"So much history," she sighs. "So much suffering."

"So little mercy," he adds.

"Hopefully it will see better days."

"*Le cúnahm Dé*. Please God."

She smiles.

"What?" he asks. She refuses to tell him he reminds her of one of the old men she has encountered in Dublin, dressed in black, leaning on a wall or a gate. The wink and the slight nod of the head. There is something about them, she has thought. In their phrases and in their watching there is a wisdom. A dying breed. Daithí, at times, seems older to her than his years.

They return to the sitting room, pull sleeping bags around themselves, and huddle on the ancient sofa, sipping the soup from mugs, watching the fire crackling in the hearth.

"Where will you start?" she asks.

He is already bringing the house back to life. When they finish the soup she holds his hand, runs a finger over his calloused palms while he talks of the chimneys he has rebuilt, he will tackle the roof next. He is trying to source traditional Bangor blue slates, he tells her, which would have been used on the original house. Everywhere he can he will use materials from the period. Repairing the external walls, replaster with lime mortar and a tinted limewash to return it to its original finish, which will kill the bleakness of its facade. Floor joists, lath and horsehair plaster, rails and coving, timber sheet the bathroom, re-enamel the cast-iron bath. So much to do before the finishing flourish, the only modern addition—a glass atrium overlooking the sea.

"It will be marvellous," he says.

"It is marvellous."

He brings a finger along her wrist, traces the veins up her arms. Her hand curls around his bicep, he bends to her, brings his mouth to hers. She breathes in the pores of his skin, his breath, brushes her cheek against the rough stubble of his chin.

"Saoirse," he whispers when he moves inside of her. There is the hush of the tides outside on the rocks, the hummocks of sea oats shivering all around the house. On one side, the sun lowers into the sea, on the other, in the far distance, the top of Mount Errigal reflecting all of its last burning light.

They have fallen asleep together on the sofa. The memories come to her in her dreams, the ones that wait for quiet, advancing from the corners like ghosts in an abandoned house.

The Bridge
Charcoal on paper

We are hurtling, every day toward a new darkness, every night toward the burning sun. A different version of me has returned from Florida. Lou senses this too. I began to wonder, on the long ride home, what would happen if I went to the police. They would not hesitate to take Léa away. Put her in a home with strangers, in a system where she will quickly disappear. And it would mean turning myself in, confessing to committing felonies, as Lou reminds me time and again, as though I was a willing participant in his schemes. Felony. The word carries a heavy weight.

When we arrive back to the farm the house is dark. Léa has fallen asleep in front of late-night television clutching her teddy bear, its glassy eyes catch the glow illuminating the room.

In the bathroom, our mother is naked and sprawled on the floor. Her drug kit and vomit strewn across the floor, mainlining Kenny's cash into her veins. There is a quiet in her, as though my mother has already left.

Lou squats down, listens to her chest. He makes a strange noise in his throat, he gathers her up, carries her out to his car. I watch until the headlights pull out of the driveway, speeding off into the distance. Something in me knows I will never see my mother again. But now it is time to go.

Upstairs, I rummage through Fleur's dresser drawer. There is her Bible with our birth certificates. Here is a pistol. Lou taught me how to fire it, practicing my shots on the steel barrel where he burnt trash. I wonder, would I use it, if Kenny appeared? Would I dare? I try not to touch it, instead, I trawl around, searching through the tiny pieces of paper, receipts, crumpled and disordered, no names, numbers with unfamiliar area codes, outside Michigan. I'm not sure what I am looking for—a number of someone I can call, someone who will help us, someone who will care enough to save us from ourselves. It is the mid-

dle of the night when I pick up the phone, dial the number. A man's voice answers on the second ring, as though he has been waiting.

I follow the man's instructions, packing an overnight bag, forging a letter from Fleur, placing Léa into his care. I open the drawer with the Bible, retrieve our birth certificates. I remove the fresh-air vent, steal a brick of cash from Lou. I have already paid for this. We will not be here when Lou returns. We will not be here when Kenny arrives. One way or another, we are never coming back.

The sun has come up in the back field, igniting the gables on the barn, blazing through the tassels of cornsilk. The clouds are moving swiftly across the morning sky, their linings on fire with the pinks and golds of the rising sun. Léa is asleep when I tuck her in across the back seat of Fleur's car, she clutches her teddy. I imagine her waking in the Lavender House.

The sun is high when we come into the city. The bridge towering, majestic, cathedral in its magnetism, pulling us toward it. I know this bridge. We crossed it, after my mother and Lou took me from the Lavender House.

And there, in front of the bridge, is the Basilica, and in the parking lot, a lone car. Exactly where he told us to wait. A tightness prickles under my arms. I smell of fear. The last reliable eyewitness, the groundskeeper, plods across the parking lot, places a box into the dumpster, then returns into the shadows of the church.

Papa Frank gets out of the car as I pull in. I park beside him. He is speaking loudly and fast. If they are going, it is better to go while Léa sleeps. Open the door—*I whisper, lifting Léa. She can sleep through everything, she always has. Let that hold true now. I lay her across the back seat, tuck the blanket up to her chin. She takes it in her hands and curls up. When she wakes, she will wake to the face of strangers.*

Like your mother, *Frank accuses.*

I am nothing like my mother, I think.

I walk back toward our car.

Wait—*he calls to me, surprised I am not coming.*

I imagine Kenny, his brutality. I am worried I may lead him straight to Léa. It is Lou they will look for, and then they will look for me. I will leave for a while, disappear.

The woman in the passenger seat calls to me. She looks older than I remember, but still a version of our mother.

I lean down into the driver's seat window.

Mama.

She reaches across and takes my hand.

Sarah.

She pronounces my name in her strong accent, and it brings me back to the Lavender House. I pull my hand away before I can change my mind.

Take her, *I tell her. I give her the documents for Léa and watch them drive away. I hope it is enough to get them across the bridge.*

Sea Cliffs

9 December 1990

The day is bright apart from an occasional, passing shower. They sleep until late morning then hike back to collect the van, driving south, away from the coast, to see where it will bring them. A hare dashes out of the fields. The land undulates, and the wet road, platinum under a winter sun, seems to wind up into the sky. They stop for lunch and continue south. At a signpost marking the sea cliffs, Daithí turns and guns the van up a steep mountain pass until it ends in a scree-strewn car park. They follow the worn path on foot as it rises through the bracken. The wind is strong at the summit. It is wide open here, remote and unguarded.

They hike along the ridge, looking down into a sheer fall either side of the trail to the reef below. The quiet is like nothing Saoirse has ever experienced. A gull rises on a current over buttresses of granite. She closes her eyes and feels envy toward flight, toward wings; toward this entity belonging to no place, no time. She opens her arms and imagines sailing into the abyss.

"Will you stay?" he asks.

The days are short this time of year and the sun is low now in the sky, outlining his face, his eyelashes reflect the bronze of the light.

"I will." She feels reckless, free to choose. He smiles and takes her hand. Something has fastened between them.

They carry this feeling back down the trail.

Later that night, walking to the pub, the music reaches them out on the road. The warmth inside is welcome, but the smell of seafood overwhelms her. She visibly draws back outside.

"All right?" Daithí asks.

She insists she is fine.

"Will we give it a miss tonight?"

Seamus has already spotted them. He raises two fingers and Daithí looks at her, letting her decide. She nods. The pub is heaving, their corner from her first night here is taken. They find a single high stool near a ledge, she sits, and Daithí stands beside her listening to the musicians furiously wheeling off a tune. A young woman, Seamus's daughter, comes out from behind the bar, carrying their pints. When the reel ends, the pub erupts with applause, but they are quickly hushed as the woman delivering the pints is encouraged to sing. She waves them away, but they insist.

"Go on, your good self," Seamí encourages, and his daughter begins a ballad, a lament of sorts. There is no musical accompaniment, but she leans against the bar and her voice fills the room, the listeners are pressed to silence by the pureness of the notes. They resonate through Saoirse; her whole body receives the song.

A Mhuire dhílis,
céard a dhéanfas mé,
tá an geimhreadh seo 'tíocht fuar,
A Mhuire dhílis,
céard a dhéanfas an teach seo is a bhfuil ann?

An air of melancholy fills the pub. It is full of a sorrow that matches the history surrounding the house, the land. Saoirse doesn't understand the words, but it reminds her she has something to forget. Without warning, she is overcome with emotion. And it is in that moment it occurs to her—it has been over a month since she expected her last period. How did that elude her? She knows, without question. Something has been happening, deep inside her, in secret, in the darkness. One mistaken night. She is pregnant. This it is not something she can want. Not right now. Not ever with Paul.

Outside, on the walk home, there is no good way to tell him, so she tells him quickly.

"I'm leaving."

In his pause, she can feel him absorb the news.

"When?"

"Tomorrow."

"You won't stay?" he asks. She feels his quiet intensity.

"I want to."

She won't look at him.

"Look at this," he asks of her. She turns toward him.

He places his hand to his chest.

"Here—" he is saying, touching different points along his body, she feels how vulnerable he is allowing himself to be. His throat, the top of his head, the back of his ears. "Here—"

She is shaking her head.

"Here—I've never felt this—here—all over, everywhere. You?" he asks and he is searching for something in her, some response he hopes is similar.

"Stop," she whispers. "You don't know me."

"I know how we are together—" He laughs a little, at the absurdity of his own words. She loves this laugh. "Whatever this is, it has gripped me. This thing has chosen *us*. You don't feel that?"

"I wish I could tell you—" she tries to finish.

"You can tell me," he says. "Tell me everything."

There are things she can never say aloud, things she wants to forget. He doesn't know the person she really is, the things she has done, the lies he will hate her for.

"Don't leave," he whispers, shaking his head. "Whatever it is we can work it out."

"I've no choice."

"No?"

She shakes her head.

"Will you come back?"

The truth is, she doesn't know. Even if she can slip away, leave Ireland for England, have the procedure—what then? She has forgotten herself. She knows she can't afford to want this. Any of this.

This is not her life.

He searches her face but doesn't find what he is hoping to see. His face is tender, and sad and full of confusion and questions. He strokes her cheek with his thumb, sighs, a long, low sorrowful note, cradling her head in his hands, pulling her to him, laying his forehead onto the crown of her head. She puts her arms around his waist, and they stand this way, for a long moment, underneath a waning moon.

Eighth Amendment

Late December 1990

Paul is outside the bathroom, tapping on the door. The skin on her fingers is corrugated with wrinkles from the water, which has grown cold now, and there is no heat remaining in the immersion. She must get out and face him, but she feels so tired. A fatigue she has never felt permeates every cell in her body.

"You all right in there?" he asks.

She clears her throat, hoping he can't tell she has been crying.

"I'm having a bath. Go away."

"I'd like a word."

Saoirse cannot bear the sight of him. When she returned from Donegal after her shortened stay, he wore an air of smugness, believing things hadn't worked out with Daithí after all. He couldn't even begin to imagine the half of it, she thinks. He mustn't guess even a small portion of it.

Mags had known immediately what her trouble was, the reason she had returned to Dublin so soon.

"I'm a woman," Mags had said when Saoirse came to the surgery during Joseph's lunch hour, when she knew he wouldn't be there. "I always know these things." She was also German, and she knew how to instruct Saoirse in what needed to be done outside of Ireland. She wasn't the first woman in Joseph's office who had reached out for help. Mags kept a hidden folder in the back of a filing cabinet. She sat with Saoirse in the empty office while she rang a clinic in Liverpool.

The woman on the phone asked if anyone was travelling with her. Saoirse immediately thought of Daithí, the comfort this idea brought—then the humiliation, of admitting she had slept with Paul all those weeks ago, the shame was too deep. She would navigate this on her own. She would have to wait until everything opened again, after the Christmas holidays. And then there was this—another international border to cross, using someone else's passport. And that was when she realised. The stolen passport expired two weeks ago.

"We'll get you an emergency one," Mags told her, and immediately started making a checklist, all the documents she would need—beginning with a birth certificate. She had a birth certificate. It just didn't have the name she needed on it.

"Lost."

"Driver's license?"

She shook her head.

"Employment number?" Mags asked, exasperated. "Love. You're running out of time."

Saoirse told her she'd figure something out. But she hadn't. Not yet.

Paul is tapping incessantly at the door.

"I'm coming in," he tells her.

Saoirse sits up in the water, folds her arms over her breasts.

Paul twists the screw on the thumb-turn lock, entering the bathroom, closing the door behind him. She freezes, her body remembering Florida. The violation. She is vulnerable here in the bath, naked; him towering over her, an air of authority has come into his face. She feels her body preparing for whatever it will take to keep him away.

It is the thing he is holding in front of him that snaps her out of her flight mode.

It is the stick from the pregnancy test.

She had known the two blue lines were coming, they were nearly instant. What she hadn't expected was for him to trawl through the rubbish. She had taken pains to hide the stick, folding it in tissue and emptying the black bag from the studio deep into the family bin.

She closes her eyes, feels a deep sickness.

He looks at the stick again, as though translating the meaning.

"Positive," he says, and a smile spreads over his face as though he is both shocked and can't contain his happiness. "When were you going to tell me?"

"I wasn't," she tells him so quietly, he must lean in.

"Pardon?"

"I'm not keeping it."

"Sarah—you don't understand."

"What don't I understand, Paul?"

"You have no choice," he stutters.

"I have a choice, Paul."

He is very still. Then his fingers tap the stick. He places it on the counter and his face brightens again. He is coming toward her. She pulls her arms so tightly around her knees, making herself as small and covered as possible.

"You have all the support you will need from us." He kneels, gripping the side of the tub. She can see he has given this a lot of thought and has an expectation of what she will say. "Look—think of it this way," he says, and she glimpses something like hope in his smile. "This can be a new start—this is a chance to make a proper go of *us*." He waves his hand at the surroundings, indicating the house, his lifestyle. "We can make a good life for this child."

She feels trapped, his face this close beside her naked body feels animal, sharp teeth coming at her through a hole. She has the urge to slap at his hands, to insist he leave at once. Instead, she recedes to the far corner, pressing her back against the curve of the bath.

"You are the last person I would ever have a *go* with," she tells him. She hadn't meant to sound so hateful. He recoils with such violence it is she who begins to apologise before she realises—he is the one who has walked in on her. He is invading *her* privacy.

She looks at her towel across the room, draped over the sink.

"Get out, Paul. I'll get dressed and we can talk about this."

Paul has stiffened. He backs away. Closing the lid on the toilet, he sits down, making a steeple with his index fingers, puts them to his nose, thinking.

"There is nothing to talk about," he tells her. "Whether you want a relationship with me or not is not the question now. Abortion is illegal in Ireland."

"I'm not asking you to perform an abortion," she snaps. "I have matters sorted. I'm not asking you for anything."

"Sarah—" He sounds shellshocked. "—have you been conspiring to have this taken care of? Conspiring from my mother's phone?"

No, you, idiot. She wants to show him the contempt he deserves. *From your father's surgery*. But she doesn't.

"It would be ill-advised to leave the country. I think you already know this." His brow turns up in a way that she knows he is threatening her.

"Stop this—" she demands. She stands up out of the water, grabs the towel off the sink. "Get out."

He diverts his eyes, runs his steeple up and down the bridge of his nose.

"This is an impossible situation. You know this."

"No, I don't know this—Paul. I want you to get out."

He ignores her request.

"You are asking me to be complicit in a number of crimes."

"Crimes? What *crimes*? You're mad—"

"Murder, for one. Or as good as."

"Don't be ridiculous."

A flash of anger crosses his face.

"I can't do this," she pleads. "—I'm not ready for this."

"It's not a question of being ready, many an Irish woman will tell you—"

She shakes her head. Furiously rubs the towel to dry herself.

"It's the legality of the thing. They would remove me from the medical register."

"No one would know. Okay." She is panicking now. "Forget I mentioned anything."

She grabs the stick from the sink. How far down in the bin he must have dug to find this, it is weeks old by now but the lines are as clear as ever.

"I'll take another test," she pleads, thinking how she'll have Mags pee on the stick, claim she has had a miscarriage.

"In Ireland, the Eighth Amendment of the Constitution states the life of the mother is equal to the life of her unborn child."

"This is fucked up." She drops the towel. He looks away from her nakedness. A wave of nausea overcomes her. She leans on the sink until it passes. He touches her back; she shakes him off.

"You can't force me to have a baby against my will."

"It is not my will or your will that matters now. You are in Ireland. You're *Irish*, remember?" Paul challenges her.

"Help me, Paul, please—" she pleads.

"I am going to help you in every way possible. But I am a medical professional—and this is the life of my child."

She thinks of lying and telling him it is Daithí's child, decides it better not to mention his name.

"I slept with you once, Paul. Which was a huge mistake, we both know. But I've been with others since—"

"None of that has relevance." He thinks about what she has said. "But when the time comes, I'm happy to take a paternity test."

"Why? Why are you doing this?"

"I love you, Sarah," he says. "But if you don't love me back, I am still morally obligated to protect the life of my child."

Oh my God, I am trapped, she thinks. A wild sense of panic overcomes her.

"Get up," she screams. He crosses his legs and remains seated on the toilet.

She hears Nuala's voice outside the door.

"Paul, are you in there? Is everything all right?"

"Yes, Mother. Go away," Paul says tersely. He turns back to Saoirse. "And fearing your intention is to harm this child—I am compelled to tell my father, and as a precaution, I am sure he will agree—I am holding your passport, which, by the way, has expired—until such a time as—"

"Get up," she shouts, this time she pushes him off the seat but it is too late. She is violently sick over Paul. All over the floor.

Darkness

Early Spring 1991

Since the time Paul announced the news to his family, they have found new ways to navigate around one another. Joseph was exceptionally cheerful whenever Saoirse entered a room, but soon made his own exit. Nuala missed her hair appointment and choir practice. She didn't get out of bed for days. But as the week went on, she had overcome her shock and it was clear she had begun the work to accept Saoirse as a new fixture in her life, an obstacle to avoid.

Saoirse made that easy for everyone. She stayed in the studio. She couldn't even paint for the first trimester and into the second. She had no will and the fumes made her sick. Her head was bent most of the day over a sketchbook, her fingers black from charcoal dust and India ink, tracing lines—remembering the silhouette of his face, rendering the feel of his hands onto the stillness of the page.

Mary had rang from Cork to give her and Simon's congratulations when they heard of the pregnancy, but when Saoirse came on the line, Mary whispered into the phone, asking her if she was all right, reminding her she was always welcome in Cork.

Vivienne's reaction, when she heard the news, surprised her most. She had scrutinized Saoirse, interrogated her.

"You want to keep this baby?" Vivienne had asked.

Paul was furious.

"Of course she does."

"I'm not asking you—I'm asking her."

It hadn't dawned on her that Vivienne might have been an unexpected ally in this. She might have helped her travel. It was too late, now, though, she knew, which made Saoirse even more despondent.

"What about your mother," Vivienne had asked. "What did she say?"

"I haven't told her."

"Why not?" Vivienne folded her arms, looked intently at Saoirse.

"I don't know where she is."

And, in a way, that was the truth.

"At least now maybe you'll stop swanning after my father."

"What?" Saoirse gasped.

"You are out of order," Paul told his sister. It was clear to Saoirse they'd had this conversation before. Vivienne moved on, turning to Paul, as though it were her responsibility to manage this situation.

"What about her people here in Ireland?"

"She isn't in contact."

"Maybe she should make contact."

"That's up to her."

"Will you marry?"

Their answers were in unison.

"Yes, of course," Paul said.

"Never."

"Well," Vivienne said sardonically. "At least you agree on something."

Saoirse had sat stoney-faced, feeling her own hatred for Paul, for his hypocrisy, coursing through her limbs.

The darkness comes down by late afternoon, along with the cold. It crawls across the glass of the conservatory, brings a chill seeping into the room. It pries itself under her muscles, sinks into her bones. Saoirse rubs her hands together, tucks them under her arms, into the warmth of the oversized woollen jumper she bought at a second-hand shop in the city centre. Her body is beginning to swell, her ankles, hands, her breasts. And she is numb. Numb with the cold, numb with the starkness of her reality.

She started a painting again, once the nausea passed. She has prepped and blocked the canvas, sketching the outline: the dunes at the strand below the caravan. The moon overhead shining on the water. But she has found she cannot enter this work. The canvas sits on the easel, unfinished.

She sits on a chair and stares out at the greyness, at the studio at the bottom of the garden. She tries to ignore the stone in her abdomen, and though it has begun to move, to ripple at times, she cannot think of it as anything other than something inanimate. A heaviness that will sink her to the bottom of the ocean. Nothing can live in this environment, the acidic sorrow inside of her.

The day he comes, Vivienne is home having tea with her mother.

She has moved in with Christopher. Saoirse is extra careful to avoid the kitchen, she makes herself tea at the studio and carries it back up to the conservatory. The doorbell rings, there are voices in the hall. Christopher stopping in after work, no doubt, to lend a cheerful nod to some decision the women are making, a decision he is not allowed to have an opinion on.

But now, someone is standing in the doorway to the conservatory. For a moment, she is lifted out of her depression.

"Daithí wants a snag list on the studio," Vivienne tells her.

"I needed to check everything is okay. With the studio."

Saoirse is alone with him now, the darkness nearly encompasses them in the conservatory, the glass reflecting what little light the room holds.

"Do you mind?" he asks, moving toward the canvas.

She nods.

"I called," he says, studying the painting on the easel. "And I wrote to you."

"I know."

"I waited. Then I worried."

"Yes."

"Then I heard."

He turns to her.

"You could have come back."

"I didn't know what to do."

"We'd have figured it out."

"It's not yours."

"I know. That doesn't matter."

"I thought you'd hate me. I hate myself."

"Don't say that. Mistakes are mistakes. You don't have to be punished forever."

"No. I know. I was—in trouble."

"You were frightened."

"Yes."

"I would have helped, if that's what you wanted."

"Mags tried to help. I couldn't—get away." He closes his eyes as if this knowledge pains him.

"And is this what you want?" he asks. She doesn't know if he means the baby, or the Byrnes. Or both.

"It doesn't matter what I want. It's too late."

He shakes his head. "It's never too late—"

Every cell within her resonates with sadness.

"This changes everything."

"It changes some things. But not everything—"

"Isn't this *my lot*?"

"It doesn't have to be."

"No?"

"Should you get out? Away from here?" He has moved in closer now, has taken her hand. She can hardly bear it. Her sketchbook is propped against the leg of the easel. She considers lifting it, showing him. He is all she thinks about.

"It's complicated."

"Isn't this worth fighting for?" he asks.

"Daithí, lovely to see you. Aren't you very good to come?" Nuala is standing at the door. Saoirse has no idea how much she has heard. "You see Sarah has good news?" They all know it is not good news, for anyone.

Saoirse lets go of his hand. She turns away and brings the edge of her sleeve to her mouth, to stopper a sob.

She feels Daithí stepping away.

"You want me to look at the studio, is that right, Mrs. Byrne?"

"Sure enough, Daithí. I'll show you myself. Dr. Byrne will be home shortly, no doubt he'll want to check in with you. And Paul, of course. Will I put on another plate?"

"Not at all—I won't be staying. I just came to check everything was all right."

"Everything is grand," Nuala says, looking at Saoirse. "You're getting on all right out there, aren't you? Anything to report?"

"Nothing," she says, knowing she hasn't managed to hide the emotion in her voice.

"Well, we'll leave you to it," Nuala says to Saoirse. "No doubt you'll want to get back to your painting." She smiles falsely, beckons to Daithí.

When he doesn't follow, she pauses at the doorway, waiting for him.

"I'll be out there for a little while," he tells Saoirse quietly. "If there is anything you can think of. For the snag list. Come and find me."

"Did Paul mention that corner is leaking?" Nuala asks.

Saoirse sits in the conservatory in the dark, watching him cross the lawn, moving past the windows he has put into place, the studio he has built. How small it seems with him inside. He leans against the counter; he is waiting for her. She doesn't move, she can hardly breathe, until he puts the lights out; he crosses the garden, stopping to glance at the house. He does not see her sitting here in the darkness, her hands clutching the arms of the rattan chair, willing herself not to betray her resolve, not to give in to what every inch of her wants: to follow him, let him drive her away from all of this.

But he cannot drive her away from herself. He might help her leave Paul, but he cannot help her leave the past, all that is waiting to be unearthed.

And so, she lets him go, hears his engine start. Waits until he drives away. Only then she releases her grip on the arms of the chair. And the weariness that sets in is so deep, she can't even weep. She returns to the easel. She covers the lines with a primer until the dunes and the moon above have disappeared. Then she begins again. This time she traces the outline of a teddy, a hand coming in from the edge of the painting, clutching its paw. She lets the darkness wash through her brush in waves. Placing her marks on the canvas. Strokes of desolation, grief. Despair.

Light in the Darkness

Late Spring 1991

The days are growing brighter, there is a longer stretch of light in the evenings. But on this day, she waits for the dark, waits for it to merge with her entire being until she can no longer tell where she begins and ends, until the darkness has clouded her mind like a blot of ink. All routes are closed to her. There can be no other way.

Paul doesn't hear her leave the house. She didn't grab a coat. She is not cold, only numb. She walks along Sandymount Strand, passing the last of the families strolling on the beach, children running toward home, toward their dinners, chasing dogs chasing sticks. It is as though these scenes exist on another plane, as though they only exist to torment her.

The Pigeon House is a shadowy presence to her left, the darkness engulfs her, she isn't afraid of it, she isn't even defiant. She finds the South Wall, and there ahead of her, far out in the sea, the Poolbeg Lighthouse only a shape now in the dark.

The ferry she might have taken to Liverpool passes so close to the pier she could wave to the passengers on deck. She wondered how many of them were crossing for reasons she herself needed to cross.

Paul, himself, had watched her every move for those first few weeks, as though she were on suicide watch, fearing she would flee to England. Now that window has closed, he has stopped watching.

"Let us turn our thoughts to the child that is growing," he tells her, as though he is a priest, or politician, selling a fate no one believes in.

The burden of secrets Saoirse carries grows with the child. She has been thinking of the real Sarah Walsh, Sasa, in the darkest hours of the night, these thoughts keep her awake into the early hours of the morning. Everything that happens from here on out is an artefact concealed in a time capsule that her old friend could very well open one day, if she ever decides to return to Ireland. The best thing to do is stop the trail now, but even this will leave a record.

Saoirse waits at the end of the pier, resigned, for the right moment, for the blackness to open, for the cold to grasp her like hands, roll her into the icy waves licking the wall at her feet. This stone inside of her will bring her straight to the bottom of the sea.

"Hey—" A voice so slight and calm wakes her from this stupor. At first, she thinks she must be dreaming.

A woman stands beside her, her face a bluish white, nearly translucent in contrast to her hair, dyed black and tucked behind her ears. Lines radiating from the corners of her eyes when she smiles. Saoirse has to wonder if she is imagining her, or is she real?

"Cold night."

Saoirse doesn't reply.

"What's your name?" The woman's gentle voice draws a pinch at her eyelids.

She whispers her own name, not trusting her voice.

"Saoirse," the woman repeats. "Freedom."

A pain arrives in Saoirse's throat.

"Catherine," the woman introduces herself, and Saoirse feels endeared to her, her briskness, her directness.

"That's Howth Head across the bay," Catherine says, as though she is not aware of the strangeness of finding a pregnant woman at the end of a pier this late at night. "I come out here to watch the lights coming on in the darkness."

Saoirse doesn't reply.

"Et lux in tenebris lucet."

"Sorry?"

"And the light shineth in the darkness."

The woman's words bring a wave of chills to Saoirse's flesh.

"Viktor Frankl. He found meaning in signs—*lights* and all that craic. Apparently, it saved his life. I'm more of a voyeur. I like to imagine who's flicking the switch over beyond from their posh sitting room. I wonder what they're wearing, what their house looks like, if they have an island in their kitchen. Kind of like walking around a neighbourhood after dark, staring into windows." Catherine laughs at the imagery she is conjuring. She will keep talking, as long as it takes.

Saoirse looks around her for the first time, as though coming out of a trance, sees the water lapping at the pier, the darkness surrounding them. She shudders.

"I'll lend you his book sometime. *Man's Search for Meaning*. It just goes to show—you never know where you'll be if you don't stick around."

Catherine checks her watch. "It's midnight," she announces. "We've survived another day. Now that's something to celebrate, don't you think? You coming?" she asks. "I'll walk with you."

She takes Saoirse's arm, and Saoirse lets her. Catherine talks to her, all the way back down the pier.

Part Two

Benefactor

Early Summer 1991

Saoirse shuffles along in front of the panels of art, scanning the work, studying the marks the young artists have made. She is in awe of the varying ways they approach a subject. Catherine, beside her, gives a running commentary that isn't entirely flattering. Saoirse shushes her.

"I'm sorry, but there is no depth," Catherine insists. "There—paint by number. They're flat and lack imagination. In my opinion. What do I know? I'm not an artist. Just a critic."

"They're students," Saoirse tuts. She wanted to come to this end-of-year show to get an idea of the level that will be expected of her when she begins college in September. "See, this is what worries me. I just want to draw. I don't want people to walk around judging my work, criticising me."

"Indeed, but I've seen your work. You *are* original. Your work *is* interesting. You'll be that one percent—this course is for you. Most of these others—the college has quotas to fill. Cash cows."

She walks rapidly past the undergraduate wall now, pointing, throwing her hand at each one as though releasing confetti. "Cash cow. Cash cow. Oh, that really is a cow—inspiring," she says dully, scanning the room.

"They're beginners," Saoirse laughs, appalled.

"Oh, look. Here's something worth our bus fare."

Catherine drags her across the room to three large panels displaying scenes of coastal erosion, cliff edges, a pocket of a ravine painted in vivid oils onto canvas.

"Now, I love these. I would buy these."

And Saoirse agrees. The work is alive, and pulsing, and they open something inside of her for a moment.

"The point is, I think you'll do well here. In fact, I know you'll excel."

"Well, it's too late now, even if I doubt myself. Joseph has paid the fees."

"Ah Joseph, bless. You have a *benefactor*! How did Paul take it?"

Saoirse raises her eyebrow in response and Catherine rolls her eyes.

"Good for you, Saoirse. More reason to get yourself here in the autumn."

"But the baby will only be what—" She calculates. "—if all goes to plan, still under three months."

"The term starts later than that, the child will be nearly four months at that stage, practically reared, see."

"I'll be tired and leaking and—"

"All the more reason. You have live-in babysitters. It's the right thing, Saoirse. Trust me. I feel it—and so do you. You'd be disappointed if you turned it down."

Saoirse knows her friend is right.

"Shall we visit the sculptures?"

Catherine throws her eyes to heaven.

"We better save something for next time. Let's get lunch. My treat."

They make their way slowly out of the exhibition space; Catherine gives her arm to Saoirse. The students are as young as Saoirse, and younger. They glance at her protruding belly and look away. Catherine tells her she is "neat" for being so far along in her pregnancy, and Saoirse feels there is nothing "neat" about her body. She has never felt so tired, so frumpy, but at least she doesn't feel as hopeless as she did that night on the pier. In fact, there is even a little spark of excitement stirring about starting the course. She looks forward to getting back to her sketchbooks once she is home from the city centre, to begin drawing out some ideas that inspired her. There is a sense of control she feels she is regaining, and she is grateful to Joseph, getting her started down this road again.

She owes much of this to her new friend, Catherine. They have become close in a short space of time, it reminds her of Sasa—the real Sarah Walsh, the way they were in Boston. How quickly they formed a friendship. How quickly it was dissolved. How quickly this could all change with Catherine—if ever she knew. In fact, all it would take is for Sasa to decide to come home. Saoirse is aware of the chain reaction her return would trigger, these thoughts do not cease to keep her awake at night.

The muscles in her abdomen clinch, seize with some unseen force and Saoirse must stop to breathe. False contractions, Braxton Hicks,

Catherine calls them. Whatever they are, she hates how they twist her insides, hates that they are only the beginning of how she envisions she will lose control—as though both she and the child are marionettes, manipulated by some unskilled hand, a puppet master pushing and pulling on the thousands of strings entwining them, deciding some unknown fate. "We won't go far," Catherine promises. Saoirse takes a breath, and the women cross the street, spotting a café on the other side. It is small and cheerful and empty of students.

Arrivals

15–17 June 1991

When the time comes, Saoirse insists Nuala should wait before ringing Paul on his rounds. There is no need to bother him. Not yet. This is only early labour. She knows the midwives will get her sorted, make her comfortable, and it will be a long wait for everyone. But Nuala is already ringing the hospital where Paul is working, giving breathy instructions for the receptionist to tell her son to meet them at the hospital.

By the time Paul arrives, Saoirse has a bed on a ward with three other women. All of them in early labour. He immediately closes the curtains around her bed, instructs the midwives to bring her fluid and requests a foetal doppler for himself. He has brought his own stethoscope and blood pressure cuff. The midwives skirt around him.

When she is in full labour, and in quite considerable discomfort, they transfer her to a labour suite and the anaesthetist arrives, she attempts to insert the needle for an epidural. Paul stands behind her, still asking Saoirse if she is sure, wouldn't she like to hold on a little longer? Filling her with statistics and outcomes she doesn't need to hear. The head midwife holds Saoirse's hand and explains what is happening, how long it will take for the epidural to kick in. She gives Paul a warning look. When she checks the dilation of her cervix, and Paul stands over her shoulder, the midwife no longer hides her annoyance.

"Sir," she tells him, "you either stick at your wife's ear, or you'll find yourself in the canteen until this is over."

Paul pulls up a chair near her head, but he is restless with impatience. The midwife is firm with Saoirse now; as things intensify, she instructs her to keep her eyes on her. "You're going to hold the urge now until I tell you to push. But when you push, you concentrate all that right here—" Saoirse concentrates on the general location she indicates.

Saoirse shakes uncontrollably, from some force working its way through her. This must be what it feels like to be in a plane coming down.

The hardness of her abdomen shifts, and in a gush, the baby is delivered. A stone coming to life—the midwife lifts the baby and places her on Saoirse's chest, and here she is, this entity, an angel slipping into her life. Saoirse folds herself around her daughter, places her hands over the baby's eyes, shielding her from the light, the air, from everything bright and loud and unpredictable in this terrible world.

Paul doesn't stay long. He is absolutely exhausted, he claims when they are stitching her up. When he leaves, the midwife brings Saoirse a cup of tea in a white ceramic mug. She has never tasted anything so nice.

"You are some woman for one woman, you know that?"

The midwife strokes her hair and kisses the top of the baby's head.

"You're going to be all right," she says. And a fresh round of tears springs to Saoirse's eyes.

In the morning, the registrar comes to her bed, to record and register the birth.

"Good morning, missus." She is smitten with the baby. She has a checklist of the documents Saoirse needs.

"Your identification, the father's identification—if you are naming him on the birth certificate, that is. I'll need your RSI number, as well."

Saoirse has never felt so vulnerable.

"RSI number—"

"Have you one, or do you need to apply for one?" the registrar asks.

"I have one—I think. I'm sorry," she apologises. "I was away for a long time."

"In America? I thought I detected a bit of an accent."

Saoirse commits herself to nothing.

"Had you employment here before you left Ireland?"

Saoirse nods, hoping the registrar doesn't ask for details.

"I'm sure you have a number, then. Right—no worries. Leave it with me."

Saoirse sinks back into the pillow.

Later, the registrar brings Saoirse the application to register the baby's birth. She has made a phone call to a friend in another office across the city and has found the RSI number, and filled it in on the form. Saoirse takes note of it for future use. Another piece of information stolen from Sasa.

That night, Joseph and Nuala come to visit. Joseph holds his granddaughter, smiles down at her with joy. Nuala sits upright, her back straight in the chair.

"What are you calling her?"

"Leah," Saoirse tells her.

"Bless. Leah, that's lovely!" Joseph smiles down at the baby.

"Will you try and let your mother know?"

"Of course," Saoirse lies.

"Will she come stay?"

"No," Saoirse tells her and reaches her arms out to take Leah back.

"Is she a Byrne or a Walsh?" Joseph asks hopefully.

"Byrne, of course," Paul says, reaching out to stroke his daughter's head full of hair.

Saoirse doesn't argue.

"Would you not worry? Different last name to your own child?" Nuala asks.

"She could marry me," Paul says.

Saoirse closes her eyes impatiently.

"Consider a deed poll?" Joseph says. He explains how she can change her name. "We know someone." Joseph winks. "In the registrar's office in the city centre."

"Who's that?" Nuala asks.

"James, of course."

Nuala nods in recognition.

Saoirse has no idea who James is, but she thinks it may be a good idea to have her name changed, distance herself from Sasa's identity—*Sarah Walsh*—altogether. She thinks of the annual showcase at the college, which no doubt she will have to enter. It's a good place to start trying out a new name—as an artist.

Saoirse Byrne.

"Maybe," Saoirse says. Leah fusses and Saoirse lifts her, rubs her back to wind her. She wishes they would all go away. She is tired. Leah is cranky, absorbing her mother's tension.

"Get me your long-form birth certificate and we'll get James on it."

"I think Saoirse is going to need a helping hand from James, there, too," Paul says.

"What do you mean, Paul?" Nuala asks.

"She loses everything." His laugh is false, his face registers exasperation. "Remember you told me you misplaced your birth cert?"

Saoirse never said such a thing.

"I'm not sure I even brought it to Ireland," she says.

"You'd forget your head."

She shrugs, puzzled.

"Not to worry," Joseph says. "James will sort you out. You have one job right now. God bless her." He rubs his thumb in the sign of the cross over the baby's forehead.

When his parents leave, Paul stays behind a moment to say goodnight. He cradles his daughter, kisses her dark hair.

"I won't be in tomorrow," he says, handing her back.

"No?" Saoirse pretends to be disappointed, but she is relieved.

"I'm on my rounds. I won't be here to help fill in the forms."

"I can manage."

"She's a Byrne," he insists.

"Of course," she reassures him.

An awful smile spreads across Paul's lips.

"Not a *Roy*."

A coldness runs through her when he mentions the name she has only ever seen on a birth certificate. She had eventually destroyed it, throwing it on the coal fire in the sitting room at the Byrnes' when Paul wasn't home. Had he somehow seen it, before?

Catherine is coming through the door, her arms full of gifts and a bundle of tulips for Saoirse.

"Well done, honey," she calls.

She kisses Saoirse's forehead as though she is her own mother. Her eyes light up as she takes Leah into her arms.

"Ah, look. She is gorgeous. You're feeding her yourself?"

Saoirse is still frozen from Paul's words.

"She is," Paul answers for her.

"Good woman. In my day, they forced the bottles on you, they nearly had me cast as a witch for breastfeeding. Don't let them shame you out of it." She looks sharply at Paul.

"Well, I'll leave you to it," Paul says at the mention of breastfeeding. "I'm off to wet the baby's head."

"Good for you," Catherine says without even trying to force a smile.

"You're very pale," Catherine tells her when he leaves. She places a hand on Saoirse's forehead, feeling for a temperature. "I won't stay long."

Saoirse can hardly reply. The shock of Paul exposing what he seems to have known all along is unrecoverable. She has no idea what he is angling at.

Catherine senses she is not in the form for company.

"I'm sorry—" Saoirse whispers.

"Don't be daft. You call me if there is anything. *Anything* you need, at all."

THAT NIGHT, WHEN THE WARD fills with the sound of waking babies, Leah sleeps soundly. Saoirse feels the loneliness and the terror of the night pressing on her. She lets it happen then—the one thing that has helped—she allows herself these few moments: imagining Daithí, the presence of him, walking through the curtains, the pressure of his weight on the mattress. His arms coming round, encompassing the whole of her and Leah. She gives in to this sense that they are safe.

Leah squirms in her arms, her little lips suck at something in her sleep, something that is not there. *Pull yourself together*, she tells herself. *I will not mess this up*, she promises Leah quietly, though she feels the weight of what is before her. Up until now, there was always a way out. How is she going to survive this, she wonders. How is she going to survive Paul? She won't decide anything now. She lets herself fall asleep, holding her daughter, feeling these phantom arms around her.

WHEN THE THREE DAYS ARE over, Paul returns to take her home, back to his parents' house. He has set up Vivienne's old room for Saoirse and the baby. He has taken down a wicker cradle from the attic, pleased his daughter sleeps where he and his siblings slept in their first weeks of life. He sets it up beside the bed.

"However things have gone in the past, we are going to make this work," he tells Saoirse, pulling back the covers and climbing into bed beside her.

There is no freezing this time, no harnessing her emotions. She has lost that control—there is a sense she is watching herself from somewhere else while her body takes flight in its own direction—her hands, her legs—thrashing at him, pushing him from the bed, a primal shriek rising in her throat.

"Jesus Christ! Calm down!" Paul shouts, a look of horror on his face. Leah has startled from her sleep. Nuala is on the landing first, followed by Joseph, both calling through the closed door. Saoirse and the child are inconsolable now, Paul shushing her, Saoirse demanding over and over *get out! get out!*

Paul stumbling from the room, the concern from his parents on the other side of the door, Paul scolding them for their fuss, declaring Saoirse insane with postpartum.

Saoirse tries to gather herself. She sits on the edge of the bed soothing her wailing daughter, ashamed and bewildered, knowing her loss of control had less to do with Paul making assumptions, violating her privacy, catching her at an unguarded moment—and everything to do with the swish of a shower curtain, the violent memory of a man entering, unwanted, into her most private space.

Incorda Volupta

Autumn 1994

When she had first started the art course three years ago Saoirse had been paralysed with fear. Between caring for Leah and tiptoeing around Paul and the Byrnes, she doubted her ability to take on the pressure of art college. It was Nuala who insisted she continue to pursue her artwork. Saoirse knew her motives were to keep Saoirse out of the house, but it worked in her favour.

Nuala devoted herself to her granddaughter, giving her a tiny apron so they could cook and clean together, minding her while Saoirse was away at college, and in the evenings, in the conservatory, allowing Saoirse time to work on her pieces. Nuala reserved a special affection for Leah and Leah followed her grandmother around adoringly, throwing herself into any task set for her. Joseph encouraged Saoirse's art practice as well, insisted she keep going as far as she could with her education, contradicting his son's insistence that Saoirse wouldn't have time for such frivolous pursuits outside of her duties of being a mother, or a *doctor's wife*, which he said flippantly.

Saoirse ignored him. She was beginning to understand this rule of communication—say nothing, or at least as little as possible. Ever since the day she had brought Leah home to the Byrnes', ever since the moment she lost control, Paul had kept his distance. He had never mentioned the incident in the hospital, or even asked her about the last name *Roy.* There were things she had discerned—that the only way he could have seen this name was on the airplane, in those first hours of meeting. She was certain he peeked at her passport, while she was sleeping or out of her seat to use the toilet—and found her original birth certificate tucked inside. Who knows how he had intended using this against her—whatever he thought he had on her—but that moment in the bedroom derailed his plan. Still, knowing he had this link to her past was terror enough for Saoirse to keep their domestic arrangement steady, for Leah's sake.

There was so little she could have, given her circumstance. She had Leah and she had her art practice. And that would have to be enough. She often thought of Catherine on the pier that night, the words she spoke about light coming through darkness—Leah and her art were undoubtedly her light, which left Paul and his family.

It would be unbearable without her secret ritual—a ritual which at first embarrassed her, even if only she herself knew of it. It had begun in the hospital, in the terror and loneliness of it all, when she had summoned the memory of Daithí. His soothing presence. She had found it dangerous at first, allowing herself to think of him, and she had tried to quit, or at least limit herself to a few moments every day. But a presentation in art history class put an end to her shame.

The lecturer presented images from his trip to Paris featuring a series of paintings and sculptures capturing the sensual poses of lovers, arched figures, uninhibited desire—the images had awoken a permission within herself, allowed her to give over to the memory of him and how they had been—in the way she now gave over to her art.

Incorda volupta. Her lecturer loosely translated: *Inconsolable pleasure.*

If she couldn't have Daithí, she could have this: the pleasure of him, the pleasure they had shared. Now he filled much of her quiet moments, not so much as a ghost, but as a companion. She carried him with her.

Liam had begun visiting the Byrne household more often once Leah was born. He gave Saoirse news of Daithí, but only when Paul was out of the room. Daithí left Ireland shortly after Leah was born and travelled through Europe and then into Africa, eventually landing in Kenya to meet his father and his half siblings. He and his father got on famously, Liam told her, and the last he heard, they were building homes and medical centres together for persons and their families affected by the AIDS epidemic, Daithí with his builder's skills and his father connecting with his medical network.

Saoirse had closed her eyes and loved him for this, wished him every happiness and also tried not to think about how this wish might devastate her one day if Liam ever told her Daithí had met someone, was settling down. The Daithí in Kenya, the man moving on with his life without her, existed on another plane entirely to the one who came to her now.

In art class, while the other students and her tutor watched over her shoulder, she imagined he was there instead, standing behind her, admiring her work as she sketched and sculpted the paint into place. The thought of him brought her confidence.

"Hmm," Bernice, her tutor, had said early in the course, watching her put the finishing touches on a still life of yam peels arranged to depict a classic female bust. "Utter chaos! I don't know how you get there, but you get there in the end."

Saoirse had relaxed after this, gave in to her painting, tried new materials and mediums. But then, in her written feedback, Bernice told Saoirse she was beginning to see an evolution in her work, and this made Saoirse feel intimidated all over again.

"Look at this part of the figure here—the relationship between these marks and the surrounding space," Bernice had said in a group critique, pointing out the floating numerical figures in her painting, the blocking. "You're onto something." It wasn't the first time she had heard her work compared to various painters, the references had led her to abstract expressionists and encouraged her research. Here she stumbled on futurists—and once Saoirse had a taste, she was burning to get to work.

According to her tutor, she was beginning to develop a recognisable style.

"Careful now," a classmate joked. "You'll give her notions."

"Is that a Degas?" another joined the banter. "Oh wait, no—it's a *Saoirse*."

She had laughed, shy at the attention, but pleased knowing her classmates were beginning to treat her as an equal, careful to bring her down a peg from the praise, just in case.

The research unleashed her process, in the way she approached the objects, the fluidity that followed. She had begun to draw imagery, buried memories, releasing them onto paper, setting them free in paint.

She entered three finished paintings in the end-of-year show.

"One to watch," Bernice told the audience at the award ceremony, with both respect and envy in her voice. "One to watch."

Solo

Winter 1996

She pays for Paul's unhappiness, his discontent. It is particularly evident when Catherine is around. He has arrived home from work at the surgery to find her friend has come to visit, *again*. He is even more annoyed to find the two women in the studio out back with a fresh bottle of champagne uncorked. Paul has accused Saoirse of treating the studio space as though it belongs to her for entertaining purposes, he accuses her of colonising his parents' house, slowly, one room at a time. She already has the conservatory for her art studio, if that weren't enough.

But Saoirse knows what really bothers him is she has taken to staying out here—painting until the early hours of the morning and falling asleep in the single bed at the back, even though Paul reminds her, he has generously allocated Viv's old bedroom to her. Living out here makes her remote, removed from his control, his illusion that she is with him. He takes no pains to hide that it makes him furious, in fact.

Now, to come home, and find Catherine. Paul blames her for everything from Saoirse's artistic ambitions to her refusing to marry him. Saoirse smiles patiently on the outside, and seethes on the inside, treading the fine line between keeping her daughter's environment stable and Paul's temper at bay.

"Entertaining, are we?" Paul asks with a smirk.

"Bubbly?" Catherine offers, just as coolly. She doesn't even try and hide her contempt any longer.

"What are we celebrating?" he asks.

Catherine throws a glance at Saoirse.

"I haven't told him yet," Saoirse says.

Catherine gives her an apologetic grimace.

"Told me what?"

"I've my first solo exhibition."

"Really?" Paul sounds surprised.

"Catherine has set it up."

"Nice one," he says unenthusiastically.

"It is nice," Catherine says. "It's really nice for Saoirse—"

Paul scoffs at Catherine calling her *Saoirse*.

"Good for Sarah," he emphasises her name. "These must be good friends of yours, Catherine."

"I had the contact, but it is her work they want. You are gaining a name for yourself, my dear." She gives a little flourish of her shoulders.

Paul raises his brow.

"Don't you want to know the details?" Catherine challenges him.

Saoirse watches the standoff with dread. She knows what it will cost once Catherine leaves.

"Where is this exhibition to be held?" he asks, and it is obvious even he can hear the elevation in his own voice and moves to temper it, coming to Saoirse to congratulate her, kissing her cheek, forcing an unnatural smile. His artful display makes her shudder.

"At the David Davis Gallery. Quite a nice place to start. A small, remote historic house. Yet, prestigious. Your one was there—who's the concept artist?"

"In Cork?" he asks.

"Indeed."

"I know it," he says pompously. "Well, I'll leave you to your celebrations."

He looks pointedly at Saoirse.

"I'll put your daughter to bed."

Catherine smiles a wide, patient smile.

When he leaves, she turns to Saoirse and shakes her head indignantly.

"Don't start," Saoirse tells her, finishing her glass of champagne.

Catherine tops her up.

"I think you're going to need this."

After Catherine leaves, and after Leah is tucked up in the house, while his parents have turned the television on in the sitting room, Saoirse does not know that Paul is watching her through the window of the studio. She sits at the little island, finishing off the last of the champagne, the radio on to keep her company, she considers the paintings she will enter into the exhibition.

She doesn't know he is behind her, creeping up on her stealthily, until he is already grabbing her, pulling her hair from the base of its skull, yanking her backward off the stool. She knows the act absorbs the surge of hatred she evokes in him; and if it weren't for short-circuiting that rage, he could hurt her very badly, she fears. He never threatens her with the information he has, but she knows this is hanging over her. It is threat enough.

He tries not to leave marks and he never would dare hurt her in front of Leah. This, in itself, is a small mercy. This is what it costs to keep her daughter safe. Safe from greater dangers, the danger of her own mother's secrets being exposed. Saoirse grips his hands, trying to relieve the pressure on her scalp.

"You should have told me—" His voice is no louder than a whisper. He hears his own panting and already despises himself. "You should have told me yourself."

When he has drained his rage and apologised and blamed it on the long hours and his jealousy at her confiding in Catherine over him, and the countless other excuses he makes for himself, Saoirse manages to send him away. Telling him she'll clean up and follow him up to the house.

First, she puts her face into her hands and sobs. She feels the arms of Daithí come around her, holding her, comforting her until she is strong enough to clap her hands together and decide to get on with it. She wipes her eyes and cleans up the studio kitchen, then takes out the sketchbook. She studies a drawing she has been working on—the blurry hours after she put her sister in the car, sent her over the bridge. It is a composition that mirrors this theme that has persisted all her life.

Escape.

Once again she is here. She needs to find a way out.

Yellow Lines

Mixed media on canvas

This is how much I trust Eddie; how little I suspect his involvement in Lou's criminal world. After I put my sister in the car, after I send her over the bridge to awaken in a house of strangers, I get in the car and drive myself back toward the farm. There is nowhere else I can think to go. I call Eddie from a pay phone at a truck stop a few miles before the exit.

Eddie tells me to stay put, he is coming for me. I hang up and breathe a sigh of relief. Thank God for Eddie, he has friends and relatives everywhere, he will know how to help me disappear. I sit and wait and wonder how much I need to tell him without getting him too involved.

The interstate doesn't stop moving, the constant whir of motion. The eighteen-wheelers pull in and leave again. Truckers stretch their legs, drink coffee from Styrofoam cups. I have only been back from Florida for forty-eight hours though it feels a lifetime has passed, and I can still feel Kenny on my skin.

When Eddie pulls in, I feel the taint of what happened even deeper. I don't know what I expected when I called him, but I didn't expect him to be annoyed.

I turn off the car, leave the keys in the ignition.

You're in trouble, *he says when I climb into his passenger seat.*

I don't answer.

His hands shake as he lights us both a cigarette. I sit back against the door and study his face.

Eddie is easy—always easy. He isn't easy now.

Come here, *he says and leans toward me, puts his hand around the back of my neck. It feels sudden and unnatural and when I won't budge, he tries to draw me toward him.*

Don't, *I tell him, pushing him away. Reaching for the handle.*

Hey—*He softens. He is studying me now.* What's the matter—what's happened?

Nothing, *I say, defensive, covering my cheek as though I am hiding a bruise. I look at Eddie and wonder how I ever let him touch me.*

He puts his hands up to show he is not coming near me. The smoke curls off the end of his cigarette. He takes a drag and holds it in his lungs, the smoke streams slowly out his nostrils. I roll down the window and throw my own butt onto the pavement.

It's Lou, yeah?

Suddenly it seems I shouldn't be saying anything to Eddie. What is this? *I ask myself. Somehow, in the past forty-eight hours, he has become a stranger. We sit there in silence. He snaps on the radio to break the tension. "Space Cowboy" blares into the car and even his antics with the song's lyrics won't make me break. He quits trying. Sweat has broken out on his brow. It isn't just me, then, I realise. It is Eddie, too. Everything has changed.*

I know something about Lou, *he finally says. And now he is being real.*

Yeah?

Whatever he was, he's no small-time drug dealer any longer. He's in the big time. You ought to be careful.

I nod as though he is telling me something new.

My old man was an asshole, but he never had me running drugs for him. I thought you'd be smarter than that.

He reaches under his seat and pulls out a brown paper bag. It rustles as he opens it. He demands I look inside. It is the pistol from my mother's drawer.

You know how I got this? Lou brought it to me. Told me to come find you. Turns out, I didn't have to look too long. You came to me.

Did you tell him I called you? *I ask, ready to bolt.* Does he know you're here? *I am reaching for the handle.*

Calm down—no I didn't. You think I want to do Lou's dirty work?

Why would he give you that?

To scare you, I guess. It's working, ain't it?

Why'd you take it?

Well, it's Lou. You don't ask questions, do you? You should know.

This feeling of unease is growing. Eddie is not telling me everything. I pull the handle now, ease the door open.

Wait a minute. *He stretches the bag out toward me.* You take this. I don't want it. *Eddie's voice is stronger than I've ever heard it.* I don't want any of this. I don't need this trouble. I'm already on probation. I'm only here because you called me.

He is right, I called him. I've brought him into this trouble.

And you want to know why I took the fucking gun? Because I didn't want you to come home and have him shoot your head off—he's that angry.

I am in the middle of deciding whether to thank him or run from him when he says it.

Don't you know, babe? I love you. Can't you see us marrying some day?

I draw away.

Oh, what. Don't, *he says, hitting the steering wheel, embarrassed.*

I'm apologetic. I didn't know he was going to declare such a thing. I'm just—

All right, *he says.* That's enough. What do you need from me? You need me to teach you how to fire this thing? Just tell me what you want, and I'll do it, *he says with passion.* I'd do anything for you. *He hands me the bag.*

I am not thinking. Not thinking like a criminal anyway. I reach in and take the pistol into my hands. Place my finger on the trigger. Feel the cold heaviness of its weight. I already know how to fire a gun. What worries me is how much I can imagine myself finding Lou. Imagining what it would feel like to stand in the field, point the barrel at his crotch, at his chest. Aim for his heart. I think there is so much I would be capable of right now.

I don't need this, *I say, handing the pistol back to him.*

He pulls his hands away.

Don't give me that thing. I don't need my fingerprints all over it. Put it in the bag.

Eddie is right. He shouldn't be involved in this, no more than I should be. It isn't fair. We are teenagers—kids, really. We should be on some back road somewhere screwing, falling in love. Falling out of love. But kids like Eddie and me, we have no future. We only have each day and the hope that the shitty options that confront us will get us through to the next one.

I put the pistol back into the bag, crumple the paper around it.

I'll take care of it, *I tell him.*

I think you and your sister should get away. *He is staring straight ahead. He won't look me in the eye now, now that he has told me he loves me.*

I don't tell him Léa is already gone.

Where are we supposed to go? *I ask.*

What about Mrs. Jones? *he suggests. There is something on his face, a look that crosses his brow.* She has connections—

JezaBelle? *I ask. I feel my own brow twist in puzzlement, then suspicion.* You didn't tell her I called you, did you?

He hits the steering wheel again, which feels like an overreaction. When would I have done that? I didn't call Lou, I didn't call JezaBelle. You called me. Remember? And here I am.

Serious, Eddie, I'm in trouble, but I'm in trouble with Lou. Don't make it more complicated.

He calms and looks at me again.

Are you scared? *he asks, seeing through my words.*

A little, *I whisper.*

You should be.

I shift the paper bag on my lap and step out of the car.

Come on, *he tells me, resigned.* Remember my cousin Red? I'll drive you to his farm. He'll let you crash for the night and then we'll work it out.

I can't leave Fleur's car here, *I tell him.*

It's better this way, *he says.* I'll send Red back for it.

I can't work it out in words, it is a look or a gesture, I'm not sure, but I sense it—something is very, very wrong.

I've got to pee, *I tell him.*

I think you can wait until Red's place, *he tells me.* It's only up the road.

I left the keys in the ignition. I'll lock up, *I insist, stepping out of the car.*

He follows me.

Inside Fleur's car, I open the glove box and put the paper bag deep inside. Take the keys out of the ignition, lock the doors.

Eddie is waiting beside the car. He takes my elbow. When I back away, he tightens his grip. I see the stress on his face and that's when I know. I am Eddie's problem to solve.

Stop it, Eddie. You're hurting me.

I don't mean to, *he says, not loosening his grip.*

I'm coming with you, don't worry. Where else would I go?

I can't believe how calm my own voice sounds, whatever this is taking over.

Get in my car, *he tells me, and his eyes look mean.*

Look—let me pee. Give me some change, I'll get us a Coke and you drive me to Red's. Okay?

A look of uncertainty passes his brow.

Give me the keys, *he says. I hand him the keys to Fleur's car.*

He looks around, sees there aren't many places I can go from here. He loosens his grip on my elbow, fishes around in his pocket, pulls out a ten-dollar bill.

I'll be right back, Eddie. This is all we can do. Right?

Yeah, right, *he says, resigned. He walks back toward his car. When I look back, he has sat on the hood, placed his head in his hands.*

The hand dryer is firing in the men's toilet. I walk in one door and straight out the exit on the other side, scanning the parked trucks, looking for some way to escape. On the far side of the parking lot a station wagon is hidden from view amongst the trucks. It is pulling a pop-up camper bearing a Massachusetts license plate. A mother in the distance walks a child toward a table, the father has laid out a picnic.

As they tuck into the picnic, I crouch at the little half door of their camper, willing it to open. This is life or death. The door opens. I tear away the Velcro straps holding the door closed. I climb inside, between laundry baskets packed with shorts, tank tops, blankets, a suitcase. I pull the door closed, shifting back, into the darkness, folding into the space. It isn't long before the muffled voices of the child and mother return. I feel the shift of their weight, the slow roll of the car.

We are moving now, low on the road. A small hole has rusted away in the floor of the camper, just above the back wheel. The faster we move, the more the air comes through this hole. The interstate is close underneath, I can make out the yellow lines passing in a blur. I am certain I feel the curve of the road as we move into Ohio, diverge away from the highway leading to Florida. We are heading east under Lake Erie. With this hole I will survive this darkness, the heat of this space, and I will emerge out the other side, a headline.

Teenager Sarah Gagneux. Disappeared Without a Trace.

Impressions

Winter 1997

Catherine has come by to help Saoirse select the paintings for her next solo exhibition. They will choose them, wrap them, and prepare the canvases for transport to the Gallery in Letterkenny, in Donegal, in the New Year. Saoirse reminds her friend their time is limited, she has to collect Leah from school just after noon.

"That is hardly possible," Catherine says, tutting at the way time has flown. Saoirse had thought four years old was too early to start a child at school, but the truth was, she wanted to keep her daughter beside her as long as possible. Nuala had insisted Leah was smart and well able for school. *She'll be grand*, she had said to Saoirse's worry. And she was. Leah loves school.

It is the day Vivienne hosts an afternoon tea for her literary circle. She borrows her parents' sitting room for the occasion, even though Paul tells her to book a room at the pub. Saoirse apologises to Catherine for not offering her tea—instead, she tells her, they'll quickly work through this and then walk to the café before collecting Leah. She won't go near the kitchen with Vivienne and her friends around.

Catherine props the paintings against the glass, lining them up to see how each sits next to the others. She stands back, studies the configuration, then rearranges them again.

"I quite like these," she tells Saoirse. She has arranged three of the earlier pieces. They are more figurative and impressionistic than her recent work. What Saoirse doesn't tell her is the figure in these paintings is Sasa, the woman whose identity she has stolen.

There is a buzz of voices in the hall. Vivienne is bringing one of the members of her circle down the hall. She is a journalist, Vivienne tells her now, pausing at the door, and coincidentally, an art critic. Saoirse is startled by her tone—it is upbeat, pleasant. Then she sees why. Her visitor stands behind her, she is interested in Saoirse's work.

"I've been meaning to say congratulations, on the new exhibition." Vivienne tells her now, even though she has had several opportunities to say this to her in the past month.

"Thanks," Saoirse says, guarded.

Vivienne's guest follows her into the conservatory. She is stout and severe, wearing a polka-dotted dress with pockets. Catherine gives a little cry of delight. She knows this woman. Saoirse is thrown off guard, suspecting the visit isn't a coincidence after all.

"Edel, delighted to see you—" Catherine greets the woman with a kiss on each cheek.

"I thought the two of you might know each other," Vivienne says.

Saoirse feels her face flush.

"I really love your work, Saoirse. I'd love to do a piece on it for the magazine," Edel is saying to her.

"Oh, no. I don't think it's like that—" Saoirse is flustered, she feels ambushed, exposed. "I'm not really into that kind of thing."

Vivienne's laugh is patronising.

"*Not into that kind of thing?*" she mimics. "It's called publicity."

Edel walks around the conservatory, studying each piece. She may as well be examining Saoirse's naked body.

"I'll leave you to it," Vivienne says. "Who's for tea?"

Catherine stands beside Edel as she makes her way around the room, examining the paintings. The two women discuss the work as though they are visitors in a gallery, as though Saoirse is not here.

"Do you mind if I take a few photos? I can have a photographer return for some proper shots. And we'll want one of the artist. These are for my own reference."

Catherine nods her approval. Edel snaps photographs of the earlier paintings, one after another.

This can't be happening, Saoirse thinks.

"These are lovely. A different style to the rest," Edel is saying.

"Her earlier pieces, but something about them works, don't you think?"

Catherine turns to Saoirse, beaming. When she sees Saoirse's face, her smile drops. She takes Edel's arm, guides her toward the door.

"Look, Edel. Why don't we set up a better time to meet—Saoirse has a school run to make and we were going through the final works." She looks at her watch for effect.

"Sure, no bother." Edel seems unfazed. "Get in touch."

She holds a card out to Saoirse. Catherine takes it.

"We'll give you a shout."

She can hear Vivienne apologising in the kitchen, telling her Saoirse can be awkward at the best of times.

Catherine watches her friend, concerned.

"I know what you're thinking," she says.

"Do you?" And Saoirse cannot hide her annoyance.

"I see it. That weapon is all over you now," Catherine says of Vivienne, she can't stand her falseness, her pretension, either. "You have something she wants now. But listen to me. Edel is sound. Top of her game. She'll look after you."

"It's not that."

"What is it then?"

Saoirse can't explain the reason for the dread this unwanted attention brings. She can't tell her friend that by making her work public, she has exposed herself, opened up a new dimension that she hadn't counted on, put herself and Leah in danger. She can't tell her how stupid, stupid, stupid she has been.

The room feels as though it is beginning to spin. Catherine notices. "Sit down." She guides Saoirse to the rattan chair. "It's okay, it's just nerves. That's normal."

Outside of her art and nightmares, it has been a long time since she has let herself think of her life as it had been. There was a time when thoughts of Sasa and the identity she has stolen kept her awake at all hours, but she has since lost herself in motherhood, in her work as an artist. The fear of getting caught has moved to the back of her mind, it has somehow become contained in the process of surviving, in becoming—in the process of turning her memories into sketches, then into objects on a canvas. Her work has created a barrier, a hermetic seal of sorts, between a young girl fleeing for her life and the woman, the artist, the mother she has become.

But here, in this series of paintings, nothing is buried. And that is what scares her. It wasn't deliberate, it just evolved—she went from painting her own daughter to describing these scenes in Boston. These are actual, recognisable people. This canvas—a bright morning in the Public Gardens, the frog pond mirroring the blue cloudless sky on its surface. She had only arrived in Boston as a stowaway, she had been sleeping rough in the city for three nights and in these scenes, these memories, she had just laid her head back on the bench, was nodding off to sleep when she was jolted wide awake by a bawdy, singsong accent.

"What's the craic, Sasa?"

She startled, unsure what was happening, if she was being attacked, or arrested, until she saw it was a woman wearing a miniskirt and black fishnet tights over her meaty calves staring down at her on the bench, blocking her view. She was too shocked to move, she only lay there hugging her backpack closer to her chest.

"Mother of God—" the woman scolded her.

Her brain, heightened from fleeing, had raced to figure out who this woman was; where her accent was from, why she was treating her as though she knew her—but no matter how she stretched to understand, she was absolutely certain she had never seen this woman before in her life.

"Sit up," the woman instructed, dropping down on the bench beside her, bawling at her now, looking her up and down. "Sarah—what in the devil—"

Hearing her own name from this stranger's mouth startled her and she had scrambled to sitting, poised to flee, but the woman continued to berate her as though they were old friends. Sarah stood, thinking she should slip away quickly.

"What are you like? The state of you. Are you on drugs?" The woman took her hand and pulled her back down on the bench, not in an unfriendly way, but to straighten her hair, remove a twig that had become tangled in the strands. "Where are the babbies?"

It was halfway through this question the woman stopped smoothing her hair; her eyes widened and she leapt away, scooting to the other side of the bench.

"It isn't yourself, is it?"

She had shaken her head. Gripped her backpack closer, but she no longer felt she needed to flee. Something told her this woman wouldn't hurt her, and maybe she would even help her.

"No, you're not herself. Jaysus—you're the spit of her!"

And when she had met Sasa—the real Sarah Walsh, a nanny from Ireland—walking toward them pushing a stroller, holding the hand of a little girl, she finally understood why she had been mistaken for her. And here, in this painting, the little girl with her skirt and patent leather shoes was unmistakable, too.

And here, on this canvas, Sasa sneaking Saoirse into the heiress's home when she realised she had been sleeping on a park bench, she had helped her get hired as the spare nanny; and here—the two of them, brazen while the Cambridge heiress slept, stealing booze and watching the northern lights on a dockside at the woman's vacation cabin in Maine. And in this last one, Sasa, on the night of her birthday celebration, slumped against the leg of the desk, taking a shot of vodka, sucking a lemon.

This is the night Sasa told her about the baby she had given birth to at the age of seventeen, pregnant from a man who was her neighbour, her parents' friend. How her mother insisted she travel to England, telling everyone, even her granny, her departure was due to enrolment on a secretarial course, *isn't she a great girl?* Sasa was sent away to live in London with a distant cousin to spare her mother the shame. How she was forced to give birth, then give the baby up for adoption.

My little boy, she called the baby, how they told her best not to hold him, how she had tried to grasp his fingers, toes, before they took him away. How she had run away to America with a group of Irish friends who all overstayed their visas. And now she is self-exiled, forever, she had declared—she would never leave America, never return to Ireland, not in a million years.

This last painting is the night Sasa broke her heart, though, telling her she was leaving for Florida, following a new boyfriend down, begging her to come with her. But Florida was a place she would never return to again, not in another million years. And here, at the bottom of the painting, at its very edge is the document she stole, the corner of a passport that has bought her a new life, freedom in a foreign land. The passport that started her on a journey to becoming who she is now—artist and mother: *Saoirse Byrne.*

"You're not even hearing me, are you?" Catherine's voice breaks through her thoughts. Vivienne, too, is standing over her, holding a glass of water toward her.

Saoirse tries to stand.

"Leah," she says, remembering her daughter's collection.

"Look, pet, I think you've had a spell," Catherine is saying.

Saoirse tries to tell her that isn't the case, but her friend won't listen. Vivienne insists she take the water, that she remain seated until she feels better. They are keeping her from her daughter. She tries to stand again, sways, has to sit back down.

"You're not going anywhere," Vivienne tells her.

"Please," she begs, panic overcoming her. "Leah."

"I'll go for the child," Vivienne says, annoyed. She hands Catherine the glass.

Catherine kneels in front of Saoirse, concern on her face.

"Here, love, can you tell me what happened?" she asks, but Saoirse is looking beyond her. She reaches for the water from Catherine, takes a sip to please her, then rises from the chair, touches the corner of a canvas.

No, nothing is buried here. Her past is on display for all to see.

What have I done? Saoirse thinks, and the way Catherine is looking at her, she knows she has said this out loud.

Cracks in Everything

Early Spring 1997

Saoirse is relieved as they drive away from the Byrnes' house. Paul had threatened to come with her to the gallery opening in Donegal, but Nuala had other plans. Since Paul is working alongside his father in the surgery now, Nuala decided it was time Joseph took a break, now that he could. She booked a holiday to Spain, bringing Leah with them.

"Sure, isn't this what your father has worked so hard for all his life?" she warned Paul when he complained.

Saoirse knows the only reason Paul had even considered coming to her exhibition was because he, too, heard Daithí was on his way back from Kenya, returning to Donegal. They heard the news at Emily and Liam's wedding. Emily had told them it was a pity Daithí was missing their day by only weeks. Liam hoped he would be his best man—but that was the way it went.

Saoirse longed to hear from him, to know what it was like meeting his half siblings, working alongside his father. She also knew if he wanted to get in touch with her, he would have done so by now. She had to let him go, let go of her habit of conjuring him. It had served its purpose, she told herself, and now it was simply unhealthy. It was time to move on.

For a moment, Saoirse feels buoyant and light as Catherine drives them along the canal, heading west out of Dublin. The gallery owner, a friend of Catherine's from college, rang her that morning before she collected Saoirse, asking her to pass on the news that Saoirse had sold every painting before the opening night.

"So, does this mean the exhibition is cancelled?" Saoirse half hopes it to be the case.

Catherine laughs.

"Oh no, it goes ahead. They will seize your back stock; they will commission your work. You will take a shite, and they will call it sculpture."

It has taken her a while to convince Saoirse that she could keep her privacy *and* hold exhibitions around the country.

"You sell the work you want to sell," Catherine had said of the paintings featuring Sasa, even though she couldn't understand why Saoirse wanted to hold on to them in the first place. "Whatever your reasons, you are in charge here, Saor. Don't forget that."

But it worries Saoirse, there has been so much attention already. She has won prizes and scholarships. The newspapers ring, wanting a story from her, or a photo, anything on her background. Vivienne has not let her forget her friend Edel wants to do a spread in the *Arts and Culture* magazine. Catherine tells Saoirse that her refusal adds to her mystique, keeps them wanting more.

Saoirse is suspicious Catherine has created this fuss, that she has instructed her friends to buy her work, selling her on sympathy.

"These are not my friends," Catherine says. "They are business associates, and there is a reason they are rich! Their sympathy might extend to attending an event and drinking the free wine, but these are people with money to burn—they are buying your work because they feel they are getting something that everyone wants but no one else can have."

Saoirse tries to fathom this information.

"Hey, I've been wanting to talk to you about this." Catherine turns serious now. "You don't have to believe in yourself. But you have to believe the art critics, believe the money. But come here to me," Catherine says. "Have you thought of seeing someone?"

"Like, dating?"

Catherine laughs.

"Let's not get ahead of ourselves. I'm only talking about counselling."

Saoirse laughs at the misunderstanding.

"Couples counselling?"

"A therapist. For yourself. Possibly with the view of getting away from *that man. That family*. They do nothing for your confidence."

Saoirse isn't sure she likes where this is going.

"And maybe someday, yes, consider dating again. You are a young woman. Tell me, don't you get lonely?"

"Of course." The words come out in a hoarse whisper. Saoirse clears her throat. She can't start thinking about Daithí, not now, not while they are driving toward him, toward his home, toward the last place they were together.

"And you?" Saoirse asks, more to change the subject than prod at something she knows is painful for Catherine to speak about.

"Well, you know how that ended. I'm sure Paul has looked into and informed you on the intricacies of my marriage?"

Saoirse doesn't deny it. Catherine glances at Saoirse.

"I'm sorry," Saoirse tells her.

"My husband was very ill. He couldn't live, as much as I needed him to. Didn't want to live like that, and I couldn't blame him. He took his own life. He was the love of mine."

Saoirse closes her eyes.

She knows what it feels like to lose the love of her life.

A quiet grows between the women.

"You've been saying you will tell me—" Saoirse says after a time. "Why were you on the pier that night?"

Catherine nods, tears come to her eyes, and she reaches for Saoirse's hand, keeping an eye on the road.

"You know why," she whispers.

Saoirse squeezes her own eyes against the sting of the memory, the kindness of her friend.

"That's where he ended his life, isn't it?"

Catherine nods.

"How do I thank you for all you've given me?" Saoirse whispers.

The sun has come out from behind a cloud. Catherine wipes her eyes and reaches for her sunglasses.

"For starters, you put your life back on track," she says. "Whatever brought you to that point—you get away. In your case, I imagine you get away from someone who has no idea of the meaning of love."

"That might be difficult," Saoirse admits.

"Difficult? In what way? I mean, of course it won't be easy. But I think it would be an investment in your future, in Leah's future, if you decide to leave the Byrnes. Besides," Catherine changes track, her voice rising with enthusiasm, "I think you are just at the start of a very successful career. And you know I've that big empty house waiting for you and Leah in Greystones, until you can get on your feet."

"You are too good," Saoirse tells her. "But—it is about Leah."

"What about Leah?" Catherine is stern with insistence.

"She needs a father."

"Oh, she will have a father. Paul will make sure of that; don't you doubt it. Tell me this—what was your own father like?"

Saoirse isn't expecting this question. She looks out the window, at the fields passing by in a blur.

"I don't want to pry. I gather things weren't easy for you one way or another. But I ask not because I'm curious. I ask because sometimes we must look back to figure out why we landed where we did. I mean—Paul? Was there something you saw in him? Something in particular? It's not just bad taste, right?"

Saoirse feels a sense of guilt, and simultaneous glee, giggling with Catherine like they are the bold girls at the back of the classroom.

"Stop, Catherine. This is Leah's father we're talking about."

When they stop laughing, Saoirse shakes her head.

"I didn't know who my father was, but in fairness, Paul is nothing like my stepfather—"

"No?"

"No. He was selfish and vile, he took advantage of every opportunity he came across, and used us in the process—"

"Yes, this describes Paul, don't you think?"

"My stepfather neglected us, put us in dangerous situations. We were poor. Always moving—Paul isn't like *that*. He is stable, and has a decent job, more than decent—and a house—kind of—but at least I don't fear where my daughter and I will sleep at night. The Byrnes are a *good* family."

"Oh, I see. You've traded up, have you?"

Sometimes Catherine is too pragmatic. Saoirse shifts in her seat.

"Maybe."

"But did you? Trade up?"

Catherine leaves the question hanging in the air.

"Yeah, thought not. Same shite, different man. You know something? You mind everyone so well. You need minding yourself. You deserve better. Leah deserves to see you break that pattern."

And there is Daithí, in their silence. The way he minded her, took care with her. Took care with everyone. And he was home in Ireland again. Needing him, wanting him, and yet, she can't have him. Not with her past.

"Catherine—"

Catherine glances at her, noticing her change of tone.

"What is it? Tell me."

What Catherine can never understand is nothing needs breaking as much as it needs shoring up. This torrent of, what—lies? Omissions? They are growing, bulging against the reservoir, already cascading down the spillway, ready to breach the walls. The only option Saoirse sees open to her is to carry on as long as she can, get Leah to a certain age. And if the dam breaks, if she is found out before then, she realises, it is taking everything with it—everything she has so carefully put into place.

"Sometimes you have no choice," Saoirse tells her. She hadn't meant to reveal so much, but it is too late. Catherine has glanced at her. She is checking her rearview mirror, putting on the signal. She is pulling into the side of the road.

"Why do I feel there is more you have to tell me?"

Saoirse feels a dangerous sense of energy circulating through her body. One part of her wants to trust Catherine—take the leap. But she knows she should not be saying these things—not even to Catherine.

"What if—" Saoirse asks.

"*What if* what?"

"What if it puts you in a position you don't want to be in?"

"Tell me, pet." Catherine's eyes are soft, tempting Saoirse to confide.

"What if I am damaged beyond repair?" Saoirse asks, fighting to keep her emotions in check. Everything is right here, if only she could begin. But she can't. She shakes her head. The kindness in Catherine's voice doesn't make it easier.

"Leonard Cohen has an answer for that," Catherine smiles.

"Leonard Cohen?"

"The way he sings about cracks and light."

Saoirse smiles sadly. She wishes she could tell Catherine. If anyone, she would understand, she would forgive her. Catherine grows serious.

"Is he hurting you?"

Saoirse looks down at her hands.

"Saoirse?"

"Not in front of Leah," she whispers. "Not where it shows."

"Jesus, love."

Catherine pulls her into her and Saoirse can only let go, sobbing into her chest.

"It's okay. Ah, now. It's all going to be all right."

Fingerprints

Charcoal on paper

It is a small headline on the front page of the Boston Globe. *The words float as though coming forward out of the newspaper box. I am waiting outside the music school with the children I mind, waiting on the Number One bus to bring us back up Mass Ave toward Cambridge. This is only a job now without Sasa. I am bored and uninterested, and passively glimpsing the headlines while we wait, the way you read a cereal box at the breakfast table. Something about the thumbnail image grabs my attention. The little girl I mind tugs at my free hand, the bus is coming. She moves closer to the street, I move opposite, toward the box to have a closer look. I have seen this image before.*

It is a younger version of me. So young I still have a constellation of freckles across my cheeks and nose. It is my seventh-grade yearbook photo, the last time I subjected myself to such a sitting. The photo accompanies a startling headline.

THREE BODIES UNEARTHED AT RURAL FARM IN MICHIGAN

I skim the rest of the column until the words bend under with the fold. The bus has pulled up and the girl is growing anxious, fearful we will miss it. Her brother kicks his legs in the stroller. I push the coins, our bus fare, into the slot, releasing the door, taking a paper. The girl is already standing on the step, boarding the bus. I rummage around in my pockets, searching for more change. The girl has a small purse and she pays our bus fare.

I have held a vision of the farm—in my version, the fields are golden with the last hour of sun. Winged things are alight, sailing inside the heat-soaked air. Lou's car is parked in the driveway. They have given up on us coming home, or perhaps they never really noticed we were gone. My mother and Lou are inside the house, getting each other high. A wasp flies into a web, the spider darts for its prey. Lou sinks another needle into my mother, collapsing another vein, liquidising, devouring her from within. How did someone so beautiful, so young, exchange her life for him?

And yet—on another level—I have known my mother was dead. I knew it when Lou picked her up, the angle of her neck, how he had placed her in the car. And I knew Lou was a sitting duck. Kenny was coming. You can't steal hundreds of thousands of dollars from the Florida mafia and go unpunished.

It is on the stifling bus I learn the shocking confirmation of what happened after we fled. The newspaper says their bodies lay in a shallow grave, undetected for weeks. My mother is dead. Lou is dead. How Kenny has been murdered, buried at the farm, is the mystery—but by the end of the article, I will understand that I am a suspect.

The newspaper says two children were initially missing. One was found safe with relatives. The second was spotted in a Detroit parking lot before disappearing without a trace and is now considered a fugitive, a minor whose full name is still to be confirmed. She is either dead or sheltering. Fingerprints found on the gun. Local teacher, accused of coordinating criminal activities linked to violent Florida gang, including sex trafficking, drug hauls, and money laundering. Manhunt underway for missing teen. Unnamed man to receive immunity for leading law enforcement to the shallow grave, claiming he witnessed slayings.

I think this must be what it is to suffocate.

In the travel agency, my whole body trembles as I tell the woman I must return home immediately, to Ireland, to see my granny who is dying. It is not hard to conjure real tears—thinking of my mother, thinking of how I have been framed. I hand the agent the stolen passport, she copies the name onto my tickets. She takes the money I have taken from Lou, who took it from Kenny. It is stolen money, but I am certain I have paid this fare.

I look at the clock behind the travel agent's head. I have six hours to get to the airport, to board this flight. Six hours will probably be just enough time.

Vigil

30–31 August 1997

Saoirse has drank too much. She opened a bottle of wine while cooking the dinner in the studio, and by the time Liam and Emily arrive, she is drunk.

Leah did not want to go back up to the house, to her own room, instead, she has fallen asleep on the bed in the little room at the back. It is her defence mechanism, Paul says, Leah can sleep anywhere, through anything.

They have finished dinner and dessert. Saoirse had served the coffee, and their guests have shown no sign of leaving so she opens another bottle. It is well after midnight and Liam and Paul are discussing music, the gigs Liam is playing, how he hopes he will be given a regular session with RTÉ. Planning for their future family will be much easier. Paul tells Liam gigging couldn't be so hard, not like a doctor's life, especially working alongside his father at the surgery now that his father is reaching retirement age.

"As a doctor you're always on call," Paul tells him, full of self-importance. His talk is drinking talk, one-upmanship. "Even in the grocery shop, someone wants to corner you, get a diagnosis, wrangle a prescription."

Saoirse resents his exaggeration, and she resents the unhappiness in Paul's voice. She wonders if she ever heard him happy, even once? She pours more wine into Emily's glass.

"You've a great run of exhibitions, Saor—where are you now?"

"Cork," Paul answers.

Saoirse doesn't even bother correcting him. She is exhibiting in Limerick, but he doesn't warrant a correction. She no longer bothers to hide her contempt for him. It has been like this now. Saoirse had taken Catherine's advice, documented everything. She lets him see she is recording every squeeze, slap, threat, it all gets logged in her book. She has threatened to go to the medical board. He had grown quiet and avoided her now as much as she avoided him. This rare occasion, having dinner with Liam and Emily, was an excuse for Paul to keep up appearances, and Saoirse to keep a connection to Daithí, to hear about his life.

Emily catches Liam's hand, she rubs it like she is giving him a massage. He pulls it back from her and places it on her knee. Saoirse imagines Emily can't wait to get out of here, to discuss her and Paul on the way home, the unhappy couple. How lucky they are in comparison, she will say. And they will touch each other all the way home, once inside the door, grope each other, make love. Maybe even fuck, if there is a difference. At first, Saoirse feels a bitterness. And then she does that thing again.

Imagines Daithí sitting next to her, instead of Paul. Imagines the touch of his hand on her knee, the small of her back, and she feels such an intense pain of longing she can hardly breathe.

"Have you seen Daithí since he's returned?" Emily asks as though she can read Saoirse's mind. Liam looks at her in warning.

"We were there last month—" Liam isn't even aiming for subtle now, giving Emily the knife across the throat—but she isn't looking in his direction.

Paul sneers. Emily doesn't seem to notice. She is desperate to keep the conversation moving.

"—his house is finished. Absolutely stunning. It is painted white on the outside. *Lime rendered* he calls it, I guess that means *whitewashed*—and he has an entire glass atrium facing the sea. It's unreal—"

"Good for Daithí." Paul's tone makes her pull back.

He lifts a stack of dirty plates, dashes the cutlery from their surface into the sink. Emily nervously jumps up to help him clear.

Liam is looking at Saoirse, stricken. And in that look, she knows—he is not here to visit Paul. He is here on a favour. It is for the same reason Seamus came to the gallery earlier in the year, to her solo exhibition in Donegal. She had been shocked to see him walk through the door. Seamus confirmed Daithí was recently back from Kenya.

"The lad would've come himself, but he wasn't sure you'd be happy to see him," Seamus had said. She had so many questions, so much she wanted to know, but Saoirse felt him searching her face, and she had seized up, not trusting herself to speak. "I've to get back to the pub," he had said and left soon after he arrived, and she wished she could start the conversation again. She wondered what Seamus had told Daithí on his return, that she was apathetic? That was so far from the truth, she wanted to cry thinking of it.

She sees this in Liam's face now, that he is here on a mission, though he would never say, he would never betray Daithí, not even to Emily.

Paul returns to the table. He picks up his napkin fallen to the floor.

"It *is* good for Daithí." Saoirse turns on Paul. "Why wouldn't you be happy for your friend?"

Paul looks like he will choke on his anger, or that he will choke her to dispel it.

"You probably ought to check on Leah," he tells her slowly.

"I'm sure she is fine," Saoirse challenges.

"I heard her stir."

"Will I check?" Emily asks, too enthusiastically. Liam places a hand on her leg. Instead, she makes a point of looking at the clock on the microwave.

"Right, so, look at the time. We're keeping you now—will we make a move?" she asks, clapping her hands together.

But Liam doesn't move. Saoirse realises he has something to say to her, but hasn't gotten her alone.

"I'll ring a taxi," Paul says.

Saoirse's head is spinning from the wine. She imagines she will be sick later. She gets up from the table, moves into the little room where Leah is sleeping. Closes the door without saying goodbye. If they would leave, Paul will get done whatever violence he needs to commit on her to relieve himself of his anger. She would die if this ever made it back to Daithí—what she has given up over him, what her life has become. Leah is sound asleep on the bed. She looks out the little window across the garden. The lights have come on in the Byrnes.

The doorknob is turning. She thought he would wait until Liam and Emily leave. Even the threat of her written record does not deter Paul. Not with this level of anger, and she knows it has everything to do with the mention of Daithí, his jealousy, the one-sided rivalry—whatever it is he holds against this man, it started well before her. But she also knows he blames him that things did not work out with her. She feels him behind her now. He puts his hand on the back of her neck in silence and squeezes. His words are nearly inaudible, but they freeze her blood.

"I have almost finished with you."

She struggles out of his grasp. "Please, you'll wake Leah," she whispers. His fingers come around her neck.

"Stop," she says, trying to loosen his grip. "You're hurting me." She doesn't think she said it so loud, but Liam is calling from the kitchen.

"You okay? Lads?"

"This is all your fault," Paul hisses in her ear. "You have ruined my life."

The television turns on in the front room. They are moving dishes around. Someone turns on the taps.

Saoirse sits down on the bed, unable to choke back the tears.

"What's the matter with you?" Paul hisses.

"I can't do this anymore," Saoirse says.

"What are you talking about?"

"You know what I'm talking about, Paul. I hoped to stay for Leah—but this just doesn't work."

"How is this not working out? For you? How could this not possibly be working out for *you*?"

"Jesus," Emily is saying from the kitchen. "Lads—"

Saoirse thinks Emily has seen Paul pushing her backward, how she has half fallen onto Leah's legs. She scrambles to get back up off the bed. The child turns over, away from where Paul is holding her forehead now so she can't lift herself off the bed.

Emily is insistent, calling to them from the kitchen.

"Stay," Paul tells her, and she can't help thinking this is the tone he takes with Bugle.

He moves toward the urgency in Emily's voice.

Saoirse rubs her neck where his hands have left a burning sensation. She sits beside her sleeping child and puts her face in her hands. This dread. All her life, this dread, this feeling of shattered glass. *I've got to get us out of here*, she thinks.

"Ah feck," Paul is saying. "Turn it up."

"I can't believe it—" Emily gasps.

"Ah, no," Liam echoes.

Saoirse can hear the headlines now: "It's been reported in the last few minutes that Diana, Princess of Wales, has been seriously injured in a car crash in Paris—"

Saoirse falls back onto the bed, lies beside her daughter, she turns her face into the pillow. She bites the feathery down to keep from sobbing aloud. She weeps until she is empty of tears and the pillow is soaked beside her. She nearly has no further strength, but she manages to move herself beside her sleeping daughter, she moves her own body around Leah, like armour, she kisses her hair, kisses her sleeping eyes, picks up her hand and kisses her fingertips.

She imagines herself moving out into the sitting room. Whispering to Liam.

Tell him to come for us.

And she feels, in her imagination, Daithí, coming through the door, lying next to her, placing his body around hers. She hears the commentary coming out of the kitchen, and she couldn't care less. There is one thing in this world and she is here, beside her. She will lie here and hold her daughter and imagine being held.

SHE DOESN'T KNOW HOW LONG she has been asleep when frantic knocking wakes her.

The alarm clock radio at the end of the bed says it is 3:16 A.M., the darkness through the skylight is beginning to show hints of the morning. It is disorientating then, to still hear Emily and Liam's voices in the kitchen, the three of them watching the television reports coming out of Paris.

It is Nuala knocking, she realises, it is her voice outside in the garden.

"Paul—" Nuala cries.

"We know, Mother," Paul says, annoyed. "We're watching the news—"

"It's not looking good for her," Emily is saying. "We can't look away."

"Oh Paul," Nuala gasps.

"Come in, Mam, don't be silly—it's not like you knew her—"

"You all right, Mrs. Byrne?" Liam asks, concerned.

"Listen to me." Nuala lets out a frightful cry. "It's your father, he's after collapsing."

"My father?" Paul cries.

Saoirse sits up. Leah startles beside her.

By the time she soothes Leah, by the time she gets back to the kitchen,

Departures

8 September 1997

e hearse and funeral car have arrived outside the door of the Byrnes' use. No one is ready to leave. Paul stands at the hearth, holding the ituary. Vivienne sits on the sofa, her head in her hands. Christopher ınds at the casket near the window, watching the street, pretending not notice the scene unfolding behind him.

"I put it in," Vivienne insists between gasps. Her makeup runs and e is dabbing at her watery eyes with the edge of her pinkie, trying to ntain the damage. "You can see, right there, I wrote it down in the otebook. I must have forgotten to say her name."

"You're an ass, Vivienne," Paul hollers.

"Stop it," Saoirse pleads. She turns to Vivienne. "I don't mind. It oesn't matter."

"It does matter," Paul roars.

"We're about to bury my father," Vivienne says, and breaks into fresh ears. "You can give me a break."

"It's okay, Viv, it really is," Saoirse nods. "Don't think another bit bout it." She takes two tissues from the bookshelf and hands them to Vivienne.

"The car is here," Christopher announces.

Paul ignores him.

"It's not okay." He turns on Saoirse. "She did this on purpose—"

"Stop it—" Saoirse says, motioning toward Leah, who has just come into the room.

The undertakers are at the door, ready for the removal.

"Granny says she is on the way down."

"We know—" Paul scolds. Saoirse takes Leah by the shoulder, smooths her hair.

"Get your coat, love."

Nuala's footsteps are on the stairs, slow and heavy, the way she has it is empty, the others have followed Nuala up the g see their shapes moving through the lighted wind closer in the distance.

She returns to Leah. There is nothing to do now her daughter and wait.

BELOVED GENERAL PRACTITIONER AND LIFETIM SANDYMOUNT RESIDENT DIES AGE 63

Irish Times, 4 September 1997

Dr. Joseph Byrne, lifetime resident of Sandymo General Practitioner, passed away surrounded by h ily in St. Vincent's Hospital after a short illness. Belo of Nuala, adored father to Vivienne (Doherty), est to Simon and Paul, who both followed him into profession. He will be sadly missed by his daughter- son-in-law Christopher, his adored granddaughters son, a host of nephews, nieces, relatives, acquaintan and friends. The surgery will be closed Monday, 8th as a mark of respect. Dr. Paul Byrne, who completed under Dr. Joseph Byrne, will take over as lead Gen tioner at the surgery. Removal and service details to been since they took Joseph from the house, and then returned him, laid out in the casket.

"You never liked her—"

"That isn't necessary, Paul, stop this—" Saoirse demands. He is out of control, and the cold body of Joseph, his grey hair smoothed at the temples, his hands folded over the rosary beads, makes her feel like she, too, has stopped breathing. Vivienne has given up defending herself and has stopped trying to save her makeup. She is sobbing into the tissues Saoirse has given her.

"It's rotten," Paul says, picking up the obituary.

"It was an oversight," Saoirse tells him firmly.

"To hell it was."

"We'll get them to reprint it," Christopher says. "They can add her name. It's not a big deal."

"It is a big deal."

Leah has come back with her coat.

Nuala calls from the hallway.

"It is time to close the coffin," she says ceremoniously. "Is Simon coming to the house?"

"I told you, Mam—" Vivienne tells her, sobbing. "They are meeting us at church."

Nuala has come into the room now wearing a black cape coat, heels, pearls. Her voice catches in her chest.

"He has every right to travel in his father's funeral car." She looks at Saoirse when she is saying this.

"Of course, he does." Vivienne sniffs. "He just didn't want to ride with us."

"Because the car is packed to the hilt," Nuala tells her, and her face crumples.

Saoirse holds Leah's coat while she pulls her arms through. She takes a handful of tissues and stuffs them into her own pocket, takes her daughter by the hand. She cannot hear any more. She takes her daughter up to Joseph's coffin. She squeezes Leah's hand. "Say a prayer for Granda," she whispers.

Leah folds her hands and looks worried. Saoirse nods. Leah mumbles a prayer she has learned at school. When she is finished, they both cross themselves.

"Good girl," Nuala tells her.

Leah bursts into tears.

Saoirse pulls her into her side. At six years old she seems so innocent to Saoirse, and fragile, and she wonders if this is because she is comparing her to her own sister at this age? Her own little Leah looks like a Byrne, but she has all the gentle sweetness of her little sister, Léa.

"Why is everyone fighting?" Leah asks as they walk out the door together.

"Don't worry, honey. Everyone is just sad."

"I miss Granda," Leah sobs.

"I know, we all do." Saoirse pulls Leah closer to her, strokes her hair. *He was the only sane one in this house*, Saoirse thinks.

"Come on. We need a bit of fresh air."

"Will Granny be mad?"

"No, love, she's too sad to be mad."

They pass the driver waiting at the black mourning car at the end of the driveway. He opens the rear door when they near the car. Saoirse lifts her hand to him.

"Thank you, we'll walk."

"Madame," he says, closing the door.

"Will you tell the others we've gone ahead?" She fights to hold her voice steady. The driver nods and tips his hat. She feels she could collapse right now on the pavement and never get up again.

They walk hand in hand to the church, along the sea road. The tide is out, the clouds are mirrored on the wet sand.

At the church, a crowd has formed on the steps and flows down into the car park and out the gates. A line of schoolchildren form an honour guard. Saoirse holds Leah's hand. She swaps her daughter's wet tissues for the dry ones in her pocket. In this crowd Saoirse feels detached, as though she is moving farther away from Paul, his family, this community that has gathered to pay their respects to Dr. Joe. She almost expects to look over and see Joseph leaning against the church, winking, sharing the joke.

Saoirse wills herself not to break down, not while she is holding Leah's hand, not when her daughter needs her most. There is a hand on her shoulder. Catherine is the first one Saoirse rang after she heard Joseph had died. The two women hug.

"Stay with me," she whispers.

"Of course."

The hearse arrives and the family car behind it.

The crowds move and the women step farther back with them.

When the coffin is removed, Catherine urges them forward, prompting Saoirse to follow the family as they walk behind Joseph's coffin into his final Mass. Simon has joined his mother, taking her arm while Vivienne takes the other. Paul walks beside them with Christopher, he isn't looking for Saoirse or Leah. Mary, waiting on the steps, holds the hand of her youngest child, half a year older than Leah. Her girls are sombre, waiting to follow the coffin into the church.

The crowd folds around Saoirse and Leah until there is no chance of catching up with the family. Catherine walks with them as they follow the congregation streaming into the church as the hymn begins.

Come back to me with all your heart
Don't let fear keep us apart

The pallbearers place Joseph's coffin on the altar. The Byrne family reach the front of the church, taking their seats in the front row. They haven't saved her and Leah a seat.

You shall sleep secure with peace
Faithfulness will be your joy

The hymn catches Saoirse, it is as though the woman, with her soprano notes, has put two fingers to her trachea and squeezed. She is startled to realise, halfway up the aisle, she is thinking of her own mother and her sister, Léa. But the more she tries to repress their memory, the more acutely she feels the eruption of emotion deep inside. She knows she will not be able to control this, not while these chords, this hymn, excavates all the pain she has buried. She turns to leave. Catherine takes her arm and pulls her gently into a pew, halfway at the back of the church. She collapses into a seat, bites her hand to contain the accumulation of all that she must mourn. She is overcome and mortified, at once, battling to keep these sounds from escaping. The harder she tries, the closer she is to losing, and she places her face into her hands and weeps.

Long have I waited for your coming home to me

A pair of hands press firmly now, into her shoulder blades, a steadying pressure, and if they don't help contain her sobs, at least they give her a focal point, allowing her to gain some control. To one side Leah's leg presses against hers. Catherine's hand crosses Leah's lap and comes to rest on Saoirse's knee.

Saoirse's breathing is ragged, but now there is space between the gasps. She rummages in her pockets for the last piece of tissue. These are not Catherine's hands holding her. She doesn't have to turn around to know they belong to Daithí, kneeling behind her. She takes the handkerchief he offers, pressing the cloth to her face, breathing in the scent of him. She is not imagining him this time. By the time the processional hymn is sung, and the congregation is seated, Saoirse has regained her composure. She reaches for Leah, pulls her close; she has strength enough now to mind her daughter, to bring them both through this grief.

The Return

Early Summer 1998

The tracks curve and the open coast comes into sight, the Sugarloaf prominent on the horizon. She is nearly back to Greystones without her daughter. It is here Saoirse begins to dread the emptiness of the weekend ahead.

In the autumn it will be one year since they buried Joseph. The same day she untangled herself from Paul. Catherine had brought her and Leah to her home in Greystones on the day of Joseph's funeral. Of all the pain of that day, Saoirse admitted, being slighted by Simon and Mary after the Mass had been the most unexpected and hit the hardest.

"Oh, they were keeping themselves to themselves, were they?" Catherine had said wryly. "I'll tell you why if it brings any comfort? They are bedding down for the battle. All is civil in love and families until there is a property to inherit. Welcome to Ireland, darling. I think your Paul has quite drawn his line in the sand."

"You will not," Paul had argued when Saoirse had told him she was leaving for Catherine's with Leah after the graveyard, but he hadn't yet witnessed the full measure of Catherine.

"Yes she will," Catherine had commanded without raising her voice. "These girls need minding. You are clearly not up to the task." She had led them to her car and Paul turned back to his mother. Saoirse hadn't spent a single night in the Byrnes' house since.

After Leah was tucked into bed that night of the funeral, the two women sat in front of the fire while it crackled and sparked in the grate.

Catherine brought out a bottle of wine and two glasses.

"Now," she said, full of curiosity. "Tell me about your man."

"Daithí." Saoirse's entire body filled with light saying his name. She had brought up her hands to cover the smile spreading on her face.

"Look at you." Catherine smiled.

Saoirse told her everything, of the time they spent, the way she had thought of him, even how she imagined him beside her all these years.

She reminded Catherine of how Seamus had shown up at the gallery opening, in Donegal.

"Ah, that tall lad with the kind eyes?"

Saoirse smiled.

"I thought it was himself you fancied."

"No, Daithí sent him."

"You dark horse." Catherine shook her head in awe. "Isn't that extraordinary. Can I ask again. What the hell were you doing with Paul so long?"

"I wasn't *with* Paul. Though I was tied to him, all right. It's complicated."

"How so?"

"You know *how so*."

Catherine nodded grimly.

"But now—not so complicated?"

"Do you really think I should leave one man and run straight into the arms of another?"

"Too true," Catherine had laughed. "You are a sensible woman. Still." Catherine held her hand to her heart. "The way he looked at you—"

"Daithí's like that with everyone," Saoirse told her, refusing to hope. "That's who he is. If he was free—why did he disappear after the funeral?"

"Oh, my love. Can't you see? The same reason he sends his man to the exhibition instead of coming himself. He has his own heart to protect."

"Well, I'm sure he will go back to America or Kenya, or wherever he goes. He probably has met someone, why wouldn't he?"

"And if he hasn't?"

Saoirse closed her eyes and pulled her arms across her heart, making a sound close to a whimper.

Catherine laughed.

"We have to do something about this. Yes, we do." She smiled and tipped the rest of the bottle between their two glasses. "But you are too right," she continued. "You need to focus on getting your daughter and yourself back on track. And my home is open to you both, for as long as you need." And Saoirse had taken her up on her offer.

THE DART IS PACKED. COMMUTERS returning home on a Friday, schoolchildren in uniform returning from the city centre, adult children coming to reunite with their families for the weekend, meet their old friends in the pub. It is here Saoirse feels the price of her freedom—leaving Leah with the Byrne family every weekend hurts. And this weekend, in particular, will be extra lonely, with Catherine travelling to Paris. Saoirse has much to do this weekend as it is, she reminds herself. Her upcoming exhibition in Dublin will be *prestigious*, Catherine had reminded her before she left the house.

"You'll be too busy to notice we are gone," she said, waving from the taxi.

As the DART comes into the station now, passengers stand and move toward the door, waiting to alight, to begin their weekend. Saoirse collects her shopping, she stays seated while the train clears. She is not in a hurry to return to an empty house.

Out the window she becomes alert to a man resembling Daithí disembarking from the train. He has the same stature, the way he holds his bag. She cannot see his face but there is something about him that makes her eyes lock onto him, follow him as he moves with the crowd, then stops again, hesitating on the platform before moving once again toward the exit. The man passes through the turnstile, and he is gone. These phantoms fill her with a charge and then leave her with an intense sense of disappointment. She must stop this, she thinks, as she steps back to allow a woman with a pram to pass in front of her. The woman blocks the aisle, calling her children out from their seats.

"Let me help," Saoirse says. She takes the handles of the pram from the woman, bustles it out the door and down the steps. The woman is still wrestling her children off the train.

"I'll leave it there," she calls to the mother.

"Thanks a million," the woman calls back.

Saoirse exits the turnstile, follows the crowd out into the night; they hail taxis, step into waiting cars, taking the buzz with them toward the weekend ahead. She feels a melancholy settling over her.

"Saoirse." Her name is called so lightly from behind, she thinks she has imagined it. She turns and he is there standing against the stone of the station, the bag at his feet. Daithí was always lean and fit—it isn't the physical sense of him that has changed—but the gravity the years have put on him. He is, she knows, registering the changes he sees in her.

"I think we were on the same train," he says, a crooked smile spreading across his face, and in it, she sees the Daithí she knows. She is frightened and thrilled at once.

"I thought I'd be waiting for a while, for the next train," he tells her when she doesn't answer. He leans down to collect his bag, slings it over his shoulder.

"You're waiting for me?" she asks.

"I am."

The truth of it strikes her—it isn't a coincidence that Catherine has left for the weekend. She curses and loves Catherine all at once.

"Are you well?" she asks, trying for nonchalance, not knowing what else to say, or what to do with her hands. She hears her own inflection, then giggles, self-conscious, at how Irish she sounds. She wonders if he hears it, too.

"I am well." He grins. "Very well. And yourself?"

"Sure, I'm grand," she says, now affecting the accent. He bites his bottom lip, and she thinks she couldn't have imagined this smile. How gorgeous it is to see; how lovely it feels to be standing near him once again.

He is moving toward her now, dropping his bag, reaching for her. Taking her into his arms.

Up in the village, they have taken a window seat at the front of a crowded pub. They ordered dinner and Daithí chose a bottle of wine and when it came and the server poured it out, Saoirse thought she hadn't tasted anything so nice in a long time. The shyness she felt, and what had seemed like an uncertainty in him, has vanished. They have fallen back into conversation, that old familiar feeling returning.

"I met my father," he is telling her.

She smiles at the weight he puts on this event, knowing it is responsible for the change she senses in him.

"I heard you went to Kenya."

"I built clinics alongside him." He shakes his head, overwhelmed. "I have a half brother, half sisters—beautiful people. And it wasn't just meeting family. It was the comradery of the workers on the building sites. The children. The generosity. The one thing that struck me: nobody could do enough for our crew—they made it clear they weren't taking charity—they gave more, whatever it was. It reminded me of the Irish welcome. We're so good to visitors. And the people who were sick, the ravages of this illness—" He is somber at the memory. "—the dignity."

The server comes to clear their plates.

When she leaves, Saoirse reaches across to him, taking his hand while he talks.

"And to be embraced into that community. It was like discovering a hidden part of me, finding out what was underneath. Or at least I've come to understand a part of myself I had never known. And my father—how do you describe his manner, the respect he commanded, the way he carried himself, I've never met anyone like him, his stoicism. I am in awe of him—"

Saoirse feels she has already met his father, this person he describes. She sees all he describes in himself. She doesn't tell him this; instead, she listens, watching something not so much as happiness, but a serenity, pass as light across his face.

"I can see why my mother fell in love with him."

"I think you've fallen in love with him." She smiles.

"I suppose I have."

Their hands are moving, sliding fingers over fingers, winding over palms and the back of their hands in a slow, perpetual motion.

"Why did you come back?" Saoirse wonders. What she is really asking—*Are you leaving again?*

"Don't you know?" he answers.

She shrugs, not wanting to venture a guess. She thinks maybe it is the boom in the housing sector, or not wanting to get left behind in the Celtic Tiger economy everyone is talking about.

"I came back for you—"

She cannot swallow the sip of wine she just took.

His gaze is intense but neither dares look away.

"I came back to see if, you know—" He laughs self-consciously, then he grows sombre. "It's a dangerous reason. You know you already broke my heart?"

"*I* broke *my* heart," she whispers. "I wish it had been different."

"You can't wish that—not for Leah's sake. She is gorgeous. I was at the Byrnes' for her last birthday—"

"She told me." Saoirse smiles thinking of her daughter meeting him. "She showed me the box you gave her from Kenya. She tells everyone *Dotty carved it*."

"Ha—now I'm a sculptor!"

They laugh at her innocence.

"You've done a brilliant job, Saoirse. You are a good mother."

"Thank you. She is special, I feel."

"When you came to Donegal—" He seems unsure whether to continue.

"Go on," she encourages.

"You told me that last night—you pushed me away—told me I didn't know you."

"Yes."

"And part of that was true—and will always be true. You're a mystery. Something tells me you'll always be a mystery."

The server has come back now with a dessert menu, Daithí politely takes it, she moves away.

He has withdrawn his hands from Saoirse's.

"This is what hurt. There is a part of you *I knew*. Certain as the bone, the flesh of you sitting here. I knew—your essence. And I believe you knew mine. You do know mine. You saw my core, Saoirse. Plain as that. I can't tell you—the jolt that gave."

She remembers it. She loves watching his face as he remembers it.

"—I never stopped thinking of you," she tells him. "I never stopped hoping—"

The pub is emptying out.

"I know nothing of your past," he says.

"I have a sister." She speaks softer now, aware of the growing quiet.

"You lost her," he guesses, reaching out to her again.

"I did. In a way. She's out there. She was younger than Leah when I left."

"Left home?"

"I suppose you would call it that."

"Tell me her name," he says gently.

She closes her eyes and shakes her head.

"Okay." He nods solemnly, accepting her refusal.

Not even her name, she thinks. How can they possibly go forward when there is so little she can give?

"There are things I need to work through," she tells him.

"This sadness, your melancholy, it comes through in the work."

She nods, her throat clenched with grief.

She realises he understands the way she processes her loss; he does much the same, with his house. His grief for his mother will be stamped there, the dream they shared. She wants to see his house again. The work he has done, the piece of art he has surely made in remembrance.

"I will tell you everything," she promises. "In time."

"When you're ready," he replies. He brings her hand to his lips.

She sniffs and wipes her eyes with the edge of her sleeve.

"Shall we go?" he asks.

"I'm ready," she agrees.

He catches the server's eye, signals for the bill.

THEY HOLD HANDS, WALKING IN silence through the now quiet village, passing the station, and once on the Burnaby Estate, Daithí points out features of the houses, the brickworks, copper cladding, the pitched roofs—marvelling at the craftsmanship of a bygone era.

At the door, she shows him her key. They grin foolishly at one another, and she turns to open the door, feeling like a teenager. Inside, he drops his bag and they are kissing, moving their hands over one another, he is bringing his knee between her legs, every part of her alive. She places a hand on his trousers.

"Okay," he says, stopping abruptly, moving her hand away. A seriousness has come over him, she thinks he has changed his mind. She moves away.

"Wait," he says, holding his hands in the air. "Just wait."

"Okay," she says, unsure.

"I need to take things slow," he tells her, his eyes to the ceiling.

"That's fair," she says. He doesn't want to be hurt again. She doesn't want to hurt him. "—we can just—" She tries to hide her disappointment.

Opening his eyes, he registers the misunderstanding and laughs out loud.

"No, babe." He is self-conscious now. "Nothing like that—it's just, it's been—how long? I won't even manage a condom—"

Saoirse covers her mouth with her hand, hiding her relief, her amusement.

"I'm about to blow in me kacks," his laughter fills the entrance hall, his shoulders shaking now.

The broken moment buys him time.

Saoirse moves back toward him, her confidence returns, she takes hold of his hips, the button on his trousers.

"We better get these kacks off of you, so," she says, kneeling now, in front of him.

He leans back against the hall table, gripping the edge, closing his eyes, he lets go.

This Happiness

7 December 1998

Today is Saoirse's twenty-sixth birthday. She marks it secretly, as she has done all these years, this time with a walk at dusk around the headland, hiking over the bracken to the EIRE sign made from whitewashed stone laid out on the clifftop.

The breeze is stiff, waves rolling, unrelenting, across the Atlantic from North America until they reach this western shore, battering the coast. To the left, sea stacks glow orange in the setting sun. To the right she searches for their house, easy to spot at the end of the bay now that it is white with limewash.

She had put on her coat after dinner, left Leah curled up in front of the fire, a little table pulled up to the edge where she fixed together a jigsaw, an image emerging of a village: lantern-lit streets glittering in the snow, somewhere in Northern Europe, she guessed. Daithí sat at the other end of the sofa, strumming a guitar, a tune she didn't recognise.

She has never felt so settled in her life as she does here in this little corner of the world. Even Catherine's house, which had been a sanctuary after the Byrnes', couldn't compare to this home they share. It was a hardship leaving every other Friday to drive the long road to Paul in Dublin. Often, if Daithí was sharing the drive, they dropped Leah off and turned right back around driving home—the seven-hour return journey worth the time together. Sometimes Paul or Viv would meet her halfway, other times, if Daithí worked on the weekend, he gave her the small worker's van and she drove her daughter all the way to Sandymount herself and then continued to Catherine's, staying a few nights.

It was painful to be at the Byrnes', even for the short time it took to say goodbye to Leah. Catherine's house held happier memories for her, of the weekend she and Daithí reunited, when they had decided to make a go of it. On that weekend, after two nights of talking and sleeping, cooking and making love, they had finally left the house early on the Sunday morning, strolling down the shingled strand.

"The house is finished," he had told her. "I want you to come, make it your home. If you want this."

"I want this—" she had begun, but hesitated.

"There are no long-term commitments. No promises need to be made, from either of us," he reassured her. The house, he said, was the reason it took him so long to find her after he returned from Kenya. He wanted to make a place that felt like home for her and Leah. He had wondered over the years, if the unfinished house was the reason she hadn't come away from the Byrnes'—the night he had waited for her in the studio. If it had been finished, would she have stayed? She had assured him things had taken the course they needed to take. But things were different now.

"Well," he said, resolved. "It's finished and ready. Come, if that is what you want. And the rest will fall into place."

Thinking of the conversation she needed to have with Paul made her stomach ache. He had grown quiet since she had moved to Catherine's, but she couldn't trust his silence, there was always the air of unfinished business with him. But to ask his permission to take Leah to Donegal with her, to live with Daithí—she couldn't imagine this could go any way but badly.

"Are you saying this is what you want, and your reservation is with Paul?" Daithí had asked.

"Yes," she said decidedly.

"There is no *asking* Paul. You don't negotiate with a man like that."

She knew this herself.

"You work out what is best for you and Leah, and then we will *tell* Paul how this is going to work."

Of course, Catherine had already investigated the legality of it. It was less complicated than she believed since she wasn't looking to take their daughter out of the country, and so Saoirse was free to live her life, as long as she came to a custody agreement with Paul.

"It won't be easy."

"Nothing will ever be *easy* with Paul," Daithí had said. "But Saoirse, you are not his prisoner, we won't let him dictate how we live."

Saoirse had smiled gratefully.

"One thing," he had said, tentatively. "Will you let me speak with him first? Given our history, it seems decent I should at least give him that courtesy." Saoirse had agreed. Paul, of course, had been livid. Daithí wouldn't go into the details of their meeting, Saoirse assumed it had been ugly. Paul had called a meeting, brought the family solicitor and asked Vivienne and Christopher to attend, along with Nuala, certain they all had his corner. Vivienne was the authority now, in the absence of Joseph. What he hadn't counted on was his family taking this as an opportunity to remove Saoirse entirely from their lives, for the most part.

Saoirse and Daithí sat quietly in the Byrnes' sitting room, watching the volley between the siblings.

"What do you care where they live so long as you see your daughter on the weekends?" Vivienne had asked.

"That's not the point—"

"What's the point then?" She folded her arms across her chest.

"It's outrageous. Last time I was in Donegal, he lived in a hovel," he accused Daithí without directing the insult at him.

"It's hardly that way now." Vivienne raised an eyebrow in question toward him.

"You are welcome to come visit, anytime," Daithí said calmly.

"This isn't right."

"What's not right?" Vivienne negotiated. "Saoirse is not your partner. You have never been a couple, as far as I know."

Paul cringed.

"What she does with her life is no one's business. And there's no fear, her part of the deal will be kept," Vivienne had told her brother. "We know Daithí will see to keeping the custody agreement. He is good for it."

"In fairness, Viv, Saoirse is good for it," Daithí corrected her. "She doesn't need me to honour her agreement."

"Right, pal," Paul had sneered.

Daithí had lifted his hands to show he wasn't prepared to argue.

"She is a fine mother to Leah, and I think she has been more than fair on you," Daithí told him.

Saoirse was surprised when Nuala had nodded in agreement.

"What about school?" Paul asked.

It made sense, Nuala chimed in then, supporting the idea Leah should learn through Irish while she lived out west—Nuala had studied teaching when she first came to Dublin and her fluency with the Irish language was fairly good. She loved the idea, in fact, her granddaughter would be a fluent speaker.

"Sure, she'll never have to struggle to learn the language. She'll just have it. And she is so smart—she is running circles around the other children. Irish will challenge her."

Paul had lingered in the corner silently raging while the solicitor took notes and left in a hurry, saying he would draw up the agreement. They had left for Donegal within weeks, to allow Leah to settle before she started school.

SAOIRSE IS PASSING THE VILLAGE school now, on her way back home, on her way back toward Leah and Daithí. Night has fallen all around the road, the Atlantic crashing on the other side of the embankment near the house. Sprays of salty sea water clear the top of the rocks lighting on her face reminding her of the first Friday Mass at Leah's school, the priest sprinkling the congregation with his silver aspergillum—this seawater is a sign: *we are blessed*. This new joy, this happiness, is overwhelming at times. And the secret she carries now—a tiny life growing, she will soon tell Daithí he is to be a father.

She pauses outside the sash windows, looking into the warmly lit kitchen. Leah is at the kitchen table now, stirring the soda bread mixture, thicker than porridge. Daithí has stoked the coals in the range. They are finishing their ritual—their routine of baking bread, putting the loaf in the oven. They will cut the first slices while still warm in the pan, slathering them with butter and washing it down with mugs of milky tea. They will wrap the remainder of the bread in a tea towel, leaving it on the table with a pot of marmalade, and Daithí will set plates and bowls out for the morning. Saoirse enters into the warmth of the kitchen through the lower door.

"Bring me the heel when it's ready?" Saoirse asks, and leaves them to it, going back down into the outbuilding Daithí has restored for her to use as her studio. She had finished the last of the *Lost Was Found* series when she was at Catherine's, and now she is biding her time for the Raymond Frank Gallery exhibition to open. And when it is over, she has decided she will move on to something new, she will reinvent herself again.

She is working in charcoal now, experimenting with shades of pastel and sometimes watercolour. Looking for a way into this new work, describing this western coastline, working to express her daughter's joy, and Saoirse's own newfound freedom. She no longer carefully signs *Saoirse Byrne* onto the lower canvas. Instead, when she has finished a piece, she simply scrawls SAOIRSE and it feels right.

There is a certain amount of protection, she feels, this name gives, evolved from its origin. That she has been given *Saoirse* by Daithí, that she rarely thinks of Sarah Walsh—Sasa—any longer. The threat of this woman, once her friend, now a stranger—coming back to Ireland and discovering Saoirse's actions, is only a remote possibility, some distant nightmare that once seemed vivid but has now receded so far to the back of her mind it is nearly forgotten.

Daithí raps on the door, opens it a crack. He is carrying a slice of the baked bread, still warm, and a mug of tea.

"This a bad time?" he asks.

When she says it is not, he comes inside the studio, places the tea on her worktable, he stands beside her easel, asks permission to look. He holds her around the waist, kisses the top of her head, admires the quick sketches she has drawn from memory after her walk—the headland, looking down onto the cove, the house in the distance.

"Leah's waiting for you. She's brushed her teeth."

"Thanks, babe." She makes another mark to finish the work.

"I'm doing the books and the bills, when you have a minute," he tells her.

"Sure, I'll tuck her in and be in."

LEAH IS READING. WHEN SAOIRSE comes up the stairs, they turn out the light and sit on the window seat underneath the sash window, watching the waves coming onto the shore, a sound they fall asleep to at night when the sea is calm, and sometimes, it is to the wind battering the house. The rooms are dry and warm and Saoirse is in love with the house as much as she is with Daithí and her life here with him.

When she tucks Leah in, kisses her forehead, Saoirse returns downstairs to the second sitting room, it is the room farthest from the sea. Daithí keeps a desk here with his files and his ledger for the business. He has a computer, with a phone connection to the internet which is very slow. He has tried to show her how to set up an email account, but she has no interest. He tells her it is a way of connecting with the outside world, if she wanted to look someone up back in America, for example, she could. He never suggests her sister, but she knows that is what he is thinking. She imagines typing in her own birth name, pressing the Enter key. She is terrified what it will bring up. No, she insists. She doesn't want an email. And he leaves it at that.

When they first arrived much of her time was filled with sleeping and reading. These bookshelves are full of his mother's own library, from the boxes he salvaged in his grandparents' garage. Saoirse and Leah pore over the nature books together. In the evenings, when Leah is tucked in bed, Saoirse devours novel after novel in front of the crackling fire, it is as though she has stepped back into another era through the words and the atmosphere of this Georgian house he has restored. She had started with *Persuasion* and then *Sense and Sensibility*. She read passages aloud to Daithí while he worked. When she needed a break from Jane Austen, she found *Lady Chatterley's Lover*, and read all the steamy bits aloud to him. He had begun to join her on the sofa—she would stretch out her legs over his lap and he sometimes rubbed her feet and listened to her read.

They had begun *Tess of the d'Urbervilles* in this way. The opening scenes, three young lads rambling across the South of England countryside filled her with such longing. It was the freedom of the men she envied. But almost immediately, as the story unfurled, she began to see a parallel with Tess and her own dangers lurking. Soon she had stopped reading aloud, turned the pages quickly, glance-reading the story to find out how it ended for the girl.

"I should have known," she had said, agitated, flipping back through the title pages, where underneath a subtitle was written of Tess, "*A Pure Woman*." Daithí had looked up, amused by her indignance, which quickly changed to worry when he saw her distress.

"All right?" he had asked.

She checked the copyright page for the publishing date.

"A hundred years and nothing has changed for women!"

"What's the trouble?" he asks of the plot.

"The *trouble* is a girl is raped, forced to have a child, the child dies, the girl finds the love of her life, and then her lover leaves her when he discovers she is not a *Pure Woman*! Ultimately, Tess is the one punished, executed! For the sins of men—*This happiness could not have lasted*," she reads, in tears. "What bollocks!" If it hadn't been his mother's book, she would have flung it across the room, thrown it into the fire.

"Babe?" he says, and he is so attuned to her in this moment, she knows, in some way, he has come to understand the nature of her own troubled story.

He has taken a handkerchief out of his pocket for her to wipe her eyes, her running nose. He folds her into his all-encompassing arms and she is comforted by the sense that his empathy is deep, that this is a glimpse of how he will respond when she is ready, ready to share the full truth of everything that needs to be told.

"What if you find out I'm not such *A Pure Woman*?" she asks, venturing a little, nearly coming out of the mood. She breaks a smile when she sees what his face suggests.

"*Pure* is not something I think I would ever accuse you of—" he says, biting his bottom lip.

She sniffs, playfully taps his arm. "What is that supposed to mean?"

"You have few inhibitions," he says admiringly.

"Do I not?" she laughs.

"Like myself—no holding back, not with you. We are well matched that way, wouldn't you say?"

"I would say—" And she had sat upon his lap. In the passion of the moment, they hadn't paused, as usual, for him to find a condom.

Now it strikes her, watching him here, at his desk doing his books, the night of *Tess* is significant for other reasons.

"What's up?" she asks, nodding toward his paperwork.

"Your license, babe," he says, putting a final stroke in his ledger, closing the book. "I've been meaning to put you on the insurance."

"My driving license?" she asks.

Saoirse has been driving since she was fourteen. Lou had taught her on the stick shift with a dodgy clutch. She could drive anything, including a builder's van, and certainly the little van she takes to Dublin every other week, but she has never held a driving license.

He turns toward the sound of her uncertainty, furling his brow.

"Saoirse, you have a driver's licence, yeah?"

He looks at her, waiting, while she considers her response, feeling her guilt is obvious on her face. It is too late to catch herself, too late to say she has lost it. She can't seem to fake it with him, to lie, the way she has with everyone else.

"Babe? You've been driving across the country at least every fortnight."

She doesn't know what can be done now, apart from being honest. She gives a small shake of her head.

He looks baffled for a moment, annoyed.

"You know that's an offence, right?"

She presses her lips together. *Offence* sounds better than *illegal.*

"Right. We'll get it sorted."

She nods but he has turned back to his desk. He hesitates, then turns back to her.

"Is there anything else I need to know, Saoirse?"

Her look tells him there is.

There is much more.

"Tell me," he presses.

"I'm pregnant."

Bealtaine

May 1999

A deep blue sky stretches above the bay, the turquoise waters from the shallow cove roll translucent onto the spit. The Byrnes have agreed Leah may stay in Donegal for all the month of May to spend time with her new baby sister without breaking her weekends to travel to Dublin. Eloise surprised them all by coming early, she is three weeks old now.

It is a warm day and they have driven to the same beach where Saoirse spent her first night with Daithí years before, only the caravan is long gone from the dunes. Saoirse thinks of that night and a current of desire passes through her. It hasn't faded. She watches him run in and out of the waves with Leah while she rests on the beach with the baby in the shadow of a granite outcrop.

All day the sun arches around the bay, clocking their silhouettes across the sand; recording their work in shadow—building sandcastles, grazing on a picnic of sausage rolls and apple tart. Eloise kicks her feet while all around her Leah has gathered a circle of spotted cowrie shells, scallops, periwinkles, laying them carefully now as though Eloise is the adorned centre point in an ancient festival. The day is coming to an end underneath the setting sun.

Down the way, the lifeguards have put away their equipment. They have gone home for their evening now and Saoirse wraps Eloise in a warm cardigan and places a hat on her head. Daithí piles the gathered driftwood atop the granite outcrop, speaking to Leah in Irish. She has nearly finished her first year of school in the Gaeltacht. Her conversations with Daithí are growing more nuanced and even Saoirse is picking up the *cúpla focal* with the other parents at the school gate, but it is no more than an effort to say hello and goodbye or a few words about the weather. Terese, the woman who runs the café, tells Saoirse not to despair—even if she was fluent, it wouldn't make a whole world of difference.

"Sure, I've lived here all my married life—forty years, nearly twice as long as I lived in Dublin. I conduct all my business through Irish and the locals still arrive in to tell me how well my language is coming on." She complains in a light-hearted spirit, telling Saoirse she can expect *her man* to be better received than she ever will be. Saoirse can see herself this is true, how fond they all are of Daithí.

"Us women will never have it easy, will we?" Terese declares.

Saoirse has long since become resigned to the fact that interactions, never mind friendships, will always be a challenge. It would be hard enough if she didn't fit in simply because she was foreign, but as long as she has this past to hide, the awareness makes it all the more difficult. The reluctance isn't with the locals—it is with Saoirse herself. But in a way, Daithí's character is like a veil that shades her. The way he is at home here, the earth and sky and sea that settles around him settles around her, too, like a placenta. She positions herself against the strength of his back at night, burrowing into his warmth. He reaches back to take her hand, pulling it around himself, and it is the closest she has come to peace in her life.

Terese is put out, in her own good-humoured way, about the computer they have placed in the corner of her café. The way the young people come in and book an hour *online*.

"They want to *surf the web*, they tell me," she laughs. "You live by the sea, I tell them. Go out and surf the waves."

Saoirse tells her she isn't interested in computers or the internet.

"I like reading," she tells her.

"Don't worry, it is a fad."

But Saoirse doesn't think the World Wide Web is going away anytime soon; even Daithí talks about helping her put up a website for her art. She dismissed the idea immediately, reminding him she had no interest.

It's not that she isn't curious. After Saoirse had finally passed her test, Daithí bought a family car—a silver minivan—and she was back on the road, driving. It was one of the grey, drizzly afternoons while she was still pregnant, she had come from town with the groceries and had little strength to go back out the road to the house before returning for the school collection. She had started to sit the hour out in the empty café, trying to read the newspaper left behind on one of the tables. The idea crept up on her and then she couldn't stop wondering, if she went online and typed in her sister's name—Léa AND Gagneux—what might pop up? Images of her sister playing a sport in middle school? A missing person's flyer? The temptation had been so great she got up to leave, waited the remaining three-quarters of an hour in the school's parking lot instead.

WHEN THE SUN TOUCHES DOWN in the Atlantic and dips below the horizon, a lavender wash fills the sky. Daithí sets the driftwood alight, describing for Leah the ancient celebration of Bealtaine, when fires were lit on the hillside this time of year to welcome the summer. Leah yawns and leans against him in the fading light, the wet driftwood smoulders and the sparks fly into the clear night air.

He guides the smoke toward them with his large hands as though cleansing them all in a ritual. "Warding off ill fortune."

And there is that unsettled feeling again. Her worries, which had sunk into her subconscious for a time, had resurfaced with the *Tess of the d'Urbervilles* reading. Registering for a driving license using Sasa's RSI number stirred her anxiety further, and with each new violation this fear that her history is a gathering force culminated with Eloise's arrival—registering her daughter's birth brought on an edginess, a sense of unwellness, she can't shake.

A terror strikes her now, looking around at the lengthening shadows on the beach. Saoirse tries to push it away. But the thoughts keep coming, unrelenting. Maybe it is motherhood, maybe it is the maturity of her age but something has recently occurred to her. She imagines her kind, vulnerable friend gathering courage to return to an Ireland she felt forced to leave—a place that robbed her of her choices, her child, her humanity—only to find what little remains of her life snatched, pilfered, picked through, appropriated for Saoirse's gain. Daithí, her girls, this community he has brought them to—they will know this about her one day: she is no better than a magpie. No better than Lou.

Daithí feels the distance grow now, too.

"Babe?" he asks.

"It's getting cold," she answers. "The girls are tired."

They put out the fire, piling it with sand and wet seaweed, smothering the flames. They pack up their things from the beach and head for the van.

Millennium

Late December 1999

At sunset, and before everyone arrives, Daithí takes the package from the hall table. It arrived over a week ago, into every letter box across Ireland for this very night. He has turned on Raidió na Gaeltachta and calls them all into the kitchen. The president is lighting the first Millennium Candle at sunset on the East Coast.

Daithí takes out their scroll and candle from the package.

"Won't you write the names?" he whispers to Saoirse, trying to coax her participation, even for the children's sake.

"Will I do it, Dotty?" Leah asks.

"Of course you will."

He hands Leah the pencil, lets her write each of their names on the scroll. She leans onto the table, the orange glow of the setting sun passes through the window and lands on the parchment, her tongue poking out of her mouth in concentration. She writes her sister's name first.

E-L-O-I-S-E she spells.

"Clever girl," Daithí praises.

Then her mother's next.

S-A-O-I-R-S-E

"Not an easy one to spell," he says.

"How do you spell *Jasper*," Leah asks, sounding out the name they have given the cat that prowls around the walls. Daithí and Saoirse smile at one another.

"Isn't this the last light now?" Leah asks when she has finished writing all their names. She hoists herself onto the sink to see out the window looking out over the cove, at the setting sun.

"It is." He winks. "The end of a millennium, and the welcome of a new—"

"That's special, right?"

"Very special."

Daithí lights a match, puts the flame to the candle, places it in the window. They pull on their coats and walk down to the rocks to watch the last of the light set down into the Atlantic, its final blaze striking the Famine Wall. They marvel at the portal of warm amber trailing toward them, the waves, illuminated with the ancient light, roar into the cove below.

"That's it, then," Daithí says as the world around them becomes shrouded in grey, and across the bay the Christmas lights begin to turn on in the hills above the village. They walk back to the house and Saoirse helps Daithí light candles in every window. She tries to muster some hidden enthusiasm, but all she can feel is dread. This night has been planned for months, but it had gone out of Saoirse's head—she hadn't even remembered until a few days ago, when Daithí reminded her to pick up supplies when the shops reopened, to make a curry for their guests. She was surprised at first, stunned, to even think of having a house full of people, she could feel her reluctance registering across her face. This was how she had been since the announcement of the art prize. She hadn't taken phone calls; she had been even more adamant at avoiding requests from the press. It was when Daithí surprised her with a website, he forged ahead, against her will—her artwork, images of herself painting in the studio—something had snapped.

"Why?" she had whispered, feeling the violation.

"This is the way it's going these days," he tried to persuade her. "Everyone is self-promoting. You *have* to have a website."

"I don't have to do anything," she had cried.

"What's this?" he asked, stunned.

"Take it down."

"Hold on. It's not even live yet, Saoirse."

"I need my privacy," she had said, trying to recover herself. She had gone out for a walk then, to get away from it all. To try and distance herself from her own reaction. The distance between them was growing.

She had been thankful for Christmas, when it came, like the effect of a snuffer on a candle, extinguishing the blazing attention of the past weeks. They had slept late and made meals together and played games at the kitchen table, the condensation steaming up the windows. They took walks out the coast road—Leah managed it all the way up the hill overlooking the sea stacks while Eloise rode on Daithí's shoulders—then down again onto the beach near the village. They waved to friends and called out *Happy Christmas*, but everyone kept to themselves, and the phone didn't ring even once. The Christmas bubble had wrapped the four of them in its quietude.

But after Saint Stephen's Day, it all started coming slowly back to life. A trickle of journalists begun ringing again, to check a fact or two, and the curator wanted to confirm the public seminars Saoirse had reluctantly agreed to give.

Drawing the girls was Saoirse's balm, but she couldn't even manage a sketch. She was restless. Daithí didn't attempt to press her for a plan after the New Year. He knew they must bring Leah to Paul for a few days before school started again. They had been planning to travel to Dublin together for the seminars she was to give at the gallery, but she doesn't think she can keep her obligations.

The last thing she needs tonight, she thinks, is a house full of guests.

The Millennium Party is in full swing. Catherine has driven over with Liam and Emily, they arrived shortly after sunset. The food is out, and neighbours, artist friends, Daithí's foreman and his family, they have all stopped into their open house, and everyone wants to congratulate her on the award. The glass atrium is lit with strings of Christmas lights. The fire is blazing in the hearth. She can't breathe. She needs some air.

Orion sits above the house where her children sleep underneath the eaves. Leah had tried to stay up until midnight, but she fell asleep an hour ago, lying on the sofa, and Daithí carried her upstairs.

Saoirse stands on the rocks listening to the waves washing onto the shore in the darkness. Across the bay in the village, most nights it is darkened by this hour, but tonight every light is on. She thinks of that night, nine years before, on the pier leading to the Poolbeg Lighthouse, and she hugs her arms to herself against the chill.

I am still here, she thinks. *We are still here*.

But time is running out, she knows, on her short-term thinking. The confessions she should have made years ago are upon her. But Leah and Eloise are still so young. If only she knew the outcome, what hardships it would cost them. How will it be when Leah learns in the school yard her Mammy has done bad things?

Bury it Bury it Bury it her mind screams.

Back toward the house, the lights flicker and then cut out. There is a collective gasp from the guests, then laughter. The power is cut in the village now, too. Saoirse stands in this blue darkness, taking in the faint glow from each of the windows across the bay, Millennium Candles shining out into the darkness.

A figure is moving down the rocks toward her, the house is dark behind him apart from the glow of candles in the windows. The sea breeze off the Atlantic has sunk into her bones and she is shaking now with cold. Daithí is silent when he reaches her. She wants him to take her into his arms, wrap his body around hers, she longs to feel his warmth flowing into her limbs. But none of these things happen. The distance that has grown between them has become more pronounced, ever since the art prize announcement, and he doesn't know what has happened, how to close this gap. He has lived two of the most blissful years of his life with her, he has told her, and this distance feels too wide, too sudden, as though an abyss has opened and neither of them knows how to cross.

He stands within arm's reach, his hands in his pockets, staring up into the sky above the sea.

"It's dangerous out here in the dark."

"I'm careful."

"I don't know what is happening, babe. You went behind a cloud."

She cannot answer for the sensation of grief closing in, squeezing around her throat.

"Are you sick?" he asks.

"No." Her voice trembles.

"The girls?" he asks.

"They are perfect. You know that."

"I know, of course I know that."

"I'm sorry."

"I can't see *you* anymore—it's like you're not here."

"I have something I need to tell you," she says, surprisingly urgent.

"So, tell me."

She looks up at his face. It is strong against the sky, resolute.

"I just need a little time."

"I'm not sure we have that any longer," he says, turning toward her. "I have done everything, *everything*, Saoirse, that I can think of to keep an open mind, waiting for you to open up. I want to give you privacy and space, but I'm worried. There is a big part of me that wonders—are we going to survive this? Me and you? If you don't let me in—I'm not so sure."

Already it feels as though he is being ripped away from her. A sound that feels like a whimper escapes her.

"Tell me."

The tide is rushing closer, more urgently, over the rocks. He has come out for one thing. He is ready to hear, and he is not relenting. And she feels angry now, violated, as though this is something she must rip herself open for, hand over this entire thing for him to solve.

The lights turn on in the house, the power is back on, and their guests' applause reaches them on the rocks. The Famine Wall is stark and haunting in contrast to the lit house. She does not want to return to the company inside, to the revellers. She has the mind to wait out here all night, until they are gone. Until it is just her and Daithí and the girls.

He shifts, she pivots toward him.

"This may be too big for us on our own," he says. She wonders how much he has guessed at her past. "Will you talk to someone? Catherine can help find the right treatment in Dublin."

She turns away, feeling betrayed by both of them. They've been discussing her. If they searched for her on the internet—what will they find? What will Paul discover if he types in a single name: *Roy.*

He hears the distress in her breathing and reaches for her, she lets him draw her in to his side, feels her shivering.

"You're home here. I promise you we will handle this together, but I need to know what we're facing. I won't let you come to harm."

You can't promise that, she thinks.

"It might give you some solace to get back to work, once the holidays are over? Return to routine."

"I'm not taking the art prize," she tells him.

But he has guessed at this, too.

"The prize doesn't matter. You and the girls, that is it, that is all there is."

His two fingers travel across the night sky and her gaze follows the line they make, above an island in the distance, to a faded star high up in the dome of the sky.

I am not who you think I am.

"Polaris," he says. "The reliable star. The constant sky."

My confession could take our girls from us.

"This is our little corner."

The truth will erase me from this place.

"No one is in danger here."

But they *are* in danger, and the danger is her. She cannot outrun this forever, yet to face the truth is to face impossible loss.

Just a little more time, she begs him in the silence. *Let me hold on to this—onto us—just a few more days.*

A cry erupts from the house, an ecstatic shouting and joyous laughter of celebration, it is echoed a moment later from the distant shore, from the village across the bay.

The new millennium has arrived.

She leans her head against his chest, looking out to sea. He encircles her, rocking her, back and forth, below the house, below the walls, in front of the wide-open ocean, steady on the rocks.

Happy New Year

3 January 2000

It is already the third of January and Saoirse needs to get Leah to Dublin for a visit before the holidays end. She rings the Byrnes hoping Paul will answer, not Nuala. Not Vivienne. Paul will take as little time as possible to convey an arrangement for Leah's drop-off. But it is Mary who answers the phone.

"Ah, Sarah!" Mary says when she hears Saoirse's voice. She is one of the only people who still call her Sarah. "Happy New Year. God, the season feels like a warped record already, if you know what I mean." Saoirse laughs conspiratorially, knowing Mary must be ready to pack up the children, flee from the oppressive company of the Byrnes. These days, without Joseph, it must be a joyless house altogether, she imagines.

"Any craic?" Saoirse asks.

"Ah—craic galore! Do you want the full postmortem of our millennium exploits, or just the highlights?"

Saoirse grins. For a moment she misses her, the way they were always on the same side.

"You know yourself; Vivienne is in there holding court, Paul is ready to kick everyone out. He has been cross all through the holidays. His new girlfriend was supposed to join us but she cancelled on him last minute. I'd say she ran away as quick as she could, back to her own country, smart woman. I've been ready to leave this house since the moment we arrived, but I can't get Simon to budge from his croissants and newspapers." Mary talks at top speed as though she has been deprived for days.

She takes a breath. There is a long pause of silence.

"Hey, how you keeping yourself? We were just reading about you in the papers."

The curator had told her about the dreaded press release, Saoirse sighs inwardly.

"Number Five of outings not to miss over the millennium. The

Raymond Frank Gallery! Very posh. You're everywhere, missus. C gratulations!"

She can picture Mary hunched over in the Byrnes' hallway, h cupped over the receiver, trying not to get caught fraternizing with enemy.

"Simon and I are secretly planning a trip into town on the way hon swinging by the gallery to see your exhibition. We're very proud of yc Sarah. Your work is stunning."

Saoirse smiles to herself. "Ah, thanks, Mary. You were always ver kind to me."

"Well, you deserve the success. Remember those pictures you painte of the girls, the weekend we met? I've them framed in the hallway a home. I tell everyone they're painted by a famous artist. You're a big deal Sarah."

"Stop, Mary. You're too good."

She was always fond of Mary.

"You must come down to Cork sometime, visit us. You're always welcome. Leah is gorgeous, you know, sorry we'll miss her this time, she's a credit to you."

"Your girls keeping well?" Saoirse asks to be polite. It seems Mary just wants to chat, it would be rude to ask her to put Paul on, she supposes. "And your little man?"

"Ah, they are grand; thanks be to God. Getting too big, too fast. Your littlest girl—what did you call her? Eloise? Lovely! Would you go again? I would go again; I love the baby stage—Simon swears he'll get the snip if I don't stop brooding over other people's babies."

Saoirse can't get a word in edgewise.

"Speaking of—did you see the first millennium baby was born in Dublin. Ah, bless. Sarah Walsh," Mary laughs. "Isn't that gas?"

Saoirse freezes. She hasn't heard that name spoken in years.

"Pardon?"

"That's the mother's name. Sarah Walsh. Coincidence, eh? We were all saying what a coincidence that is, you have the same name. Well, the name you were formerly known as—as Vivienne says—before you *reinvented yourself.* Hah! Vivienne. What a weapon, huh. Bet you don't miss her."

"No, I suppose I don't," Saoirse says, shifting in the hall. Looking to

see if Daithí brought the papers in from his trip to the shops. "Common enough."

"Vivienne, common?" Mary delights in hearing the two words positioned so closely to one another, as if.

"Not Vivienne. The name. Sarah Walsh. I suppose it is common enough, no offense."

There is a pause before Mary continues.

"We were trying to remember, how, and when, you changed your name to Byrne. You know Vivienne, *investigative*." Saoirse can feel the roll of Mary's eyes. "Was it a deed poll? Vivienne thought Joseph had helped you get a deed poll."

Saoirse doesn't like to hear they've been discussing her in this way.

"God almighty, I'm so ready to leave this house," Mary says, exasperated.

Saoirse's mind is racing.

"I'm holding you up here," Mary laughs into the quiet on the line. "I'll get himself now for you, will I? Unless you want me to pass you around to say hello?" She laughs again.

"Just Paul, please, Mary. Thanks very much."

"Sarah. Saoirse—"

"Hey Mary—"

"Happy New Year, pet. The house isn't the same without you. Or Joseph."

Saoirse's voice cracks when she answers.

"Ah, thanks, Mary. Happy New Year. Take care."

"God bless."

"God bless, Mary."

Homecoming

6 January 2000

The coffeepot on the hob gurgles, steam pressing through the safety release valve.

"Damn it." Saoirse has just sat down, Eloise in her lap, eating her breakfast. She bangs the spoon in reaction to her mother's frustration, porridge flying everywhere.

"Monkey," she says affectionately, rising to turn off the hob.

"Stay where you are," Daithí tells her, coming into the kitchen. His work boots are on his feet, unlaced. He turns off the pot. Fills her mug and dribbles milk into it. He places it in front of her. She takes a sip, avoiding Eloise's hand reaching up to touch it.

Daithí has been out to the shops again; he brought home the papers for her. He managed to get the shopkeeper to search the storeroom for the back-dated copies.

"I thought you were avoiding reading those," Daithí says. "I would have grabbed them for you the other day."

The front page is full of images of the millennium celebrations from around the world. *Let Us Step With Hope into Our New Century* the headline leads.

She tries to read around her daughter, she shifts sideways to turn the page, and there is her exhibition again, the article Mary mentioned.

Top Ten Things Not to Miss in the Millennium. Mary is right. She is number five. It mentions the prize and her public seminars. The tour she is supposed to give of her exhibition.

She had Daithí send two emails on New Year's Day, one cancelling the seminars and the second one refusing the money for the art prize. She worries now, her refusal will bring more unwanted attention, more complications. She curses whoever put her name forward for the prize. Daithí rubs her shoulders behind her. She jumps at his touch.

"All right?"

She quickly folds the page over. She doesn't want to bring this all up, yet again. She has hardly slept in days. She knows the dark circles under her eyes are worrying him. He is reluctantly returning to the building site today. She has arranged to bring Leah to Paul on her own, but the drive feels too long, Daithí convinced her to make the shorter drive and catch the train from Sligo to Dublin. Eloise has finished eating. She lifts her arms to her daddy. He takes her, spins her around, sets her on the floor. She has only begun to take steps, and her lack of balance now makes them both laugh. She reaches for the bench to hold.

Leah has heard them talking from the other room. She runs into the kitchen now, jumps into his arms, begs him to come with them to Dublin. He swings her around, and when he sets her on the ground again, he reaches into his pocket, takes out a mobile phone. He has been trying to get Saoirse to take it with her when she leaves the house. He tries to show her again how to use it. She waves him away.

"Show me," Leah demands. Daithí humours her, shows her the little symbol of the phone, how to turn it on, how to disconnect, how to ring his number.

"At least keep it close, Saoirse. I might want to ring. Hear your voice."

"We'll be grand," Saoirse tells him.

She is looking forward to a change of scenery. Maybe even a break from him. She will stop into the exhibition after dropping Leah and get that over with, then she and Eloise will spend the weekend with Catherine. She has been considering rummaging around in the boxes she left behind. Bringing home her sketchbooks—using them to guide her story with Daithí when she does begin to confide in him. She made him a promise. She will talk to Catherine while in Dublin, ask her help finding a therapist, perhaps make an appointment before she returns. The plan has taken the pressure off for the moment, if nothing else it has lengthened a looming deadline.

His own phone rings. Leah giggles.

He lifts it out of his pocket as though he doesn't know who is on the other end.

"Hello? Hello? Hello?"

"Hello, Dotty, it's me."

Eloise laughs with delight at their mischief.

"Hello," he says into his own phone. "Can I speak with the cleverest girl in all of Donegal?"

"Speaking," Leah laughs.

Daithí scoops her up. Kisses her.

"I can always count on you, *mo shióg craiceáilte*. You're in charge of the phone."

Leah puts it in her dress pocket, delighted with herself.

Saoirse smiles distantly, turns back to her coffee, back to the newspaper. An article catches her attention, a feature on the first millennial babies born across the country. It annoys her to see Edel's name in the byline. Vivienne's friend who badgered her, relentlessly, to do an expo on her art. But it isn't Edel's name that keeps her attention—or the way she manages to make the article all about herself—it is the name underneath the caption. Saoirse places her mug back on the table and reads the article in full.

IRELAND WELCOMES THE FIRST MILLENNIUM BABY

Irish Times, 3 January 2000

As the last of the evening light faded, and the New Millennium crept closer, Dublin's streets filled with revellers making their way to celebrations across the city. But for Sarah "Sasa" Walsh, celebrations were the last thing on her mind. Hours before midnight, Ms. Walsh, originally from Wexford, and recently returned from the US, boarded an ambulance at the home she shares with her extended family in Kilmainham, accompanied by her sister Ruth.

"It wasn't an emergency," she explained of the ambulance ride she took across the city on New Year's Eve just passed. "The midwives brought her in as a precaution," Ruth interjected.

Sasa described the scene from the eyes of a returned immigrant.

"Everywhere you looked, candles burned in windows, streets still lit with Christmas lights. I forget how much I missed Christmas in Ireland. Where else will you get an entire country closing down for two weeks? You barely get the day in America. Here, it's magic."

When I found the sisters the morning of the New Year, they told me how they had passed the night, awaiting the new arrival.

When Baby Faye arrived with the New Millennium, the women had forgotten the day, and certainly had forgotten the hour.

"It seemed in that moment, all of Dublin just exploded outside our window. There was roaring and shouting and clanging and popping off fireworks. It was like it was all for Baby Faye," Ruth told me. "Then Sasa's midwife says, 'Sweet Jesus—I think you've just won a lifetime supply of nappies.' We had no idea what she was talking about until she pointed to the clock. The three of us just burst into tears *and* laughter."

Faye, born nine seconds into the New Year, has lovely smooth black locks. She is healthy and has all ten fingers and toes, the sisters happily reported. Quieter of the two, Sasa, the proud mother, posed for a photograph. A joyous and momentous occasion on anyone's calendar, and noteworthy in itself. But things haven't been smooth sailing for the new mother. When I met the sisters and heard the tale of the first Irish citizen of the millennium, Ruth told me how happy she is to have her sister home from America. "It's taking her a while to get back into the swing of things, but we are so proud of her. Our lives were put on hold without Sasa. I had to beg her to come back, insist this country has changed for the better." Ms. Walsh agreed with her sister's analysis, though reservedly.

Ruth mentioned her sister's trouble signing on at the local social services office right before the holidays. Officials believe Ms. Walsh's identity may have been stolen.

"We're really not supposed to go into it," Sasa explained. "The guards are sorting it. But I'm hoping it'll be fixed once everything reopens in the New Year."

"She doesn't have to worry," her sister told me. "All she has to do is look after this little one and we will look after her." As if on cue, Baby Faye woke and it was time for her feed. Sasa's attention moved off of me, and back onto Baby Faye.

"She was always going to be okay," Ruth told me, beaming at her sister.

And with this reassurance, I pulled the curtain and left the newest citizen of Ireland in very capable hands.

On the Road

6 January 2000

Saoirse checks the date of the paper again, turns back to the article, her eyes move over the image of this woman cradling her newborn daughter. She'd know those sad eyes anywhere. Sasa is home.

The kitchen turns grey as the cloud comes in from the Atlantic, crossing the headland, darkening the sky. A wind hits against the window, spitting darts of rain at the glass.

"You sure you're all right, babe?" Daithí is asking. "I can delay another day or two, and drive with ye to Dublin?"

She shakes her head, not trusting herself to speak.

He turns the lid on the flask, puts his boots up on the bench, ties his laces.

"Don't get up," he says, kissing Saoirse's hair.

"Look after your mammy," he says to Leah, and the girls together push him out the door, their customary goodbye.

Saoirse hears him pulling out of the driveway. She should have walked with him to the van, given him a proper kiss on his first day back from holidays, especially since she won't see him now for a few days, but she is beginning to tremble. She rereads the article for the third time, searching to understand how this is going to come out all right.

She can hear the girls' feet across the floor upstairs. Leah is playing mother again to Eloise, dressing her baby sister for the day. Telling her about their car journey to Sligo and then how they will take the train to Dublin. She mimics the way Daithí speaks, telling Eloise she will have to be *a good little baba.*

SHE DOESN'T KNOW HOW MUCH time has passed. She has put on a load of laundry, stacked Leah's clean clothes on her bed, ready to be packed. She found herself distracted quickly, and has been sitting at the table now in a fog. They need to get on the road if they are to catch the train. And now she hears Daithí's van return. She looks around to see what he has forgotten and wonders if he is back because of the rain. It is drizzling, grey and cold, and there is some wind, but he has worked through worse weather.

She admits to herself there is a sense of relief he has come back. She feels outside of herself right now, not trusting the day ahead. She thinks she might ask him to stay, after all, drive them up to Dublin. Once she delivers Leah to Paul, she will have to find a way into this with him. It seems very clear in this moment—he will know what to do next. They will move ahead one step at a time. She curses herself waiting this long. She moves to meet him in the hallway, and at the same time, there is a knock at the door.

Saoirse is surprised to find it is not Daithí on the other side. It is a woman, she is familiar, Saoirse has met the intense focus of these eyes before.

"Sorry for the intrusion. You probably don't remember me."

"Edel," Saoirse says, remembering the pressing sense she had from this woman the first time they met in the conservatory at the Byrnes'. Now, Saoirse feels like an animal who has been tracked, besieged at her own front door. Beyond Edel, Saoirse sees the car she arrived in, pulled all the way up to the far side of the house. There is a man in the driver's seat, the engine is running.

"That's right. Viv's friend. You're an impossible woman to nail down, I've been endlessly ringing your phone."

Edel is moving closer, expecting to be invited into the house. Saoirse stands firmly, blocking the door.

"I was in touch with Paul—we go way back—he thought you wouldn't mind if I called in instead, sure—I was in the neighbourhood. I hope you don't mind."

"I *do* mind," she says, battling to keep the fright out of her voice.

"Ah, sorry now, I wish you had picked up when I rang. I thought I would chance it and pop in—"

Edel tries for nonchalance, but her eyes are bright and piercing. "Paul thought it would be okay," she repeats, unblinking.

"It's not okay."

Beyond Edel, the bay is stirred up, the wind flings sea spray over the embankment.

"I told you before. I'm not giving interviews—" Saoirse moves to close the door, but Edel puts her foot into the frame.

"Ah, no worries. I'll just have coffee," she says determinedly, her body pointed to walk through the door. "I might use your toilet, if you don't mind, before I head on my way."

"Who is it, Mammy?" Leah is coming down the stairs, holding Eloise's hand.

"A lady about the exhibition, love. Take your sister to the kitchen. Make some toast."

"Actually, I'm not here about your work. Saoirse—I am wondering if you are familiar with a woman who immigrated to Boston, in America, for several years and returned home in recent weeks. Her name is Sarah Walsh?"

Saoirse is astonished, as though she has been struck, as if Edel has reached in and swiped an artery, sank her pointed teeth into her flesh. A current runs through her. She cannot speak, she cannot move away from the door.

"I'm wondering, Saoirse, where did you say you were from in America? Michigan?"

The current becomes a surge. Saoirse kicks at Edel's foot, pries the door away from her fingers. Edel is losing her grip, her voice strains as she pushes against the door.

"Paul tells me you were known as Sarah Walsh—when you first arrived—"

Saoirse uses her shoulder to bodily push Edel out the door. Leah hears the skirmish and has come quietly out of the kitchen, watching.

"Answer my question—" Edel demands, holding on to the doorframe. "Are you familiar with a woman called Sarah Walsh?" She has turned her heels and is pressing against the door with her bottom, her words raw with the physical struggle.

"She had a baby a few days ago, it's in the papers. I published a feature—it was a happy news story, Saoirse, but it appears she has some trouble. Her identity has been stolen and my sources tell me the guards have traced it to a woman living in Donegal with two dependents. I'm not supposed to reveal this—Saoirse, but I thought if we could talk. Maybe I could help—"

Saoirse is suffocating, there are pinpoints of light, everything is turning fuzzy. She gives a final hoist and Edel falls out the door onto the step.

"Can you explain how you came to take the Byrne name—" she asks, scrambling to her feet.

Saoirse slams the door.

"What is it, Mammy?" Leah is in a panic now, too. Eloise toddles behind her, Leah turns and places her arms around her, protecting her. The tableau of two sisters, frightened, standing in the doorway, elevates Saoirse's urgency.

"What have I done—" she says aloud, bringing her hands to her mouth.

"What have you done?" Leah cries. Eloise buries her face in her sister's arms. Saoirse goes to them, tries to take their hands. Leah pulls away.

"Come here, come here, babies. Come here." She leads them into the sitting room, sits them on the sofa, kneeling in front of them.

"What is it, Mammy? What's the trouble?"

"Help me, Leah—we have to go—you have to be a good girl and help me."

Leah nods stoically.

"Will I ring Dotty?"

"No. No, honey. Not yet. I'll take care of this."

"Is that a bad lady outside?"

"No," Saoirse says, recovering a small sense of control. "She is Auntie Viv's friend, but she is nosey and making us late. We need to get out of here, get you to Dublin. That is all. Pack your books," she tells Leah. "And a toy for Eloise."

"Okay, Mammy. I will. Will we take the train?"

"No. There's no time. We'll drive." Saoirse decides there in the moment.

"Will that lady follow us to Dublin?"

"Stop asking questions. We just must go. Go now."

Leah flees up the stairs. Saoirse hears her scrambling from room to room.

Eloise watches Saoirse.

"Okay, baby. It's okay. I'm going to get us out of here."

Edel is pushing something through the letter box.

"Saoirse, we need to talk. Does Kirkhill, Michigan, ring a bell? Saoirse? Or shall I call you Sarah? Sarah Roy?"

Edel's voice shakes with emotion from the confrontation.

"I'm looking at a newspaper article here going back a few years, Saoirse. There is concern for you. For the girls."

Saoirse pulls Eloise to her hip, she runs to the door, grabs the folded paper, shoves it into her pocket.

In the kitchen, she opens a cupboard and throws boxes of crackers, biscuits, apples, bananas into a cloth bag. Edel has followed her around to this window, she raps at it, Eloise leaps in Saoirse's arms. Saoirse returns upstairs.

She places Eloise into her cot. She cries out and tries to crawl back into her mother's arms, but Saoirse must keep moving. She pulls a suitcase from under the bed, packs Leah's clothes from the bed, empties Eloise's clothes from her drawer. Down below in the driveway, Edel has returned to her car. She speaks to the man in the driver's seat. Behind them, the wind has picked up, the waves pound the shore.

Saoirse's body is remembering now how it feels to flee for her life.

"Are we leaving for Dublin?" Leah asks when their things are piled at the lower door.

"We are."

"I have the phone," Leah tells her, trying to sound brave.

This stops Saoirse short. She considers calling Daithí. He'll be at the building site by now. Forget Dublin. She'll get on the road, she'll drive to him.

"Good girl," Saoirse tells her. Leah is following her now to Daithí's desk. She is reaching inside the biscuit tin, lifting a roll of money, peeling bills off the top. Leah tries to hand her the phone.

"You hold on to that. Dotty said that's your job, remember?"

The minivan is parked at the lower door, pointed in the direction of the road. Saoirse gives Leah instructions, turns the lock, Eloise poised on her hip. She holds the suitcase in her other hand, Leah's arms are full of bags and teddy bears.

The telephone in the hall begins to ring.

"Ignore that. On the count of three."

On three, she opens the door, and they run out onto the packed earth of the driveway. The car door is already unlocked, Leah opens the door and scrambles in. Saoirse puts Eloise into her car seat and climbs into the back with the girls, closing the door, reaching over the front, locking them in.

The man is scrambling out of the driver's seat, running toward them with a camera. Edel struggles to open the passenger door, dropping her phone. Saoirse buckles the girls, then crawls into the front seat, starting the engine.

Edel recovers her phone and runs toward them now, too, knocking on the driver's window, trying the door.

Edel is shouting for her to open the door, the man is standing in front of the windscreen, his shutter snapping.

Saoirse revs the engine to warn him, she puts the minivan in drive, nearly knocking him to the ground. He jumps out of the way as she shoots out the driveway and onto the road. Her heart beats like a bird caught in a house, bashing against windows. She can see them in the rearview mirror, running back to their car. She is flying up the coast road now. Her girls are crying, but she is driving, moving, moving them away from danger.

Saoirse had met the main road and changed her mind again. At her speed and knowledge of the local roads, she is certain to have lost Edel. She won't go in search of Daithí, after all, she decides. It would make sense to get Leah to Dublin. It's what Leah expects, to be driven to her father's house. She can bring Eloise to Catherine afterward, and then they will deal with this. Somewhere along the road they have driven out of the storm that was buffeting the coast. The road is dry and her thinking clearer. It is through this clarity it hits her: Paul has set this trap in motion. It is Paul who sent Edel.

Everyone in Sandymount must know what she has done. The gardaí are onto her. They will be waiting, she imagines, to arrest her, if they don't intercept her on the road. Paul won't consider the girls, won't think of the stress it will cause to see their mother arrested. She made a mistake turning around. She changes her mind again. She must get to Daithí. Daithí and his clear thinking. He is the only one still in the dark, the poor man has no idea this storm that is driving toward him, but in everything, he will measure it up, he will know what to do. She will get the girls to him and then deal with what needs to come next.

She looks for a place to pull off. There is a small boreen up ahead, off the main road, she turns her signal on and checks her mirrors, drives a little way until she meets a lane leading into a farmer's field. The clouds are banking in the distance, moving at them from the direction of home.

She places her forehead in her hands and rubs her brows with her fingers. When she looks up into the rearview mirror, the girls are staring at her, watching for what comes next.

She steps out of the car, releases them from their seatbelts. Kisses their foreheads. They walk out into the field. Leah must use the toilet, and she helps her find a hedge for cover. Back at the car, she opens the boot and lays Eloise on a blanket, changes her nappy. The three of them are calmer now, they eat their snacks leaning against the gate, sipping their juice boxes. If she wasn't thinking before, she is now thinking again.

"Come on," she says. "Let's go find Dotty."

Leah jumps into the back seat, fastens her seatbelt, looking straight ahead. She has the phone Dotty gave her pressed to her ear, Saoirse can just make out the ring tone. Saoirse recognises the look of sheer terror. "It's okay, babe. Call Dotty, that's a good girl. Tell him we are on the way."

Leah's lower lip begins to tremble, her eyes fill with tears. She brings the phone down, places it on the seat beside her. "He won't answer," she says and bursts into tears.

THEY HAVE DRIVEN BACK INTO the darting rain, the January sunshine that was bright over the field has disappeared and the water on the road hisses under the wheels. Saoirse floats somewhere above herself, not quite in her body. They must be twenty minutes out from the town where Daithí is working on the restoration of an old Victorian house now turned into a museum. She doesn't know exactly where it is, but she knows if she can keep the van on the road, reach the village outskirts, she will follow signs for the museum, she will find him. That much is clear in her head.

They are approaching a petrol station on the left, the fuel levels are low. She curses herself and slows the car. The girls have both fallen asleep somewhere back along the road. She hopes they will continue to sleep. Eloise sighs in her sleep. Outside the car, she places the nozzle into the tank, leaving it to fill. The girls will be hungry again soon. She moves into the shop, moves through the aisles, looking for sandwiches, fruit, bottles of water—anything that will keep them going once they wake.

She remembers her sister Léa now, the morning they left the farm, and the emotion almost overcomes her. Saoirse can see her sister stretched out on the back seat. How terrified she must have been when she woke to the faces of strangers.

Her hands shake as she pays the attendant. Back at the car, her breathing is shallow and quick. She sits into the driver's seat, tunes the radio to the classic station, lets the soothing notes pass over her, but the music has shifted now, the intense opening bars of the news on the hour blare out of the speakers. She reaches and turns it down, so it does not wake the girls. The announcer's voice is barely audible, but the headline grips her with a new bout of panic.

"Gardaí are asking for the public's assistance in tracing the whereabouts of a woman, who was last seen in the airport region outside Letterkenny, believed to be moving in the direction of Dublin. She is driving a silver minivan with registration plate number—"

Saoirse knows they are describing her vehicle even before the registration is read out, even before they describe the occupants of the car as children—a thirteen-month-old toddler and a seven-year-old, both girls.

"An Garda Síochána have serious concerns that there is an immediate and serious risk to the woman and her children. Anyone with information is asked not to approach them but to contact gardaí on 999."

She clicks the radio off, starts the minivan, puts it in drive, removes the hand brake. There is the muffled sound of a phone ringing in the back seat. She thinks she must be hallucinating.

A loud knock startles her. The angry face of the petrol station attendant has appeared at her window. He is knocking harder now, shouting to her, banging on the roof, trying to open her door.

"Hey, hey—" he yells. "You'll rip the pump out."

She sees in the side mirror; she has forgotten to remove the nozzle from the tank. She lifts her hand, apologising. She waits for him to remove it, replacing it in the cradle, and she pulls away, her tyres squealing.

There is a moment she tries to orientate herself at the edge of the road, she can't remember from which direction she has come, confused by which way she needs to go. She turns onto the road and drives.

She has had years to prepare for this moment, and of course she is going to fuck it up. She fucks everything up. Lou is sitting next to her, now. She smells the leather of his jacket, his aftershave. *Don't fuck this up*, he is laughing. She turns to the passenger seat, to face him. The seat is empty. The girls are sleeping in her rearview mirror.

Breathe, she tells herself. *Breathe and drive.* She will get these girls to Daithí. That is all she will think about for now. That is all she must do.

A MOUNTAIN RANGE RISES IN the distance, familiar on the landscape. She knows these mountains. She knows this summit. This is not the way to Sligo. She is moving back toward Donegal, she realises her mistake, she has become turned around.

Leah is shifting in the back seat. Eloise will soon wake, too. They will be stiff from sitting in these seats all day. Eloise will cry until she is soothed. Saoirse drives toward the familiar landscape, the landmark, the mountain range on the horizon. If she can find a place off the road, somewhere to pull in, she will figure out what to do next. She rolls her window all the way down, the cold air helps to clear her head.

The sun, when it does appear, never gets so high this time of year and it is lowering already. The brightness sits across her vision. Leah stirs in the back seat.

"Are we almost there?" she asks.

"Almost, baby, almost there," Saoirse tells her. "Lay your head down, and when you wake, we'll be home."

It stands to reason, she thinks, looking at the clock, that Daithí has been informed. He probably will be waiting for them at the house. That is her new decision made. She presses on toward home.

They pass a town. She is acutely aware of the people here, who have walked and worked and lived here for generations. Living, normal, breathing people. People who are not in trouble.

She knows this village, this road.

And there is the left-hand turn, a sign for the sea cliffs, the track leading to the summit. She has been here before. She turns, drives up into the shadow of the mountain. The light is still bright at the top, though the sun is dipping quickly. She pulls into the scree-strewn car park. There are no other cars. No hikers. She is on her own with the girls. The track rises a little farther, she pulls ahead, closer up the ridge. She hasn't been back here since the first weekend she spent with Daithí all those years ago.

The sun is setting rapidly, a streak of red like a scar across the horizon, enveloped in a sky that is darkening.

"I want to go home," Leah says.

Saoirse is afraid to answer. She feels it in the tendons of her neck, she is ready to break.

Outside the minivan, the storm earlier has passed, ushering in air that is sharp and cold. She breathes deeply, feeling wide awake. She forgot about this quiet.

"Wait here," she tells Leah. "Mind your sister."

She leaves the girls, following the bracken a little farther up the path. Here are the gulls now, gliding out over the buttressed cliffs. It is as though this is the only place in the world, in this moment, the only thing that exists.

Here there is so much peace. Here there is freedom.

She can finally think.

She stands on the ridge above the sheer drop. She closes her eyes, places her hands in her pockets. The piece of paper Edel pushed through the letter box is there, folded.

She takes it out, slowly unfolds it. Begins to read.

FORMER TEACHER CHARGED

TEEN SUSPECTED OF MURDER PRESUMED DEAD

Lansing Journal, March 14,1995

Today, former art teacher Isabelle Jones (48), a central figure in a major crime ring exploiting teenagers to further their criminal activities, was handed a life sentence for her role in orchestrating a Michigan-to-Florida drug haul that resulted in the deaths of at least two individuals.

A former student of Jones, Edward Doyle, testified with immunity, providing crucial information that contributed to the conviction of Jones.

Doyle was apprehended after found in possession of a vehicle belonging to one of the dead men. The jury found former teacher, Jones, hired Doyle as an agent for the purpose of recruiting other teenagers as mules for the transfer of drugs and large sums of money.

When questioned, Doyle led police to a shallow grave near the farmhouse rented by one of the dead men, where they made the grim discovery. The site was secured, and a forensic examination concluded with the cause of deaths of Kenneth Lord and Louis Gagneux, found to have suffered catastrophic injuries indicative of gunshot wounds, and a third body, identified as Fleur Roy, was due to a drug overdose.

Two children were believed missing in the wake of the investigations. One child has since been located and remains in the custody of relatives. A second child, Sarah Roy, also known by the last name Gagneux, was last spotted in the parking lot of the Basilica in Detroit where it is believed she handed her sibling into the care of relatives, after which time she disappeared. Fearing the young woman was trafficked into the Florida drug ring, her photograph, see inset, was featured on a series of milk cartons in a missing child campaign. However, recent testimony from Doyle, a key witness, has shed new light on the case.

According to Doyle, Kenneth Lord paid a visit to the farm to recoup money owed. The teenage girl lay in wait at the family's farm, murdering the two men, including her stepfather, and allegedly threatened the same fate for Doyle if he did not help dispose of the bodies. Fingerprints on a firearm recovered from the scene confirm the girl's involvement. The girl then fled with cash received from the drug transaction. After a nationwide manhunt, police are following two lines of inquiry: that the missing girl left the country, most likely for Mexico, or she is presumed dead. The later scenario is the most likely, according to a source, as the Florida crime ring is known for its brutal approach in situations where transactions go wrong.

Doyle, in exchange for testimony, has been granted immunity on charges of drug trafficking, money laundering, aiding and abetting and accomplice after the fact to murder. More arrests are expected amongst the Florida crime gangs. With Ms. Jones's sentencing concluded, it is expected Doyle will make himself available for trial in the future in the event the missing suspect is apprehended.

Saoirse's hands shake. She reads the headline again.

She knows her story. This is not her story.

She paces the ridge.

Maybe she knew it all along. It was Eddie who brought this to their doorstep. Eddie was tight with JezaBelle all along. Eddie was the beginning of the food chain that is now about to devour them all. Everything of his demeanour that day at the truck stop comes back to her. The way he made her believe Lou had sent him—how he handed her the gun—

how she had placed her fingerprints all over it while at that moment, Lou and Kenny were probably already lying dead from a bullet fired from his hand, from this gun. She walked herself right into his trap—wanted for double murder.

Immunity. This is what Eddie gets for keeping his head.

Stupid, stupid, clever Eddie. He has outsmarted us all, she thinks.

She crumples the paper, sails it off the cliff.

This narrative, this lie, has filled a void, one she isn't there to defend—no one will believe her now, what she endured. At the hands of Lou. At the hands of Kenneth Lord.

Eddie, her friend. Her betrayer.

The red is gone from the horizon, the steel of the Atlantic below meets the lavender of the sky.

She screams into the night, it echoes on the cliffs, fills the gulf down to the reef, echoes back to her.

The crying continues in the distance. Saoirse thinks it is her own echo, or the seabirds mimicking her distress. But it comes to her, then, it is Eloise. She has woken.

Behind her, at the minivan, Leah's face is pressed against the glass, watching her mother out on the ridge. Saoirse shivers uncontrollably. She turns back to face the cliff edge.

The wind picks up on the summit.

One more step, she thinks, and I could drop from this height. All this running, over in a moment.

The lavender clouds cross swiftly in the darkening sky. They dissolve and reassemble themselves into new formations, new shapes, the colours shifting all the time.

There is movement behind her on the ridge.

Leah has climbed out of the van.

An image flashes into Saoirse's mind. An image of her own mother, lying on the bathroom floor.

Is this what you want to leave your daughters? she thinks.

And in that moment a calm takes over. It is the calm she recognises from the morning she left the farm. The same presence of mind that allowed her to find the number to her grandparents' house. The calm that helped her decide to put her sister in the car and drive her to the bridge.

"Leah, good girl," she calls to her daughter. "Leah. I need the phone."

But Leah is already holding it, speaking into it.

"We are very high up," she is saying, "Mammy is here."

She is reaching out to Saoirse, her phone outstretched in her hand.

A faint voice in the distance calls her name.

"Saoirse."

It is Daithí on the other end.

"Say hello, Mammy. Say hello into the phone," Leah instructs, her voice heightened.

Saoirse takes it to her mouth and turns away.

"I did this," she says into the mouthpiece. "I did this to us."

"Saoirse. Listen to me. Saoirse." Daithí's voice is calm and firm on the other end.

"I did this to the girls."

"Mammy?" Leah's voice trembles. She is shaking in the cold, darkening night.

"All lies, Daithí. Those are all lies about me."

"Tell me where you are," he says.

Her whole body is wracked with shivers as though she has been plunged into a cold sea and surfaced again into the wind.

She crouches to her knees. She can still hear his voice.

Leah stands beside her, shivering. She puts her hands around Saoirse's neck.

Saoirse wraps her free arm, holding her around the waist.

"I'm cold. Mammy, I'm so cold."

"Protect them, Daithí. Whatever happens next."

"I'll protect them, Saoirse. Of course I will."

"You have no idea what happens to girls like us."

The wind is picking up on the summit.

"Tell me exactly where you are."

"I'm so tired, Daithí." Her voice is weary. "So tired of it all."

"I know," he whispers, his voice is breaking. "Tell me where you are, for God's sake, Saoirse. I'm coming for you."

"I want you to come and get the girls."

"I'm on my way, Saoirse. I think I know where you are."

"Daithí?"

"Saoirse."

"'*This happiness could not have lasted.*'"

"Stay there, babe. I'm coming for you all."

AMERICAN WOMAN ARRESTED IN DONEGAL, MISSING PERSON FOUND ALIVE AFTER NEARLY A DECADE ON

Irish Times, 8 January 2000

In a stunning development, a Donegal resident has identified herself as a missing person who disappeared from the USA nearly ten years ago and has been presumed dead.

The unfolding case took an unexpected turn when gardaí aiming to establish the identity of the woman discovered evidence to suggest she is an American connected with a double murder and a missing child case over a decade ago in rural Michigan in the USA. Though the woman has been held for over 24 hours, she has not yet been remanded in custody, as authorities seek additional time to investigate the complexities surrounding the facts of the case and verify the woman's background. A source close to the investigation says gardaí have not ruled out charges in relation to fraud and the unlawful detainment of children. The source also confirms international interest in interviewing the woman on allegations of murder. Gardaí are cooperating with American law enforcement. Updates to follow.

Lost

8–10 January 2000

The doctors have come into her room, day and night, to her bedside. They have told her she has been transferred to Dublin, to a psychiatric hospital. They have poked and prodded her. They have requested her body fluids, blood and spit, a hair sample—and she has conceded to all their requests. They have concluded their psychiatric evaluation, and everyone, she can tell, is being very careful with her.

The doctors clear out and the gardaí move in.

She gives them, in as much detail as possible, all the events leading up to that night. They have asked her the same questions again and again, and she has answered, consistently. She hears her own voice in monotone.

She has told them everything.

I am Sarah Gagneux. I have never been known by the name Roy, though I know it was my mother's name. I read it on a birth certificate.

I am her.

I am Sarah.

I am alive.

Though everything about her is dead. Or dying.

A GARDA IS STANDING AT her bedside, gently calling her name.

"Saoirse Byrne?"

Saoirse doesn't answer.

"Sarah Roy," a man with an American accent insists.

The garda lifts her eyes, annoyed, but appeases him.

"Sarah Roy. I'm arresting you for identity theft. You are also being charged with unlawfully obtaining and using someone else's personal information. You are under arrest for passport fraud. You are under arrest for filing false documents, traffic offences, obtaining employment under false pretences. You are under arrest for unlawfully detaining children using false information."

The American man steps forward.

"And you are wanted in the United States of America for questioning. On charges of murder."

THE FOG SHE HAS BEEN under lifts as the sedatives leave her system. She has stopped waiting for Daithí. Why would he come? Now that the girls are safe and he has the full picture of her deceit. A fraud and a fake and someone he believes could have hurt the children.

The last moments on the clifftop reel through her head. Saoirse had sat with the girls in the van, waiting. The headlights breached the arc of the mountain, Seamus's car pulled up the track and Daithí stepped out of the passenger's side, casting a silhouette across the summit. Leah jumped out when she saw him, she ran toward him, ran into the safety of his arms. Saoirse had stepped out of the van, moved toward him. She didn't know what to expect but she hadn't expected him to stretch out his hand, halting her in her tracks.

"Eloise?" he asked gravely, handing Leah off to Seamus. Leah held Seamus's hand, she let him lead her back to the van, he opened the door while she climbed into the back seat. Daithí had opened the other door, took Eloise from the car seat, checked her over, kissed and cradled her head with sheer relief.

"They're fine, they're all right," Saoirse told him.

"Jesus Christ, what the hell were you thinking?" he asked.

Saoirse had stumbled backward.

"Here now, lad—" Seamus said gently.

The gardaí reached the summit by then and had each taken an arm to steady her.

She had moved willingly with them as they escorted her into the garda car. She had nothing left in her in that moment, as she watched Daithí place Eloise back into her car seat. As she saw Leah's face pressed against the window, watching the gardaí drive her mother off the mountain.

SHE EXPECTED TO BE CHARGED with crimes against Sasa and illegally entering the country. But questioned for murder? Unlawfully detaining her own children?

"This isn't right," she begs. "My children. My children need me."

No one will help her. Not the nurses or the constant change in gardaí stationed at the door. They can't tell her if the girls have been separated from one another, if Eloise cries for her, if Leah is being sheltered from the awful things they are saying about her mother. The nurses pat her hand, and the gardaí give her looks of sympathy, but no one will tell her anything.

Saoirse is weak when she climbs out of the bed, paces the room, tries to think beyond the unbearable, but she is nearly wild with regret. For what she has done. For missing the opportunity to make things right. For taking responsibility of her past and her children's future before she lost all control of both.

The nurse has come in to say family has arrived to see her. *Daithí*, she thinks. Her breath leaves her. She will face him now, she will plead with him to try and understand, to listen to her first.

But it is Vivienne who steps into the room, lips tightly drawn, followed by Paul.

They block the doorway; Saoirse backs toward the bed, startled by their presence.

Paul is wooden and stilted, as though his throat is lined with cork.

"I don't know what to say, Sarah."

She detects the insincerity in his tone.

"We have been advised to say nothing," Vivienne reprimands her brother. "We have no idea who this woman is, what else will come out of this investigation."

"I'm sorry," Saoirse whispers.

Paul's face flushes with resentment.

"You've made a fool out of me and my family," he tells her. "You've ruined my life, Leah's life."

"Leah?" Saoirse whispers, desperate. "Are the girls together?"

Vivienne hasn't heard Saoirse's question, or she ignores it.

"Look, we aren't here for the chats. There is no forgiveness for what you have done. We are serving you these." Vivienne hands her an envelope, *Sarah Roy* printed on a label across the front.

"We want our family exonerated from any wrongdoing. We want the public to know we have no involvement in your crimes," Vivienne says coolly.

Saoirse feels the room spin. She wants to explain from the start, tell Vivienne everything, take responsibility. But Vivienne won't stop talking and there seems to be no coherence to her words. Saoirse's vision is narrowing to a tunnel.

"It's for Leah's own good," Paul says.

"The important thing," Vivienne says, "is we have custody awarded to Paul for his daughter and that further—"

"And *no*, to answer your question," Paul cuts across his sister. "Of course the girls are not together."

His words feel like a punch to her gut.

"Am I a babysitter? Would we leave Leah with *him*?"

Thousands of colourful dots blot out his face.

Saoirse moves her lips to form her daughters' names but a sound of unspeakable despair escapes instead. To this, there is only a startled wonder from Vivienne, derailed from her mission, her voice losing confidence.

The dots merge and it is as though a black veil has been lowered over her eyes. She does not reach out to pull off this darkness, there is nothing to grasp at, not even a single light shining on the distant plain.

IDENTITY UNRAVELLED: IRISH ARTIST'S ARREST TAKES STARTLING TURN AS TRUE IDENTITY EMERGES

Irish Times, 9 January 2000

Award-winning Donegal-based artist known by the name Saoirse Byrne has been charged with identity theft and passport fraud under the name Sarah Roy. Known by the aliases of Sarah Gagneux, Sarah Walsh and now Saoirse Byrne, Roy is a missing American teenager presumed dead for nearly ten years. An artist and mother of two, it is believed Roy was living in Ireland under an assumed identity for at least eight of the ten years she was missing and presumed dead. The investigation is considerably complex as it spans two continents and a decade, intertwining the worlds of art and crime, and investigators continue to probe further alleged crimes. Two minors are involved, their identities and nationality under question. Roy is remanded in custody at the Central Psychiatric Hospital, where a full medical evaluation was ordered while the minors remain in the care of relatives.

Prominent writer Vivienne Byrne, a spokeswoman for one of

the families affected by the crimes, expressed shock and betrayal at Roy's arrest, stating, "You couldn't make it up. She is a fraud and a fake. She has preyed on the kindness and decency of the Irish people. The family ask for the media to respect their privacy at this time while they deal with the children involved and work to repair the damage caused." Inside sources claim Ms. Byrne is directly involved with the family concerned.

To further complicate the saga, late in 1999 Roy, under the name of Saoirse Byrne, won the prestigious Margaret Dowling Art Prize which comes with a £50,000 award.

The Margaret Dowling Trust released this statement earlier in the week:

"In light of recent developments surrounding the Margaret Dowling Art Prize conferred in November, the administrators wish to clarify that, although the integrity of the art awarded is not in question, concerns have been raised regarding the ethical conduct of the artist in relation to her identity. The administrators further wish to confirm that the Trust was contacted in the weeks preceding the arrest of the artist, in which the artist, known to us as Saoirse Byrne, expressed a wish to decline the award. It is important to highlight that recipients of the Margaret Dowling Art Prize do not approach us but are selected through a process based on the merit of their work. The administrators unequivocally state that the controversy surrounding the artist does not bring into question the authenticity of her artistic contributions. Additionally, the Trust wishes to confirm they have accepted the artist's decision to decline the award. The runner-up of the prize has been notified of their success."

Found

11 January 2000

Saoirse wakes in a hospital bed, the curtains drawn around her. She has little recollection of being transferred, sedated again, hooked up to this IV. It is quieter here than the last hospital. There is only one garda stationed at her door.

She asks her again about her children.

The garda takes her hands, squeezes them to reassure her.

"They are where they need to be, your girls are safe."

Her girls, she fears, are gone from her, forever. Her life here in Ireland, her life with Daithí, is over. The waiting is agony. If someone could confirm this, she could step beyond this wall of curtains, and step off into the abyss. Close her eyes and never wake again.

A nurse pops her head in.

"Hello, pet. Visitor?"

She has a vague recollection of Catherine at her bedside. She had spoken about Leah, she remembers, and Saoirse tried to reach out through the fog, to grasp what she was telling her. She could only reach the word "safe." And she held on to this. Catherine wouldn't lie. But her fog is lessening now. She doesn't feel as drugged as in recent days, she feels she is returning to the world of the living, an excruciating sensation of despair.

The nurse parts the curtains. Daithí stands behind her, solemn.

Saoirse is overcome at once, she puts her face into her hands. He pulls the curtain closed and comes to the edge of her bed. She cannot bear this strangeness between them.

"I'm sorry it took so long—" he tells her. "I needed time—"

"Don't," she whispers, and it feels like her chest will collapse with the sorrow of it all. "Please don't—"

"It's a lot to take in all at once—and there is so much to sort out for the girls."

"The girls?" she asks.

"Leah is grand, taking it all in her stride," he whispers. He is overwhelmed with the strangeness between them, too. "And Eloise is her usual self, full of beans. The girls are fine."

She sobs. Daithí speaks more quickly, reassuring her.

"Leah is asking for you. I've been to the house. Nuala is keeping her very busy, baking and whatnot."

Saoirse brings the sheet up to her face to catch the tears, to wipe her nose. Daithí takes a tissue from her bedside locker, places it in her hand.

"You saw Catherine, she didn't know if you knew she was here."

She nods, hearing the tiredness in his voice.

"I visit Leah twice a day, I'm allowed, thanks to Liam—I've called in a favour." She can hear the wry smile in his voice. "Who can say no to Liamo? In fact, Eloise and I have just come from there and Leah sends you the biggest hug. And this card."

She takes it from him.

Mammy come home! the card demands. There is a picture of two figures, one big and one small. The larger one has *Mammy* written over it.

"Daithí—" she whispers. "I'm so ashamed."

"Come here to me," he tells her.

"You'll never forgive me. The girls, they'll never forgive me. What have I done to us?"

He sits down on the edge of her bed now. She can feel him shifting, his hands don't know where to go, what to do if they can't reach for hers.

If she has lost him, she thinks, it is better not to prolong the visit.

"Daithí, you don't have to do this—"

"Hey—listen to me. I told you, and I meant it. We will do what needs to be done. The worst has happened. And now the worst is over."

She shakes her head.

"I was shocked, Saoirse, on the cliffs. All day, waiting to hear, I feared the worst." His voice breaks. He clears his throat and gathers himself. "Some of the misinformation coming in was terrifying, I was frightened and when I saw the three of you, unharmed—I've never felt such relief. But there were still so many unanswered questions. All I could think of was getting the girls off that mountain, getting them home. The gardaí advised I let them see to you, to give you the medical attention you needed. I'm sorry, so sorry the way I spoke to you."

She closes her eyes and lays back against the pillows. Of course, he was always going to end this gently. She can't look at him, waiting for him to deliver his final verdict, hand her papers, the way Vivienne and Paul did. The only thing left to say is he will seek full custody of Eloise.

She waits.

But no such words follow.

"And I'm sorry. I'm sorry I wasn't here sooner—"

She opens her eyes and studies his face.

"I am here now," he tells her again when she doesn't answer. "Can you believe me when I tell you the worst is over?"

"It's not over." Her voice shakes. "I'm going to jail. Goddammit, Eddie. He was my *friend*." She is sobbing now. "I don't know why he's done this to me. But you have to believe me, I didn't do what he is accusing me of—I did some things wrong—a lot of things, in fact—but not that. And they're sending me back, I know it. The Americans came from the embassy—" She can hardly breathe.

"Listen to me, listen to me." He is determined that she hear his words. "I believe you."

His words stop her short.

"There are many people, in fact, who believe you. This feels like a big problem, I know. But it's a lot of little, solvable problems, and *we will* solve them. One by one."

"If I had told you earlier—"

"Yes, but you didn't."

She lets him place his hand around the back of her neck. She leans into him and he takes her fully into his arms, cradles her head, kisses her. He releases a sigh full of emotion, full of relief and empathy.

"It's like restoring a house," he says into her hair. "One thing at a time . . . let's get the scaffolding in place. Yeah?"

"They'll never forget seeing their mother lose it."

"The girls? What is done is done. The best possible outcome for them now is to see you get better—you are very ill, babe. You have suffered major traumas—the doctors are talking post-traumatic stress—but babe, there is nothing *post* about this yet. But you are here, you haven't gone anywhere. You stuck around, see? And Saor—you're in the right place."

He holds her shaking body.

The nurse is back.

"Are you ready?" she asks Daithí. "Or I can give you a minute," she says when she sees the state of Saoirse.

Daithí hands Saoirse another tissue. She blows her nose.

"I think we're ready," Daithí tells the nurse.

She leaves and then Saoirse hears her return, rolling something across the floor.

"Another visitor," she says cheerfully. "You've a busy room today."

She pulls the curtains open. Saoirse cries out when she sees Eloise in the cot being rolled forward, to the end of the bed. Eloise has pulled herself to standing, she is shaking the bars, lifting her arms out to her mother, calling to her with a crankiness Saoirse adores, one she reserves for her mother, demanding her attention.

Daithí lifts her, her feet and legs flailing—he brings her to Saoirse, places her into her arms. The relief is as though she has just given birth all over again. She holds her daughter to her, Eloise burrows into her neck. Daithí and Saoirse laugh through their tears. Eloise looks up at them, smiling.

Saoirse has made room for Daithí to slide in beside her, and Eloise eventually falls asleep sprawled across the two of them. The nurse brings them tea and biscuits. The arrangement, Daithí is telling her quietly, is for Leah to stay with Paul. Daithí and Eloise will stay at Catherine's until the investigation is finalised—then they'll figure out the next steps.

"Child Services are involved now; you have to know."

She nods.

"There's a lot to figure out." He looks tired again when he says this. The weight of his burden is great, she thinks.

The gardaí will guard the door until further notice, he tells her, until the extradition order is decided.

The word strikes fear in Saoirse.

"To the US?"

"There is only a small possibility of it. Catherine is on to everyone she knows. She has our backs. There are a lot of people working on this, all of them on your side," he reassures her.

Saoirse nods and swallows.

"You know, I think I met a friend of yours during the week, when I was in Dublin getting things sorted."

"Tell me."

"I went to your exhibition. It is swarmed now, but I went before your name was released. I wanted to get in early, before the news broke. I wanted to understand—"

He is watching her now, waiting for her to lift her eyes to him, to connect.

"There was someone else there. A woman about your age."

"Yes?"

"She had her newborn daughter with her."

"Oh."

"I think I might have met Sarah Walsh."

Saoirse is quiet.

"I think she suspected who I was. We were very Irish about the whole thing. Neither of us admitting to one another, this thing we were skirting around, but we both knew we were there for the same reason."

Saoirse takes a deep breath and holds it. How much she has taken from Sasa, from all of them. Her head hangs lower. *I am no better than Lou*, she thinks.

It's as though Daithí understands where her thoughts are going.

"It seems to me what you did, you did to survive. To keep everyone alive."

There is so much she wants to tell him. And she will. But now she can only sink into this relief that the truth is out. And he is still here.

"I think you'd understand something she said."

"What did she say?"

"She was chatting gibberish with Eloise, you know the way you do, getting her to smile—and I was admiring her wee one—she's just a newborn, a couple weeks at most."

Saoirse's throat squeezes over. She thinks of Sasa, and the reason she left Ireland in the first place. Her eyes fill with tears for her, tears of happiness. And then again, the shame for all the trouble she has caused at such a vulnerable time.

"You know what she said to me?"

Saoirse shakes her head.

"She looked so intently at me and said, 'You'd do almost anything to protect them, wouldn't you?'"

Saoirse closes her eyes.

Of all of them, Sasa would know. She would know exactly how far you would go to protect your own.

After a time, Daithí clears his throat.

"I have a confession."

She waits.

"Catherine found your sketchbooks. We went through them."

Saoirse doesn't respond.

"I didn't expect—" His voice breaks again. "There's so much in them, Saoirse. They are much more—graphic—than your canvases."

"They aren't meant for you, or anyone else—" she whispers.

"No. We could see that."

She covers her eyes.

"Daithí, I'm so ashamed. How can you even look at me? How can you not despise me?"

He places his mug on the bedside table.

"I can stand you. I can more than stand you. Look at me now," he demands.

She does as he asks. He takes her mug, places it on the table.

She is trembling. He pulls a tissue from the box and gently wipes away the tears from her chin, the tears that have spilled onto Eloise's cheeks.

"The things people—*men*—have put on you. Expected from you. *A child*. Saoirse. You were a child. I fear—I fear for what *I* wanted—all this time, how did I not see you were in trouble?"

"I didn't want you to see."

She places her hand along his jawline. He takes it, holds his against hers.

"I'm sorry, babe. I'm sorry so much has happened to you."

The emotion on his face moves her.

"But when I saw those sketchbooks, I thought of those moments in the Byrnes' kitchen again, and seeing you paint in the garden. Saoirse, I never told you this—but when we met, I wasn't long back from New York, it was after leaving a relationship, and the way I left I am not terribly proud of. Someday I'll tell you—but the point is, I felt so vulnerable back here in Ireland, in a place that had never quite felt like home. And there you were—vulnerable, so real, reaching out to the world in this quiet, wonderful language—

"And yeah, I wish you had told me. Trusted me to help you. But I can see where you were at now, why you couldn't. And all this does complicate things," he says.

She breathes in sharply.

"Complicates things," he repeats. "But it doesn't change things. I love you, babe," he tells her. "Just to be clear what I am saying—I'm never losing you again. I love you more than ever before, if that is possible."

They sit in the quiet of his words.

After a time she sighs.

"We'll go forward?" she asks.

"One day at a time, okay?"

It is all she can ask.

"The sketchbooks—"

"That's what I wanted to tell you. We've handed them over to the gardaí. I had no choice."

She nods.

"We copied them first. A professor from a research group in Art and Gender Studies at Trinity College contacted us through Catherine. She thinks people need to know your case, to know what you've been through to understand. I'd like you to consent to her having copies, examining them, looking at your story through your art—"

It feels like a piece of her is detaching, navigating away from her control. She swallows it back.

"She won't publish them?"

"No, no, nothing like that."

She thinks about it for a moment.

"I trust you," she whispers.

"I think it could help—with public sentiment."

"Oh God, this is messy."

"It is messy," he agrees. "One thing at a time. Scaffolding, babe."

"Scaffolding."

"You've been through worse. A hell of a lot worse."

Frankie: Are you saying Saoirse Byrne, pardon me—Sarah Roy—was not a vulnerable individual? Did you see her paintings?

Vivienne: Of course I have seen her paintings. She painted them right under our noses. She used my grandmother's heirloom easel—

Professor: Sorry, if I can cut across you there—but have you really seen them, Vivienne? It is clear she has dealt with a variety of trauma-related issues through the medium of her art. The work—I mean she won one of the most prestigious votes of confidence for form and composition—the Margaret Dowling Art Prize is not something to be sniffed at—this woman has talent. But not only talent, it is clear she was employing her creativity to deal with the pain and trauma, to somehow communicate what she lived and feared—and I have had a look at some of her sketchbooks, which are beyond traumatic. It is all very overwhelming, and I think we must look carefully—

Vivienne: What you're saying only further suggests to me her intelligence and ability to manipulate—

Frankie: Wait a second though—we are talking about a child—a vulnerable teenager who arrived on your doorstep.

Vivienne: No one knew that, Frankie. She told us she was twenty. She presented herself as an adult.

Frankie: I'm not suggesting you knew her circumstances or her age, but there is a symmetry here between the trauma she endured, the decisions she made as a consequence, and the . . . the survival mode she must have been in. The dual life she was living in her mind and the mental toll that must have taken. Have you examined these elements?

Vivienne: There are crimes involved here. If you read the American newspapers, they are making her out to be a monster. Another Lizzie Borden.

Professor: (Groans) Right, lets believe the tabloids. Look, she has admitted to some crimes, the authorities will ask her to answer to these in due course—

Frankie: Sorry to cut across you, Professor, but the point I'm making, Vivienne, we all agree there are serious allegations of fraud here, but can you remove yourself from the scenario and look at this with a degree of empathy?

Vivienne: (Laughing) I know what you're doing, Frankie, what you always do. Playing devil's advocate. But we are talking about a conniving, manipulating—and now the whole of the country wants to see her exonerated because she painted a few pictures—

Frankie: Well, she won't be exonerated, as you say, but the courts might take into account the mitigating forces that caused her to go to such extreme measures.

Professor: Let me ask you this, Vivienne, are you not disturbed? And when you know the story—this was a child—not a woman—a child, who had been abused, who had seen things no one should see—I know you stand up for women around the world, Vivienne, I read your work, and the letter campaigns, but what I am suggesting to you is that this woman arrived from what was, to her mind for all intents and purposes, a war-torn environment—her sister in danger, forced to deal drugs, forced into sex, and I can confirm—she was fleeing for her life—and are you telling me you can't see why she acted the way she did—

Vivienne: I am not on trial here.

Frankie: No, no one is saying you are. Okay, maybe we'll go to break.

Professor: No, wait a minute. What I am saying is can you not give her the same benefit—empathy? She has two children, her life is destroyed, they want to extradite her to the US—can you not even concede that there is a small piece of redemption you want to imagine for this woman?

Silence

Frankie: Okay, well, let's go to break. Yes—we're going to go to commercial break. We'll be back.

Misadventure

17 January 2000

"We've been through all the options," her lawyer, Barbara, is saying. They are sitting at the table just inside the door of her hospital room. "And it is my wholehearted recommendation, Saoirse, that you plead guilty to the lesser charges: identity theft, fraud. I am afraid it will go to trial otherwise; you'll be dragged through more psychiatric evaluations; you'll have to relive the trauma—"

Saoirse nods.

"You don't want this dragged out."

"No."

"For your sake or the children's."

She agrees.

"But—the good news is, I do believe there are mitigating circumstances, and I do think, maybe—we can somehow hope for the victim impact statements to be minimal."

Even the words, *victim impact*, make Saoirse feel weak.

"Who will give those?"

"Well, Sarah Walsh, for one. Maybe Paul, his family. This is the unknown."

"Would he do that to Leah?" Saoirse asks Daithí.

Daithí can only shrug. He can't honestly say what Paul is capable of.

"Any progress on that front?" Barbara asks.

Daithí shakes his head.

"I've a liaison, one of the lads is intervening, a mutual friend—"

"Good. We can also approach Paul's solicitor."

"Let's see how far we get with Liam?"

"Fair enough."

"And then there is a possibility that Paul's family will sue for damages. Even if you get off with a light sentence."

Saoirse feels the colour drain from her face. She imagines going into this with Paul, Leah in the middle. Maybe even Daithí's house at stake.

"And custody?"

"Again, what Paul is putting in his arsenal remains to be seen."

"Will I lose Leah?"

"It isn't my specialty, but the family courts here in Ireland usually rule in favour of the mother. However, this is a little different—"

"Extradition?" Daithí asks.

"I can't go back there." Saoirse's voice breaks. Daithí takes her hand.

There is something she is dreading to ask.

"My sister?"

"Now—" Barbara begins. "I have brought someone along to speak with you about all this. Is that okay? Can I bring her in?"

Saoirse feels a stab of terror.

Daithí squeezes her hand tighter.

"All right?" he asks when Barbara moves to the door, steps out of the room.

She nods. But she isn't all right, not really.

Barbara comes back, accompanied by a woman in a suit. She carries a folder, and Barbara introduces her as Juliette Mason, an official from the Canadian Embassy to Ireland. She shakes Saoirse's hand and then Daithí's. She sits across from Saoirse.

"Ms. Roy," she says. "May I call you Sarah?" She pronounces it the way Mama did.

Saoirse seems unsure.

"I think we are comfortable with Saoirse," Daithí says. Saoirse places her hand on his knee, grateful.

"Of course. Saoirse. It is important to start with saying I am so sorry for the impossible challenges and circumstances you have faced."

Saoirse smiles weakly.

"What I have come to tell you is this: Saoirse, you are a Canadian citizen." She opens the folder and shows her a copy of her birth certificate.

"You were born in Canada to a Canadian mother. Unfortunately, your grandmother never learned from your mother the name of your biological father. She was quite certain Fleur may not have known herself. Nevertheless, you were brought to the US illegally by your mother and Lou somewhere between the age of three and five from what I can make out—"

"Three," Saoirse says. "I must have been three. I remember—"

"I don't know how your parents got away with it for so long, but here we are now. Importantly, you are now under the protection and jurisdiction of the Canadian government. And the happy news is, Saoirse, we do not support any petition for extradition given the circumstances."

Saoirse brings her hands to her mouth. They are shaking.

Daithí audibly breathes a sigh of relief.

"And my sister?" Saoirse asks when she trusts herself to speak again.

"She is alive and well and with your grandparents and also under the protection of Canada."

Daithí squeezes her hand. Saoirse breaks into tears of relief.

"You need to know something—the law enforcement failed you and your sister, Saoirse, on so many accounts. If they had acted on initial reports of your trouble, and we are finding there were many—teachers, principals, even a pharmacist in one case—then police and social services could have intervened on your behalf years before the night in question. They would have had your father in custody long before the damage he inflicted."

"Lou was not my father."

"No," Juliette apologises. "He wasn't.

"We also feel it was unacceptable to give Edward Doyle immunity, to give him a platform in the absence of your own testimony. He should never have been allowed to take the stand, and he should be serving a life sentence. Evidence points to, and Isabelle Jones also alleged, that Mr. Doyle murdered Kenneth Lord and Louis Gagneux under instructions. And I understand your own sketchbooks corroborate with Ms. Jones's version of that night. We also have reason to believe you were to be targeted, and your sister."

She hesitates.

"You are aware, then, that your mother died from an overdose?"

Saoirse nods.

"It's a lot to take in," Daithí tells the woman.

"We can take a break."

"No, I'm fine. I want to hear," Saoirse says.

"It is our opinion that what you did, calling your grandparents, taking that risk to put your sister in safe hands—you should be commended. You saved your sister's life, Saoirse. You are the only person, as far as we can see, who made intelligent decisions in this long chain of misadventure. And as far as I'm concerned—that is the Canadian government's position on this—the US has no right to seek this petition for your extradition. We are petitioning for immunity on your behalf. They let you and your sister down, very badly. Your parents let you down. I don't believe the US even has the right to question you any further, but if they do, we have found a young woman you knew from the state of Florida, she went by the name Jane—though she is now in witness protection—who will testify on your behalf. She understands what happened to you in Florida."

Saoirse's eyes well up remembering Jane. It hadn't occurred to her she was in trouble, too. How vulnerable they were. How many girls believe they are to blame? Unprotected children playing grown up.

A weight that has been sitting on her chest is lifted.

"We are here to protect you, there are a lot of people on your side."

"That is good news, very good news." Daithí manages a smile for the first time in days.

"Finally, Saoirse, we have been in talks with the Irish government. Both parties are satisfied that your running was justified. You were a dead woman if you had stayed a day longer. But that is something you don't need me to tell you."

"Does my sister—does she know I'm alive?"

Juliette smiles.

"She does indeed, and when you are up for it, we will organise for you to speak on the phone if you want. And I would like to send back photographs, of you and your children, if that is okay. For your sister. She is eager to know you are well."

"We'll think about that," Daithí tells her. He is holding her hands protectively in both of his own now.

Barbara tells her they are diligently preparing her hearing, highlighting aspects of coercion, death threats—it will be compelling and robust—but Saoirse has stopped listening to Barbara telling them they have to hope that when her case comes before the hearing next week, that the impact statements of those affected, the women involved in the identity theft, won't be as impactful—that her Irish sentencing will be lenient—but Saoirse is standing up from the table, moving toward the bed, Daithí is supporting her, thanking them, telling the women they may leave, they'll be in touch.

When the door closes, she puts her head into his lap and they both cry tears of relief, joy, grief—all of them, every single kind.

ASK FRANKIE LIVE NATIONAL RADIO BROADCAST

17 January 2000

Frankie: We are back, and I'm on the line with Vivienne Byrne and I have Professor Jenkins in studio discussing the captivating case of Sarah Roy, alias Saoirse Byrne. We have some callers on the line. Niamh from Limerick wants to ask this:

Niamh: Hello, Frankie.

Frankie: Hello, Niamh, what is your question?

Niamh: It is this, Frankie. This girl was a child. Why didn't anyone ask questions? Why didn't the family wonder where her parents were or if she had family.

Frankie: Good question. Vivienne, did you ever wonder about meeting her parents? Her family?

Vivienne: This is how good she was. She was a con artist. She had a story for everything. She is good at deception, as you are witnessing here. And to set the caller straight, she didn't look like a child, and she certainly didn't act like a child.

Niamh: Well, she is not denying any of it—she is pleading guilty to identity theft—

Vivienne: As we've been hearing. Point made, Niamh.

Niamh: I mean, what a cold fish—cut her some slack.

Frankie: Okay, thank you. Next caller. Do we have Tom on the line from Dublin?

Tom: I hear a lot of people defending this girl, but what your one is saying—this woman had two children, she knew right from wrong. Why didn't she walk into the garda station when she first arrived. She waited to get caught. It all sounds a bit premeditated. And I ask you this—what if this happened in America? You think they'd give the Irish this preferential treatment? You bet if it was you or me, we'd be put straight back on the next flight home—

Vivienne: Fair point.

Frankie: Hmmmmm. Okay, Sandra calling from Leitrim.

Sandra: Where were those people—why didn't they ask questions—I don't care, you're dealing with a child. That woman sounds so far up her own arse—

Frankie: Okay, thank you, Sandra, next caller. Betty from Donegal.

Betty: Well, Frankie. This is what I have to say. I've seen this woman's art up here in Letterkenny. Stunning. Here was a woman trying to deal with traumas, life blows, and where did these blows come from? Her own parents. It beggars belief. Release her, give her babies back to her, and let her get over what was done to her. You give her our best wishes.

Frankie: Will do, Betty, will do. We have Sasa from Dublin on the line now. Go ahead, Sasa.

(Silence)

Frankie: Sasa, are you there?

Sasa: Hi, Frankie, yeah, I'm here. Look, I'm listening to this. I am the woman whose identity was stolen, and I have something to say.

Frankie: Sasa, let me get this straight, are you saying it was *your* identity Sarah Roy stole?

Sasa: Yes, she did, and your station manager was onto me, so he knows who I am.

Frankie: Okay, yes, I'm getting confirmation, we've this verified. Okay, Sasa, go ahead, what do you want to say?

Sasa: Look. I knew this woman. She was a teenager, like everyone now knows. We worked for the same family, and she stole my passport. I didn't know she was in trouble, or at least this much trouble. She flew to Ireland using my passport. She gets a job, meets a man, has a child using my name. I know all of this now. And I come home from the US of A, I was there undocumented for a time, I'll add—and I find out someone is using my identity, they have even changed it and changed my address and used my RSI number. And it was inconvenient, not just inconvenient—it was a pain in the hole.

Frankie: Okay. And are you angry? Do you want her prosecuted?

Sasa: That's why I'm ringing you. Because I'm sitting here listening to your callers, and your woman in studio, running Saoirse down. Calling for a lynch mob. Wanting her to pay for the sins of the adults in her life. But you know what? Saoirse—that is what she goes by now—Saoirse was doing what many women in this country have done for years. She was running away. She was fighting for survival—by whatever means she could. How many women have had to be run from this country? Unwanted pregnancies, rape, marriages they can't leave because it is not even in our constitution, poverty—I'm so sick of hearing people like your one there preaching to us, virtue signalling on one hand, and then so bloody ungenerous on the other. If Saoirse could have made a different decision at the time, don't you think she would have? I forgive her. And I'll tell you what—I'm going to say so in my victim's impact statement.

Frankie: In court?

Sasa: (Go away, Ruth)

Frankie: Sorry?

Sasa: Sorry, speaking of running someone out—it's just me sister here, making a nuisance of herself. But yeah, in court. I get to make one of those statements.

Frankie: And you'll say you forgive her?

Sasa: Yes, I do. Yes, I will.

Professor: Good woman, Sasa.

Sasa: And you know what else I'll say? I'll say I'm glad she took my name—maybe it was a lifeline, maybe it is why she survived and didn't get herself killed in the first place. Because you know, it's coming out now, she was running for her life. I am just so sick of women having to run all the time—and if they're not running, they're defending themselves. I'm so fucking sick of it—

Frankie: Oops, Sasa, are you okay? Careful, we're on national radio. But listen, Sasa, this is very emotional for you, I can hear.

Professor: Good on you, Sasa, aren't you brave to come on here? You get in touch with me, Sasa, when this programme is over, will you?

Sasa: And come here to me. Why is the sister of that man here? Why isn't the man here, answering for himself? He sends the woman to take his fall—can't you see this? I'm sick of it all.

Frankie: I can hear that. Thank you, Sasa, you have been eloquent and generous. And I hope you are getting everything sorted with the bureaucracy and welcome home, can I tell you that?

Sasa: Thank you. It is good to be home, actually, despite it all—

Frankie: Have you anything to say to this woman, the one who stole your identity, if she is listening?

Sasa: Well, I think I've about said it all—but she goes by Saoirse now, and you know what? I think that is appropriate. You know what Saoirse means, right?

Frankie: Freedom.

Professor: Freedom.

Sasa: Right. Freedom.

Frankie: Well, Professor Jenkins, Vivienne Byrne, thank you for joining us, that is all we have time for. Sasa, you are some woman. We wish you all the best—is that a baby I hear?

Sasa: It is indeed. My daughter. Sort it out, for God's sake, for her and the likes of her.

Professor: Get in touch, Sasa. We'll sort them all out.

Frankie: Ah, Sasa, good luck with it all. And to Saoirse, if you are listening—we wish you just that. Here is to your Freedom. We'll play you out with this one from George Michael.

Vivienne: Jesus Christ, you've got to be—

Partings

22 January 2000

Saoirse paces the room. She pokes her head out, trying to see around the garda stationed outside her door. She is grateful when he moves a distance from the door, leaning on the nurse's desk to chat. Her palms sweat, soaking into the teddy Catherine brought for her to give to Leah.

The door opens at the end of the corridor. Leah spots her mother and runs toward her, throwing herself into Saoirse's arms. Saoirse picks her up, puts her face into her hair, walks into the room with her, the two clinging to one another.

"You are so tall, my love," she tells her.

Leah holds her, she won't let go, and Saoirse won't let go either. It feels they will hold each other like this forever.

"I'm sorry, Leah. I'm so sorry."

"Were you frightened?" Leah asks.

"I was, of course I was. But I was mostly sad because I wasn't sure when I would get to come back to you."

"And come back to Eloise?"

"And to Eloise."

"And to Dotty?"

Saoirse laughs.

"Yes, all of you."

"But you're coming home now."

"I am, love, I'm coming home soon. Come sit, we'll have a chat."

The teddy Saoirse has been holding is smashed in between them. She gives it to Leah, and lowers her into a chair. Leah strokes it while they talk.

"I was sad when you were gone," Leah tells her.

"Did you have a chat? With your dad? Did he explain anything?"

"Some. And Dotty did too."

"Do you want to tell me—"

"And Gran. Mostly Gran."

"Oh—"

"She told me about you and that bad man. And she told me *Isn't Mammy amazing gone through all that and still a wonderful mammy?*"

"She said that?" Saoirse's eyes fill with tears. She tries to imagine Nuala saying these things.

"She said I can come home to you and Dotty and get back to school soon—when you are feeling a little bit better—and I'll come to her and my daddy on the weekends."

Saoirse is sniffing. Wiping her face on her sleeves.

"Is that what you want?"

Leah twists up her face like her mother is crazy.

Saoirse laughs.

"Of course. Of course, you do, baby. And I can't wait for that to happen."

"I made a card for you, Mammy. Did you get it?"

Saoirse can't see through her tears.

"I did, honey. See it there—on my bedside locker?"

WHEN DAITHÍ COMES BACK TO the room, Saoirse and Leah are on the bed, Leah is plaiting her mother's hair, twisting it into a new style.

"Lovely," Daithí laughs. "It suits you."

Saoirse smiles.

"I'll take Leah down for a sandwich. Eloise is down there with Catherine now. And Catherine, of course, wants to come up and visit, if that's okay. But Saoirse—Nuala is here—she wants to have a chat."

Saoirse hugs Leah, then gives her a little push toward Daithí.

"Is that okay?"

"Of course," Saoirse says, though a little spark of fear jumps in her chest at facing Nuala.

"Go see your sister, sweetie. You'll come back together, the two of you, yeah?"

Nuala puts her head in the door. Leah hugs her gran and skips out of the room. Daithí squeezes Saoirse's hand and follows.

"Come in, sit down," Saoirse says, moving off the bed.

"I'm not staying," Nuala says. "I need to sort a matter or two with you."

Saoirse doesn't say anything. She stands in the middle of the floor, crossing her arms.

"There are two things I want." Nuala stands tensely in the doorway. "First I want to say I'm sorry for your troubles."

It takes a moment for her words to sink in, they don't exactly match her stance.

"Thank you."

"I am not happy with any of this business, and especially the way it has brought our family into the spotlight, spilling our business onto the street. We have always had a good name—"

"You have been so kind—"

"I wish I had known; I wish Joseph—" Her voice breaks.

"Come here—" Saoirse tells her. "Sit down."

Nuala takes the seat she offers at the table.

"Joseph would have known what to do. He also would have known how to help you. If only you had come to us—"

"I know. I was so frightened, and one thing led to another. Nuala, I am sorry." Saoirse feels the tears coming to her eyes again. It seems all she does is cry these days. Nuala makes what sounds like a little hiccup, but Saoirse can see she, too, is beginning to cry. She puts her face into her hands, her back is quaking. She is trying with all her might to swallow back her emotions.

Saoirse doesn't know whether to reach out and comfort her—she doesn't think this is the right move—and she is overcome herself now with sadness and regret, how much trouble this woman must feel for something that isn't her fault, something that has happened to her.

"We did our best—did you have to blacken the family name? Joseph's name." She is shaking now, making a deep weeping sound. Saoirse can only sit with her hands between her knees. She rises and gets the box of tissues at her bedside; she brings it back to Nuala.

Nuala waves it away, she takes a package of tissues out of her bag. Takes one out, wipes her face. Sniffs. She gathers herself.

"I'm furious about this. But at the end of the day, the truth of the matter is, Leah needs her mother, and she needs her sister."

Saoirse nods.

"Thank you—she told me you said very kind things."

"Of course I did," Nuala snaps. "What else am I going to say? I love my granddaughter."

"I know."

Nuala straightens her back; it is clear she can't bear Saoirse's company a moment longer. She gathers her strength, puts on a stoney face.

"You spoke of Paul as—" She hesitates, searching for the words. "Ill-treating you."

"I won't take it back," she tells Nuala. "It is what happened."

"I know. It is inexcusable."

Saoirse folds her hands in her lap.

"He is agreeing, we want two things," she sniffs. "Leah must carry the Byrne name, and you must drop it and never use it again. In papers, with your art, in court—"

"Fair enough."

"Sentencing dependent, we will ask the court to sway their verdict to leniency, and you and Paul may share custody. It isn't right to have the child away from her school, away from her friends, away from her mother—"

"Nuala, it's more than fair. It's gracious, I—"

Nuala puts her hand up.

"We will only deal with Daithí from here on out. Daithí may communicate any of Leah's needs. Paul will pay for her support, but he isn't paying you a single pound. As for Leah's schooling, Paul has equal say in all matters related to her. But we'll let the men deal with it between themselves."

"Fair."

"Saying all of this—you are a good mother, Sarah. Saoirse. You have done a decent job despite all you had to overcome, and Leah is a credit to you. Paul, for what it is worth, needs you in her life, but I want you to know he has made that call. It could have gone otherwise."

Saoirse nods, overwhelmed, but she cannot speak, she cannot say what she wants to say, her eyes burn with tears. She wants to reach out, kiss this woman's cheek, kiss her hands. Hug her. But she knows her display of gratitude will be met with a stoney reception.

Nuala gathers herself; she takes her bag and pushes in her chair. She leaves without a backward glance. Saoirse feels that pain in her throat, the squeeze of partings, the pain of goodbye.

ARTIST'S HEARING ENDS WITH COMMUNITY SERVICE AND NEW BEGINNINGS

Irish Times, 7 July 2000

Sarah Roy, the missing teenager who reemerged in Donegal, adopting the alias Saoirse Byrne, has received the maximum two hundred forty hours allowed under the community service order. Ms. Roy pleaded guilty at her arraignment earlier in the year and was granted bail with special conditions. The hearing, presided over by Judge Harrow, highlighted the complexities surrounding the artist's arrival and residence in Ireland. She considered various mitigating factors, including Ms. Roy's guilty plea, clean record, community standing, artistic achievements, psychological evaluations and two compelling victim impact statements advocating leniency.

Harrow imposed a community-focused sanction as an alternative to a prison sentence. The judge highlighted Roy's commitment to employing her creative background in aid of victims of domestic abuse, also noting the artist's intention to begin studies on a master's degree in art therapy in the autumn.

The revelation of Roy's Canadian citizenship and illegal US border crossing as a toddler adds a further layer and Judge Harrow empathetically acknowledged the systemic failures she suffered as a child. She emphasised Roy's resilience and the potential for a new start going forward in her adopted home of Ireland.

In a statement, the artist dispelled concerns regarding her right to remain in Ireland, revealing her plan to marry long-term partner and Donegal native, Daithí Gallagher. Going forward, the artist will be known by the legal name of Saoirse Gallagher. The artist thanked her partner, children, friends, community and gave particular attention to the exceptional generosity shown her by the Byrne family for their ongoing support.

Part Three

Home

Summer 2003

When the music reaches the open window, Saoirse looks away from the mirror where her sister, Léa, finishes applying her makeup. The girls are sitting on the floor, careful not to spoil their dresses. Out over the bay, Léa spots a truck moving slowly along the coast road. She squeals with delight, filling the bedroom with laughter. Saoirse will never tire of her sister's spontaneous happiness, but she groans to think what this might mean, this cacophony moving up the road, coming toward the house.

"I think your groom is arriving," Léa tells her sister. The girls run to the window and Léa hurries Saoirse into the simple dress she insists on wearing. The three of them had tried to move her toward lace and flounce and buttons, but Saoirse had put her foot down.

"Something simple," she insisted. "For me, anyway." She didn't want to entirely spoil their fun and Léa and Leah chose dresses for the three of them, full of frills, but she didn't mind. She has given in to this day for them. But mostly, for Daithí.

She had happily married him a few years ago, quietly, in the Registry Office in Dublin. She wanted to marry him, but it was also practical as it meant she could stay in the country. Liam and Catherine came as witnesses, but Saoirse didn't even want to go for a drink and certainly not dinner afterward. She wanted to leave the city immediately, return straight to the girls and their quiet life in Donegal.

But it was on their visit to Canada the following year, Daithí had taken advantage of the mutual affection he shared with his new sister-in-law, Léa, and the enthusiasm from the girls. He had asked Saoirse, in front of them all, to let him marry her properly.

"It won't be a big thing, babe. Just our best mates, a little celebration. It doesn't have to be a proper wedding of sorts. We'll just have a party, at our house. And a great excuse for your sister to visit Ireland." Her sister and daughters had started planning the day even before she said yes and they were so happy, she had given in to their demands. They shopped for their wedding clothes on that visit, Léa overseeing the fashions, taking the train from the Lavender House down to Toronto for a few nights.

VISITING CANADA WAS RISKY, DAITHÍ had felt, but she convinced him it was the thing she needed to do, to travel to them first, to reunite with Léa and Mama on her own terms. Saoirse spoke with her sister often on the telephone and they saw one another on web cameras, but her therapist agreed, visiting the epicentre of her childhood would help her face what she had lost, what she had left behind.

When they arrived, Léa emerged from the doorway Saoirse left twenty-six years before, when she was three years old. The Lavender House was Saoirse's first memory, and in this memory, she was small and frightened and alone, and that part of her, standing there, so many years later, remained. Léa wasn't even born when her mother took her away from here, so she was startled to realise as she was analysing her sketchbooks and paintings as part of her graduate studies, that it was her sister she often rendered into these scenes, never herself. Her tutor on the art therapy component of the course believed this was a significant discovery; one she was still encouraging Saoirse to explore.

Léa understood therapy. She had overcome so much herself, but she had a few years' start on Saoirse, and had been protected from the worst of it, thanks to her youth, but mostly to her older sister. Léa was confident and beautiful, she reminded Saoirse of a younger, healthier version of their mother. She had graduated top of her high school class and was halfway through her studies, becoming a psychologist. She joked about being a therapy junkie, hooked after the number of interventions and services she received once she was rescued from *their circumstances*, as Mama called their years of abuse and neglect. She had held Saoirse's arm, worried if she was receiving proper help for her own lived traumas. Saoirse reassured her she was, but mostly she knew, she worked things out through her art, the way she always had done.

Léa described the informal case studies she had compiled on their mother and Mama over the years of university, the diagnoses she had assigned to them, but it was a futile exercise. Their mother, Saoirse was shocked to discover, had only turned sixteen when she became pregnant with her. Saoirse never imagined her so young, so unprotected herself. Léa told her of Mama's regret, her grief, how failing to save her daughter, failing at letting her granddaughter slip through her hands, had affected her.

Léa thought of Mama's words as a metaphor, but Saoirse could still physically feel her grandmother's hand on her wrist, the day Fleur and Lou drove her away from the Lavender House. How Saoirse had wrangled herself away, slipping out of her grandmother's reach. Léa's empathy, her understanding of how young, how vulnerable their mother had been, how she had been born with these struggles, clearly unfit to raise children unsupervised, opened something new for Saoirse in her own struggle to understand how a mother could let her children down so badly. Maybe, eventually, she too would find it in herself to forgive, but she wasn't there, not yet. If it had been any other way, she knew, there wouldn't be a Léa or a Leah, an Eloise or a Daithí in her life. For them, she would pay this price a hundred times over.

In Canada, the girls had followed their newfound auntie around the lake, they plaited her hair and filled it with daisies from the grass as they sat by the water, and Saoirse knew they had already fallen for her, her all-encompassing love, and had immediately established Léa as a fixture in their lives.

Papa Frank was gone now, he had died years before, and Saoirse wished she felt different about it, but she couldn't help feel unease around Mama those few weeks on their visit. She certainly couldn't stay in the house, and they had rented a place up the road but came each day to sit by the lake. She couldn't shake the sensation that some part of her three-year-old self was here still, somewhere, downstairs in the basement alone and afraid. And to watch her sister and her daughters, Saoirse knew she was the only child she had not managed to save.

While Léa and the girls swam and sunned themselves on the dock, Saoirse unpacked her ink pens and watercolours. She sat in the shade and drew one sequence after the next as it came to her, and before she realised, she had found her way in to the work.

Each scene featured a little girl, the setting developing around her. The first background was the Lavender House and lake, then this setting washed into a suspension bridge looming in the distance. The girl found herself at the edge of a frog pond, crossing the ocean in a swan boat, landing under a dome full of stars above rolling dunes. Twin chimneys, striped red and white, rose out of a bay like candy sticks, and the girl walked a long pier and came to a red lighthouse. She next found herself on a green train line heading down the coast, the Sugarloaf prominent on the horizon, before taking shelter in a fancy house in a sleepy village. Finally, she arrived at a cove on the back of a whale, all around surrounded by walls. By now the little girl had grown weary.

At the limewashed house above the cove, just inside the door, a woman painted, placing strokes on a canvas, her work upon the easel. With her brush, the artist has drawn this house, she has tucked the little girl in to a bed under the eaves, the moon shining on the rocks and the waves below. Orion lifting high his bronze club above the sleeping house.

As the plane left the tarmac, departing Canada, Saoirse knew the drawings in her portfolio case in the overhead bin were more than illustrations. The little girl from the Lavender House was coming with her, she was coming home.

A wordless picture book, the publisher had called it. The cover included a bilingual title along with her name, written in the way she signed off all her work nowadays.

Sa Bhaile ag
Cuan na Míolta Móra
Home at Whale Bay
SAOIRSE

The dedication took her some time to decide. She wrote many sentences, trying to express the depth of her gratitude, but in the end, only two words felt right and she hoped the gesture was enough to express all that couldn't be said.

For Sasa

SAOIRSE PEEKS OUT THE WINDOW as the music draws near. She sees the wedding guests assembling on the embankment above the cove, some are moving out onto the rocks. There are no strangers amongst them—Sinead and Emily have gathered with the others. Emily steps out of her high heels, slings the straps around her finger and carries them down onto the rocks.

Catherine has arrived, she has collected Daithí's father and sister, Hamisi, from the hotel. They wear brightly coloured clothes in the customary tradition of their home which Hamisi had described to Saoirse the night before when they had come together at the hotel for a dinner. They had arrived in Ireland six days before from Kenya and Daithí was keen to introduce them to everyone in his life. They toured the towns and beaches and ended in Seamus's pub—which Michael remembered from his time with Kitty.

Liam is bringing Daithí from the village, but there is no Gus or even Seamus or the other lads, she is surprised to find, and she feels a pang of anxiety for him.

But now she recognises Daithí's flatbed truck moving closer, coming nearer the gate pier, there is music blaring through speakers rigged to its side. She groans, and then laughs, to see it is a moving stage, filled with Liam and the lads, they make up a multipiece band, including a trumpet section, an uilleann piper, even a piano strapped to the back of the cab, these are the songs she first heard around a fire circle many years before, under the stars.

"Ready?" her sister asks. "You are amazing—" she tells her as she affixes a long plain chiffon scarf to the crown of her head. It is longer than Saoirse is tall—and she can't believe she has agreed to this, but Léa has tears in her eyes now, and they are springing up in her own, threatening her makeup. Saoirse swats at her, playfully, telling her to give her a minute. Léa kisses her cheek.

"Let's go—" Léa rallies the girls. She gathers her dress and leads the charge down the stairs. No one seems to worry the girls will upset the wreaths of flowers freshly placed on their heads—Leah's matching her auntie's dusty pink dress, Eloise's a soft mauve. She can hear them below, Léa throwing open the front door and the girls following her out. They dance around the hard earth of the driveway, barefooted, their frocks lifting in the light breeze off the sea. The day is bright and lovely and perfect for what is ahead.

The girls are calling up to her window now, telling her she must come down—Dotty is arriving. She fixes her hair in the mirror, overwhelmed by happiness, and this is what she does not want: to be awkward or unrefined, or burst into tears from it all—and these doubts and hesitations follow her down the stairs and out the door into the sunshine.

Seamus pulls the flatbed alongside the embankment—a stage pointing out to sea, and the guests move, dancing on the rocks below. Across the bay some of the villagers have come out to the strand to wave from the beach. Liam counts in a song from the Waterboys about love lasting as long as the stars.

And there is Daithí climbing out of the cab, casual and handsome in a white linen shirt and chinos. No one on the truck seems to be wearing shoes. He is biting his lip and when he sees Saoirse, standing on the step, looking bashful and uncertain, he holds his hands in the air and swears the music, the mode of transport—none of this was his idea. And he is laughing and the joy on his face is immeasurable.

"*Mo chuisle*," he says, as he moves toward her up the driveway—going down on one knee, hand over his heart. "*A chuisle mo chroí*."

Pulse of my heart.

She feels this must be the most precise expression of love in any language. She takes his hand, pulls him to standing. Stepping out of her own shoes, she leaves them there in the driveway.

They are a picture from the shore, walking beside the walls, the girls' dresses flowing out behind them in the sea breeze, her daughters and Léa pick bunches of ragwort flowers along the way. When they get a certain distance, near the edge of the cove, and only the rocks and sea are below, Léa holds the girls back and they watch while Daithí and Saoirse step down from the edge, he holds out his hand and leads her, they jump barefoot from rock to rock until they are a little way out, where even the music is washed away by the sound of the waves. Saoirse's veil streams behind her in the breeze. Daithí squints in the sunshine. No words are needed. Nothing is left to be said.

Back at the house, the dinner is served in the atrium overlooking the sea. Speeches and toasts are made, Liam has set up for the music. The sun sets and the tables are cleared, and Saoirse and Daithí have moved around, talking to everyone, thanking them all for coming—the dancing has begun, and Saoirse feels it is getting too much—she needs air. Daithí has caught her eye across the room, and he is taking a bottle of champagne from the bar, and two glasses, he grabs a coat off the back of a chair. He takes her hand, and they walk out into the night, leaving the girls on the dance floor with Léa.

Down on the rocks, he has spread the coat for her, he pops the cork off of the champagne, and they watch the fairy lights from their house sparkle onto the water. Across the way, the village twinkles with light, and under this clear sky they look to an island in the distance, watch for a glimmer of light in the darkness.

And Saoirse imagines far offshore, somewhere deep inside this night, someone unknown wonders about these pinpoints of light; watching how they shine, so brilliantly, from her own vast horizon.

ACKNOWLEDGMENTS

My heartfelt gratitude and admiration to Gráinne Fox at United Talent Agency for her influence on this book and her tireless support. All my thanks to Deb Futter for her enthusiasm and keen editorial vision and also for making the process such an absolute dream and pleasure, along with the incredible team at Celadon Books, especially Margaux Kanamori, Jeremy Pink, Christina MacDonald, Rachel Chou, Christine Mykityshyn, Jaime Noven, and Anne Twomey. The wonderful Deirdre Nolan, editor and friend, and assistant editor Lisa Gilmour, who gives attention to every detail, and the entire Eriu / Bonnier team, especially Sophie Orme, Zoe Yang, Sophie Raoufi, Clare Kelly, Marina Stavropoulou, and Emily Peyton. Also Declan Heeney, Simon Hess, and Helen McKean at Gill Hess. Thank you to artists Emma Cownie and T. S. Harris for the gorgeous cover art. I'm thankful to Felicity Blunt and Flo Sandelson—what a pleasure to receive your ideas and enthusiasm, which certainly shaped this story, these characters. Much gratitude to Madison Hernick for your insights, and also Geritza Carrasco and all at UTA and Curtis Brown for the fantastic support.

This book found inspiration in Irish Landmark Trust's research and in their loving restoration of built heritage. An award received from the Irish Arts Council enabled research in visual arts processes. My admiration of visual artist Melissa O'Donnell (Solomon Gallery) and poet and literary scholar Jonathan Locke Hart. Melissa's painting *Plaisir Inconsolable* was vivid in my mind for the scene "Incorda Volupta," whose title and subsequent translation (inconsolable pleasure) were influenced by Jonathan's poem "49" from *Faire Irlande* (French version) and *Making*

Ireland (English version). Residencies at Heinrich Böll Cottage, Cill Rialaig Arts Centre, and the Tyrone Guthrie Centre were crucial in providing the space and solitude needed to develop my work. Time at Annaghmakerrig, in particular, provided unparalleled nourishment and camaraderie with fellow artists. My thanks to Federica Sgaggio for sharing her insights on humanity, Sandra Clark for her music and the craic, and Kevin Rafter for his encouragement and wisdom. Thank you to many artists who gave me a glimpse into their process.

On friendships that have endured and sustained me: Sinéad Catherine Ní Chofaigh, you have been my constant. Always Jen Jansen and Karen Morgan, no matter time or distance. Thank you to Barbara Barclay, and also Jenny Powell. To Janetta Johnson, for believing. Linda Darbey, Sue Reardon, and Conor O'Reilly for your enduring friendship. Aoife Kavanagh and the Round Table Book Club, for your support. Michelle Gallen for the sisterhood, Mehdi and boys for the sheltering. The gals of the Misfits, we don't Pop-up or Gin so often, but much gratitude for your support. The generosity of readers and booksellers. Remembering Lisa Dowling Scott, who was here with Saoirse at the start and whose laughter will stay with me always.

It is wonderful to have the support of a loving family, no matter the distance. Thank you, Mary and Benny. Theresa O'Donnell, who reads every word carefully and closely. Sandy and Mary and partners, a special thank you for the time—past (and future)—at the Hurtubise Nature Retreat. Sarah, the heart and hearth of our family. Julie, who packed our lunches and made all the fun. Kathleen, the light; Laura, the love. Larry, the kindest of men. Thanks, Rye Cat, nieces, nephews, partners, new grandbabies. Love you all. Remembering with awe and love my creative mom, my hardworking dad.

To Liam and the lads—for the music.

Conor for your support and friendship in raising the greatest gifts life has offered us: Dearbhaile, Donnchadh, and Ruaidhrí: mo Ghaeilgeoirí, mo sióga craiceáilte and my three Great Loves.

When I arrived in Ireland twenty-five years ago, I wasn't alone. Sue Dible, always up for mischief. *Saoirse* is for you.

ABOUT THE AUTHOR

Charleen Hurtubise is a novelist, essayist, and artist. She is the author of *The Polite Act of Drowning*, published in Ireland and the UK in 2023. *Saoirse* is her US debut. She holds an M.Sc. from Trinity College Dublin and an M.F.A. in creative writing from University College Dublin, where she has facilitated creative writing seminars. The sixth sister in a family of nine, she spent much of her childhood in Michigan and her early adult years in Boston and has now lived half her life in Ireland, which is home. Though she lives in Dublin with her Irish family, the pull of Donegal continues to influence her drawings and writings, including *Saoirse*.